Lincoln Township Public Library
2099 W. John Beers Rd.
Stevensville, MI 49127
(269) 429-9575

The ICING on the CAKE

Center Point
Large Print

Also by Janice Thompson and available from
Center Point Large Print:

Weddings by Bella series:
  Fools Rush In
  Swinging on a Star
  It Had to Be You

Weddings by Design series:
  Picture Perfect

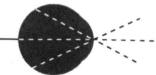

**This Large Print Book carries the
Seal of Approval of N.A.V.H.**

Weddings by Design, #2

The ICING
on the CAKE.

Janice
Thompson

Lincoln Township Public Library
2099 W. John Beers Rd.
Stevensville, MI 49127
(269) 429-9575

CENTER POINT LARGE PRINT
THORNDIKE, MAINE

This Center Point Large Print edition is published
in the year 2013 by arrangement with Revell,
a division of Baker Publishing Group.

Copyright © 2013 by Janice Thompson.

All rights reserved.

Scripture used in this book, whether quoted or paraphrased
by the characters, is taken from the Holy Bible, New
International Version®. NIV®. Copyright © 1973, 1978,
1984, 2011 by Biblica, Inc.™ Used by permission of
Zondervan. All rights reserved worldwide.
www.zondervan.com

This book is a work of fiction. Names, characters, places,
and incidents are the product of the author's imagination
or are used fictitiously. Any resemblance to actual events,
locales, or persons, living or dead, is coincidental.

The text of this Large Print edition is unabridged.
In other aspects, this book may vary
from the original edition.
Printed in the United States of America
on permanent paper.
Set in 16-point Times New Roman type.

ISBN: 978-1-61173-796-7

Library of Congress Cataloging-in-Publication Data

Thompson, Janice A.
The icing on the cake / Janice Thompson. — Center Point Large Print
   edition.
pages ; cm
ISBN 978-1-61173-796-7 (library binding : alk. paper)
1. Wedding cakes—Fiction. 2. Weddings—Fiction.
   3. Large type books. I. Title.
PS3620.H6824I35 2013b
813´.6—dc23

2013014903

CPLP 131105

To Lauren Giles,
bride extraordinaire and forgiver of
"the great cake faux pas."
Bless you!

The ICING
on the CAKE

1

Half-Baked

Families are like fudge, mostly sweet with a few nuts.

Author unknown

I've never understood that expression about how you can have your cake and eat it too. I mean, if you eat it, it's gone, right? What would be the point otherwise? And if you're one of my customers—really, I hate to brag, but how can I resist?—you're probably going to scarf it down in record time anyway.

Then again, I can always bake up another yummy one lickety-split, in any flavor you like. German chocolate with homemade butter pecan frosting. Lemon chiffon with raspberry filling. Strawberry shortcake with juicy, fresh-picked berries. You name it, I can bake and decorate it. No event is too large or too small. Weddings, birthdays, baby showers, bridal extravaganzas . . . I've created cakes for all of 'em.

Okay, now I sound like I'm doing an infomercial for my business. But no one would blame me for gushing, I suppose. Cakes *are* my business, and they're the tastiest on Galveston Island. Ask anyone. Even Bella Neeley, the island's most popular wedding coordinator, recommends me to her brides at Club Wed. Not that I'm prone to bragging, of course. That would just be wrong. Still, I don't mind admitting when things are going well, and right now I'm living a sweet life—pun intended. For the most part.

I pondered my good fortune as I headed to my newly refurbished bakery on the Strand on the first Saturday in May. I mean, finding one of the hippest spots on the island to place Let Them Eat Cake, smack-dab in the middle of Galveston's business district? Primo! And in May, no less! Talk about perfect timing. Just enough time to set up shop and then prep for all of the June weddings I'd booked. Oh, and get my act together for the church's big fund-raiser, which I'd been talked into chairing. Surely it would all come together. I hoped.

I pulled into a parking spot in front of the bakery and paused to glance at Parma John's pizzeria next door. I still couldn't believe I'd managed to land the space next to Galveston's favorite eatery. I could almost envision the restaurant's patrons loading up on pizza and then heading over to my place to have dessert. At least that's how I hoped it would all go down. In an ideal world. At about the same time I earned my own cake decorating show on the Food Network. Oh, and won the lottery.

Not that I'd ever purchased a lotto ticket, mind

you. My father's latest sermon on the woes of gambling shied me away from the temptation to buy one, thank you very much. Still, my future looked as shiny as a new penny right now, and I couldn't help but think the best was yet to come, golden ticket or not. And garnering patrons from Parma John's was the key to the equation.

I'd just started to celebrate my upcoming successes by heading into the pizzeria to grab a thick, gooey slice of the Mambo Italiano special—heavy on the cheese—when I realized my mother was standing outside my new bakery. She wore the same concerned look on her face I'd seen hundreds—no, thousands—of times before. Yikes. This could only mean one thing.

I released a slow breath, offered up a rushed "Lord, help me!" and got out of the car. Seconds later, as I fumbled through my stash of keys to open the bakery, my arms filled with bags from the superstore, Mama lit into a frantic conversation, her words as choppy as the Gulf of Mexico during a category 5 and nearly as fast as the wind that took the roof off of our little church during Hurricane Ike.

"Scarlet. I'm. Glad. You're. Here. Aunt Wilhelmina's. Looking. For you. And you know. How she is."

Yes, I knew how she was. Still, I wouldn't have a cake business without Aunt Willy. Of this I was reminded daily.

"She called. My cell phone." Mama paused for breath. "Three times. This morning."

"Oh? Weird. Didn't get any calls from her." I stepped inside the bakery and felt my burdens lift right away as I took in the ambience of my new place. Ah, life! How divine! How sweet! How—

I turned back to my mother. She paled and released a slow breath. "You must've overlooked her calls. Wilhelmina said she tried to reach you. But you wouldn't answer your cell phone. This won't set well with her. You know?"

My confidence soared right out the window as I thought about the fact that Auntie was mad at me. Her ability to fund Let Them Eat Cake had been key to my success, and her willingness to build out my new facility on the Strand was a huge blessing. My gratitude often bordered on obsession with trying to keep her happy, and that wasn't easy. She was, after all, our state's most adored cake diva. Emphasis on diva.

"I really don't think I've missed any calls. That I know of, anyway." I reached into my oversized purse and came out with my new iPhone, the one with a hot-pink case. Oops. Sure enough, Aunt Willy had called three times in a row. I would pay a heavy price for missing her calls. She hated it when I didn't answer.

In a flash, I realized what I must've done. "I guess I left my ringer off after my meeting at church last night. We had a get-together with the kids who are going on the missions trip so we could talk about the fund-raiser. Sorry 'bout that. But what's so important?"

"With your aunt, whoever knows?" Mama's eyes narrowed to slits, and her voice lowered. "But she's on the island. That's really all I came by to say. She should be arriving at the bakery any moment. Just wanted to give you a heads-up."

Ack.

I walked up the four steps that led to the main level of the bakery, my arms still loaded down with bags from the superstore. Mama followed on my heels, talking the whole way. When she paused for breath, I managed to sneak in a few words.

"Sorry, Mama. I had to go into town to pick up some supplies. I've got cake samples to bake before the grand opening, and you can see for yourself that I'm nowhere near ready to start baking yet." I placed the bags down on a table and gestured to the room filled with unopened and half-opened boxes, bins, and bags. "This whole place is a mess, and we open in two days."

"Right." Mama glanced around, wrinkled her nose, and nodded. "Well, better get busy, honey. Your aunt is liable to be upset that you're not ready for clients yet."

I reached for a knife and slit open the tape on the closest box. "Aunt Willy's bound to be upset no matter what I do."

Ain't it the truth, ain't it the truth.

"Maybe, but please don't let her hear you calling her that," my mother cautioned. "You know how she feels about nicknames."

I turned to face Mama, frustration setting in. "Then why does she call me Sticky Buns?" I set the knife aside and ripped open the box, pleased to find my kneading machine inside.

"It's a term of endearment, Scarlet."

"Sticky Buns? A term of endearment?" More likely a twisted attempt at humor—Aunt Wilhelmina's way of pointing out the vast size of my backside. Not that she could possibly understand my weight issues, irritating as they might be. Auntie tipped the scale at 103, dripping wet. Roughly. Maybe 104. I made at least two of her. Okay, two and a quarter, but who was keeping track?

I turned to face my mother, who grimaced. "Honey, let's give her the benefit of the doubt. If anyone knows her buns, it's your aunt Wilhelmina. She's been baking longer than you've been on planet earth. Almost double that time, in fact. She's considered to be the best in the state."

Thanks for the reminder. As if I could forget.

"I know, Mama." With the box now fully opened, I reached down to grab the kneading machine, which I used routinely to make so many of my breads.

"She knows her stuff." Mama knelt down to

14

help me. We hefted the machine beyond the glass display cases to the kitchen in the back. "And she's got the best reputation in the state."

"For her cakes. Not her sticky buns." I settled the kneading machine into place. *And certainly not for her good attitude.*

"Yes, for her cakes. And there's a reason for that. She built her business from the ground up. Hit the road straight out of culinary school and never looked back."

I leaned against the countertop, ready to admit defeat. "I know, I know." How many times had I heard this story? Aunt Willy was known across the state for her fabulous cake designs. She was our very own Ace of Cakes. Our Cake Boss. Our Cupcake Champion. Our Best in Show.

I sighed and then repented for the images that last one presented.

Mama clucked her tongue and gave me the usual motherly look. "I'm just saying that she's got a lot of advice to offer."

"And does so freely." An elongated pause followed my words. "But I'm not complaining."

"You're not?" The look on my mother's face let me know that she didn't quite believe me.

"No. Not really." I paused again as I thought through my response. "Okay, maybe I am. It's just that she's not easy to please. And I wonder if I'm going to spend the rest of my mortal life trying to prove myself to a woman who's never going to think I'm good enough. You know? That would be a terrible way to live."

"Honey, calm down. Take a deep breath." Mama patted my arm and offered a look that only a mother could give—half sympathetic, half guilt trip. "Ask yourself, 'What would Lucy do in a situation like this?' "

"Huh?"

Mama reached for a dust rag and went to work on the kneading machine. "Haven't you seen every episode of *I Love Lucy* a dozen times?"

"Two dozen." But I still couldn't figure out what that had to do with anything, at least where Aunt Willy was concerned.

I headed back to the front of the store to finish unpacking. Mama caught up to me. "So again I ask—what would a good Scottish girl like Lucy McGillicuddy do?"

"She would probably . . ." I found myself distracted by my mother's McGillicuddy reference. What did any of this have to do with being Scottish? Some link to our own heritage, perhaps? I shrugged. "She would probably start her own business and make a mess of things, then admit defeat. After trying to weasel her way into Ricky's show at the Copa Cabana, I mean." I knelt to slit another box open and pulled out a stash of large mixing bowls. "Is that what you're suggesting? I should put on a show?"

"No." Mama shook her head. "Not the kind

you're talking about, anyway. Just a show of affection for the woman who's invested in you, and a promise to yourself that you won't quit, no matter how tough things get."

I felt the wind go out of my sails at her words.

Mama lit into a conversation about how my father never quit the ministry, even when the congregation dwindled down to a handful of parishioners. How he kept going, even when folks headed out to larger megachurches.

Gee, Mama, this is really cheering me up.

She patted my arm—using the hand with the dust cloth. "Maybe you don't want to learn from Lucy's failures, but you can certainly take a little something from her tenacity. She never gave up."

"Never ever," I admitted. Rising with the bowls in hand, I nearly lost my balance. I caught a glimpse of myself in the ornate mirrors behind the glass shelves and noticed my messy hair and plump cheeks. Ugh. If Lucy looked like me, she'd give up, all right.

Mama paused alongside me to gaze at my reflection, a smile lighting her lovely, non-chubby—albeit wrinkled—face. "And she never saw herself as anything less than a star, honey. Never."

I sighed and turned away from the mirror, because the reflection staring back at me proved I was anything but. "I'm not sure that's completely true, Mama. Remember that episode where she thought she had no talent at all?"

"Okay, okay. But you get the idea. She kept trying to weasel her way into the show—your words, not mine—and managed to become a superstar in the process. To her fans, anyway. And you need to do the same."

"I will. I mean, I've got that big gig coming up at Club Wed next month. Hannah is counting on me. It's her special day."

I smiled as I mentioned my best friend's name. Hannah's wedding—a lavish Irish affair—would be the proverbial icing on my cake, career-wise. What a gorgeous June bride she would make! Just thinking about it got me excited. And it didn't hurt that the event would take place at Club Wed with the infamous Bella Neeley coordinating. If I played my cards right, the pictures might even end up in *Texas Bride* magazine. One could hope, anyway. And one could also hope that the magazine might sneak in a photo or two of my new digs.

I thought about my aunt's reaction should my name appear in print. She would swoon with delight, no doubt. Right after taking the credit. But who could blame her? She had made all of this possible for me. And with her help, I really could achieve my dreams, one sticky bun at a time.

Yep. We made the perfect team. And perhaps, if I kept her happy, I really could have my cake and eat it too.

2

A Spoonful of Sugar

I'm pretty sure the secret to world peace is
hidden somewhere in the smell of coffee and
baked sweets.

Author unknown

Pushing all concerns about Aunt Willy aside, I
headed to the car to grab a large bag of sugar I'd
inadvertently left there. As I lugged it into the
bakery, my thoughts slipped back to Mama's
comments about Lucy. I couldn't help but smile.
There were no words to explain my fascination
with the quirky redhead. Her antics always kept
me entertained. Up one minute, down the next,
Lucy braved every challenge and kept me
laughing each step of the way.

And talk about a hard worker. If Lucy could
overcome her status as a talentless nobody, I
could too. And I supposed it didn't hurt that
McGillicuddy was a Scottish name, all things
considered.

Several minutes later, Mama cleared her throat
and gestured toward the door. Through the glass
panels, I saw her.

Auntie.

Petite. Slightly hunched. Dressed to the nines. And judging from her tight-lipped frown, none too happy. Maybe the support hose had cut off her circulation. Or maybe she'd just come from paying another installment on her funeral, like last time. I always found those discussions so cheerful.

To call her a crusty old soul might seem insensitive, but it was the most accurate description I could come up with as I stared at her through the glass. If my life were an *I Love Lucy* episode, Aunt Wilhelmina would be my Fred Mertz. Every story needed a curmudgeon, after all. Upped the ante. And having your ante upped was a good thing when you were in business for yourself. This I had discovered firsthand.

The jingling of the bell above the door rang out, along with her familiar, shaky voice. "Why doesn't someone do something about that blasted bell? It's getting on my last nerve."

Well, hello to you too, Aunt Willy.

"I swear, getting into this place is more complicated than cracking the safe at Fort Knox. You wouldn't believe what I had to go through to get a parking space. And these stairs!" Off she went on a tangent, railing about my stairs.

Ha! Stairs—railing!

I pushed aside the laughter and watched as she wrangled her way up the four steps to the bakery's main level. From the looks of things, she'd just had her hair done. Or, as we used to say back in Lufkin, where I hailed from: "Had 'er hair did."

The soft curls that framed her face were a shade or two darker than usual, with a hint of auburn. And the makeup! Honestly, for a woman in her seventies, Aunt Willy certainly knew how to spice up her appearance, albeit with a shaky hand. The eyeliner was a little cockeyed, and the lipstick strayed outside the usual lines, but she'd given it the old college try. You had to give it to her for that.

She drew near and grunted a hello to my mother, who scurried into the kitchen.

Coward.

Not that Mama had ever shared a normal relationship with my dad's much-older sister. To my way of thinking, she'd always been a little scared of the old gal. Okay, a lot scared. Then again, we all were. But why? What harm could a precious elderly woman do, especially one so focused on dying? The rest of us had plenty of life left in us.

I gazed at Willy's face, wrinkles as soft as tissue paper and eyes so blue they rivaled the sky above the gulf. What really got me, though, were the pink cheeks. No, she hadn't spent time in the sun. She'd gone a little crazy with the blush brush. Should I tell her she'd overdone it or just look the other way?

21

Fortunately—or unfortunately—I never got the chance to speak. She lifted a shaky finger and pointed it at my face. "Scarlet, I've been trying to reach you all morning."

"Oh yes, ma'am. I—"

"When I call, I expect you to answer, especially now that we're doing business together." A tremor punctuated her words. "When you make me come and find you, it robs time from my busy day. Besides, I wouldn't have funded this venture if I'd realized you would end up ignoring me. I don't want to go to my grave with you owing me money."

Ouch.

"I'm not ignoring you, Aunt Willy. Wilhelmina," I quickly corrected myself. "I promise. I've been so busy moving in that I didn't hear the phone. That's all."

"Suppose I'd been an important client? Then what?" Her gaze narrowed, and I knew this was a test question. I'd better get the answer right, or . . . or . . .

I wasn't sure what the "or" would be, actually.

"Well then," I said after a moment's thought, "I would have called you back and offered you the deal of a lifetime." I gave a confident smile, one I hoped she would find convincing.

"Don't be so free with my money, girl." She glanced around the room, her nose wrinkled. At least I thought it was. At her age, who could tell?

"I thought you got this place set up last week."

"No, the movers couldn't come until yesterday, but they did a really good job getting everything loaded up in a timely fashion and—"

"Slackers." Just one word, but with the tremor in her voice, it sounded like two or three.

"Oh." I tried to think of the right words. "No, not slackers. The foreman's wife was having a baby, so—"

"Sure she was." Willy rolled her eyes, obviously not convinced.

"No, really. It's true. They had a baby girl, by the way. I saw the pictures. Pretty little thing. She—"

"Scarlet, you've got to stop letting people take advantage of you."

Um, okay.

"You give people an inch, they'll take a mile. Before you know it, you'll lose all control."

Tell me about it.

"Giving up control is not a good thing."

Point well taken. I shall tattoo that on my forehead—backwards, so that when I look in the mirror, I will see it in all its glory.

She took a few steps closer, and the makeup became even more of a distraction. "I need to make sure you get everything done that I've asked of you. The new recipes, the éclairs . . . everything."

"Oh, I will. But I already have a full schedule

this month. And Hannah's getting married in six weeks, remember?" Sweet Hannah! If anyone deserved a happily ever after, my BFF did. She'd beat me to the altar, but I didn't really mind that much.

"That's the Irish wedding at Club Wed?" Willy asked as she settled into a chair at the closest table. "Your photographer friend?"

I nodded. "Yes."

She put her designer purse on the table next to an open box. "Happy to see that you're getting more business from Club Wed. That's good. That wedding coordinator, Bella Neeley, has made quite a name for herself. Linking your business to hers is key. People will sit up and take notice. It's all about networking. That's what I always say."

I had to give it to Aunt Willy. Seventy-five years old and still focused on the bottom line.

Thinking about bottom lines reminded me of my ever-blossoming backside. The words *sticky buns* slipped through my mind, and I flinched. Oh well. At least Auntie wasn't focused on the size of my bottom today. No, judging from the look on her face, she was far more preoccupied with scrutinizing my new digs and rambling about business stuff.

"How do you think I made Crème de la Crème the success that it is today?" She shook her finger at me. "Not by hiding my light under a bushel."

Her cheeks practically glowed in the dark

today, so I could not dispute her on that point.

"And certainly not by giving away too much product," she continued, the tone of her voice intensifying. "You've got to cut back on the giveaways, Scarlet, and focus on making great connections."

"I'm just looking at new ways of doing things, Aunt Wil—"

"This is what I'm talking about." She pointed to the decor—the luscious, wood-trimmed mirrors and the glass cases that would eventually hold the cakes, cupcakes, and pastries. "Too much froufrou. You need to focus on the products, not the shelves that house them. I didn't invest my hard-earned money so that you could buy top-of-the-line cases. Why in the world you couldn't make do with regular cases is beyond me."

"Hmm. Well, the glass cases came with the place, remember? This used to be a candy store, and the owner had really nice taste." *And I, for one, happen to think the cases are gorgeous.*

She did that nose-wrinkling thing again. "Still, it's the cakes you need to focus on. And the cookies too, I suppose, though I never saw much value in a cookie."

I bit back the sigh as the thought, *You never saw much value in anything,* ran through my brain. How my dad had put up with her all of his life was beyond me.

Giving myself a mental slap, I forced myself to

25

focus. Surely she did see the value in hard work. And in me. Otherwise she never would have funded this venture, right?

She lit into a conversation about the importance of keeping my glass shelves stocked with the things that customers had come to expect in a bakery, and before long I found myself wanting to doze off.

Time to think more like Lucy.

As I gazed into Aunt Wilhelmina's baby blues, as I took in her ever-softening skin, a smile worked its way from my heart to my lips. She probably wouldn't win any personality-of-the-month awards, in spite of her willingness to fund my latest venture. Still, she was my auntie and I loved her.

Best of all, she believed in me. Believed in my business. In that respect she'd proven to be as reliable as those funky support hose she always wore and as consistent as her overworn story about how she already had one foot in the grave. Maybe she didn't have a motherly personality, but I had no doubt in my mind that time would prove her to be more friend than foe. I hoped.

Besides, we were more alike than I'd realized. She loved sweets. I loved sweets. She'd orchestrated a successful business. I planned to orchestrate a successful business. She was loopy with the eyeliner. I . . .

I glanced at my reflection in the ornate mirror

above the counter and groaned. I had forgotten to put on any eyeliner. Or any lipstick, for that matter. Oh well. Who needed makeup on a day like today?

Aunt Willy rambled on about the messy state of affairs in my new bakery, and I shifted my focus from my own imperfections to those facing me in the room. No point in worrying about it, really. The room would clean up just fine. And—now I encouraged myself to think like Lucy—so would the woman in the mirror.

3

Pie in the Sky

Seize the moment. Remember all those women on the *Titanic* who waved off the dessert cart.

Erma Bombeck

I've always been nuts about my BFF, Hannah. For one thing, she's the most brilliant photographer ever. But it's not her talent that draws me in, it's her personality. She's sweet and kind to a fault. She's also incredibly loyal. A thousand times over she could have—probably should have—ditched me as her best friend. I mean, I've always been very vocal. Speaking my mind comes easily, and I've shared my opinion about her work, her love life, her diet . . . pretty much her everything. But she's borne it all like a champ.

And it doesn't hurt that her photography studio, which she shares with her fiancé, is less than a block away, on the other side of the Strand. We see each other every day. Sometimes two or three times a day. And now that she was in full-out wedding-planning mode, I couldn't seem to shake her. Not that I wanted to, of course.

After Aunt Willy huffed off, Hannah entered my shop, her ever-present smile offering hope. I stopped working long enough to give her a welcoming smile. "Hey, you."

"Hey." She plopped down in a chair and gazed at me, brow wrinkled. "Did I just see your aunt leaving?"

"Yep. She scared off my mama half an hour ago, but I had no choice—I had to stay put and listen to her." I sighed, though I didn't mean to. "Kind of glad she's gone now, to be honest. Is that awful?" If anyone would understand, my best friend would. She knew my heart better than anyone.

"No, it's not awful." Hannah paused and appeared to be thinking. "Would it be wrong to say that I do what I can to avoid her? She scares me."

"She scares me too. A little. In fact, I think she scares pretty much everyone she meets, which is really odd, considering her tiny size."

"Funny how someone in such a small package can be so intimidating." Hannah chuckled. "Still can't figure out how your aunt Willy and your father came from the same gene pool. Someone must've been swimming in the shallow end at some point along the way."

"I know, right?" The very idea that my precious father—all six foot three of him—had grown up with such an aggressive older sister seemed impossible to me. I'd just opened my mouth to say more, but the words to a childhood song flitted through my mind: *Oh be careful little mouth what you say.* I shrugged instead.

"Well, I couldn't wait any longer," Hannah said. "I've got a gig and I need some sugar." She pointed to the empty cases. "What? No cake balls? No samples?"

"Haven't had a chance to bake the past couple of days, but . . ." A grin curled up the edges of my lips. "I do have a few hiding in the back. I made them last week and froze them, but they're almost thawed. Just haven't had time to get them into the cases. I don't officially open until day after tomorrow, you know, and I still have a lot of work to do."

"Right, right. But a girl needs her sugar in the afternoon, especially a girl in wedding-planning mode." She leaned her elbows on the table, nearly knocking off a box in the process. "This whole wedding-planning thing is for the birds. If not for you and Bella, I would've snapped like a twig already. I need my daily bread—er, cake."

"Have I ever let you down?" I gave her a little wink and went to fetch the tray of cake samples.

She dove in like a woman without a caloric care in the world, finally slowing when she'd eaten five or six bites of the near-frozen cake. "Mmm!" Not exactly a full-fledged sentence, but close. "I like 'em this way."

I sighed, my thoughts shifting to my buns. My overly inflated sticky buns.

She gave me a funny look. "You're not having one?"

I patted my exaggerated backside. "Do I look like I need one?" I went back to work on the room, lugging boxes from one corner to another.

"I've never paid attention, to be honest. But I've also never noticed you avoiding sweets before. Are you on a diet kick or something?" Her brow wrinkled as if this very idea made her nervous. Why would she care if I lost weight? She'd never cared when I gained it.

"It's Aunt Willy."

"Aunt Willy's on a diet?" Hannah's perfectly mascaraed eyes widened. "Whoa. Never saw that one coming."

"No." I couldn't help the groan that escaped as I thought back to a recent conversation I'd had with my aunt. "I'm just saying she wants me to trim down. Maybe she thinks my hips are a distraction to the customers?"

Now Hannah looked downright angry. "Are you serious, Scarlet?" she asked. "Tell me you're not."

"I am. Serious, I mean."

"Ugh! I'd like to give that woman a piece of my mind." Hannah—all 110 pounds of her—took another cake ball and popped it into her mouth, then spoke around it. "Besides, I would think your backside would be a walking advertisement for

31

the product." She slapped a hand over her mouth, her eyes widening. After a moment she pulled her hand away and muttered, "Um, sorry. Not sure that came out the way I meant it."

"It's fine." With a wave of my hand, I dismissed her concerns. "Besides, I'm not blind. I see the image in the mirror. I'm the funny fat girl. Well, funny most of the time. Just not today. Don't really see much to laugh about, with all this work to do. But maybe it's time to change my image into something more serious." I deliberately turned my back to her so that she couldn't see the tears in my eyes.

"Fat?" Hannah's voice rang out behind me, her words laced with frustration. "Scarlet, you're not—"

"Don't say it, Hannah." I dropped a box on the table and turned to face her, my temper rising. "You'll never know what it feels like to be . . ." I bit back the word *chubby*. "According to the Wii Fit, I'm obese."

"According to the Wii Fit, *I'm* obese." She released an unladylike grunt. "You can't go by that. And who cares if you're a little . . ." Her hands waved in the air. "Fluffy."

Fluffy. Perfect word for a girl who spent her days whipping up cream cheese frosting so light and airy it could practically float like a cloud.

"When you find the right guy, your fluffiness won't matter anyway. It'll be like icing on a cupcake—just the right sweetness." She grinned and cocked a brow.

"Easy for you to say." My dieting initiative took a hike. I reached for a cake ball and shoved it down, the sugary bite causing me to offer up a deep sigh of satisfaction. Cake always made things better, especially lemon delight with fresh raspberries.

Hannah crossed her arms at her chest and glared at me. "If it really bugs you, then do something about it."

My eyes popped open, and I glared back at Hannah. "So you *do* think I'm fat."

She groaned and slapped herself on the forehead. "I can't win for losing, can I?" A frantic "how can I possibly get through to you?" conversation followed. She did all the talking. I did all the listening. Well, mostly. I spent about half the conversation eyeing a piece of carrot cake on the tray.

I wiped the sugar off of my fingers and reached for the carrot cake. "Sorry. I think I'm just bummed about being the biggest bridesmaid at your wedding. The other girls look amazing in the dress that new designer created. All of your sisters are so trim and pretty. And I look . . ."

"Perfect. And FYI, you're not a bridesmaid, you're my maid of honor. So if you want to go with a different dress, I'm okay with that, as long as it's in the same color scheme. My sisters won't mind a bit, I promise. No one will. And Gabi, the designer, is the best on the island, so I know she can make whatever we ask for."

I swallowed down the carrot cake. It did little to ease my frustrations. "Yes, but . . . don't you see? If I wear a different dress, then I'll really stand out. It'll be the three trim, fit bridesmaids and the one chubby—er, fluffy—maid of honor. The one who had to get a different dress because the one everyone else was wearing wouldn't wrap around her big"—I pointed to my bottom—"sticky buns."

"Sticky buns?" A familiar voice called out, and I turned to see Bella Neeley, Galveston's most illustrious wedding planner, entering the shop. "Are you open for business already, Scarlet? If so, I'll take a dozen sticky buns to go. Everyone in my family thinks yours are the best on the island. You can't believe how many hours we've spent talking about them. That's the primary reason we're so excited about your new shop opening. Aunt Rosa even had a great idea for how you can draw more attention to your sticky buns. I think she's going to come by and talk to you about that one day soon."

I did my best not to groan aloud. Hannah, however, seemed to find humor in Bella's remark. She busted out with a belly laugh.

Bella looked confused. "What did I say?"

"Never mind." I reached for another cake ball

and swallowed it down whole. Strangely, it didn't taste as good that way. "Let's just say my sticky buns have been a hot topic today."

Bella nodded and flashed an encouraging smile. "Well, no doubt. They're the yummiest on the island."

This really got Hannah going. She doubled over, laughing until I thought she might have to excuse herself to go to the ladies' room. Not that the ladies' room was company-ready yet.

"Mmm. Cake balls." Bella grabbed one and ate it, then joined us at the table. "What are you two girls talking about? Besides baked goods, I mean."

Hannah managed to get her giggles under control. She placed her hands on her size 6 hips and gave me a "you should know better" look. "Scarlet thinks she's fat."

"Fat?" Bella—gorgeous, trim Bella—gave me that "are you kidding me?" look that skinny people always give fat people when they're too embarrassed to admit the truth. "What brought this on, Scarlet?"

I'd just opened my mouth to say something brilliant when Hannah spoke up. "Her aunt Willy."

"She called you fat?" Bella's nose wrinkled. "Where is she? I'll give her a piece of my mind. That is, what's left of it after dealing with two small children and a wedding-planning business." She chuckled.

"She didn't call me fat. She just—oh, never mind." I took a seat and leaned my now-aching head on the table. These girls would never get it. How could they? They had never walked a mile in my size 8½ extra-wide shoes. Unless maybe they'd been to fat camp as toddlers or something. If so, they'd both seen great success—something that had eluded me during my one stint at Camp Hug-a-Belly in the sixth grade. The only thing I'd lost that summer was my CD player.

An awkward silence rose up between the three of us. Hannah gave me a pensive look. "What's really bugging you?" Her gaze narrowed. "Is it Kenny?"

I tried not to flinch as she spoke my assistant's name.

"Kenny?" Bella took the seat to my left. "The guy who works for you? What's up with him?" She glanced around the shop, no doubt wondering why she hadn't seen him. Kenny and I were inseparable, after all. Cinnamon and sugar. Peanut butter and jelly. Cookies and cream.

Stop with the food analogies!

"Yeah, why isn't he here?" Hannah leaned back in her chair. "Are you guys still taking a break or something?"

I paused to think through my answer. "Yes, but that has nothing to do with my weight. He's never cared about that, trust me. It's the farthest thing from his mind."

"Then what?" Hannah asked.

How could I tell her what I'd only recently discovered myself? That dating Kenny—kind and funny as he was—was just the filling between the layers of my proverbial cake? Our relationship wasn't the real deal. Never would be. I loved him—just not like *that*. Only, he didn't know. Working up the courage to tell him hadn't been easy. Besides, we were both distracted with the new bakery opening.

"He still works with me," I said after a moment, "though Aunt Willy's not keen on that fact. She thinks he's a . . ." What was the word she'd used again? Ah yes. "Deterrent."

"Why?"

"I don't think she likes his facial hair."

"To be honest, I'm not keen on it either." Hannah's thinly plucked brows elevated. "Didn't want to tell you, though. Thought it might hurt your feelings. Or his. So I've kept my opinion to myself." She giggled. "Till now, I mean."

"Same here," Bella added. "But it wasn't my place to say so. I think he looks a little like Shaggy from *Scooby-Doo*. Nice guy, but pretty scruffy. Not that scruffy's bad, mind you. Some people like that look, just not me." Her nose wrinkled. "Sorry. Is that too honest?"

"No, I guess not." Still, I couldn't believe they'd kept this from me. I drew a deep breath. Actually, now that I thought about it, Kenny did look a little shaggy. Rough around the edges. But I'd always found his casual outlook on life oddly endearing. "How come you guys never told me?"

Hannah shrugged. "Never came up, I guess. But I have to say I'm with Willy on this. Kenny's a great guy, but I'm not convinced he's the guy for you. So I'm cool with you guys taking a break." The edges of her lips turned up in a smile. "Not that you asked my opinion or anything."

"Or mine." Bella's cell phone beeped, and she pulled it out of her purse. "But just in case you ever wonder, I like my guys clean-cut. D.J. tried to grow a mustache once, and I made him shave it off. Scratched my lip when he kissed me."

She glanced at a text message on her phone, then lit into a conversation about how all of the men in her family were hairless—on their faces, anyway. Apparently Uncle Laz had the hairiest back in town. And her older brother had the hairiest legs. She lost me about midway into a conversation about her brother Armando, whose recent attempt at a goatee had sent the whole family into a tailspin. On and on she went, talking about how ridiculous he'd looked and how relieved they'd been when he finally shaved it off. To be honest, I felt a little sorry for the guy after hearing his woeful tale.

Bella laughed. "There I go, sharing my thoughts out loud."

"Hey, I've always offered my opinion pretty

freely," I said and then sighed. "You might as well tell me what you're thinking too."

"I'm thinking it's okay that you and Kenny are on a break." She gestured to the shop. "And I'm thinking this new place is fabulous."

Hannah didn't look as convinced. "*I'm* thinking you might be over your head trying to handle a grand opening at the same time your dad's got you working on this fund-raiser at church. But that's just me."

"Fund-raiser?" Bella glanced back down at her phone as another text message came through. "What's that about?"

I tried to look confident as I responded. "It's pretty inspiring, really. Our little church has a team going to Managua in a couple of months, and we're trying to raise money to get them there. We're doing a talent show to raise money."

"Managua?" Bella's wrinkled brow clued me in to the fact that she didn't have a clue where that was.

"Nicaragua," I explained. "Central America."

"Ah."

"Are you singing?" Hannah gave me that motherly look she'd become famous for.

I snorted. "Seriously? You think I should sing?"

Bella looked up from her phone. "Wait. You sing, Scarlet?"

"No. Absolutely, definitely not. Ever. Under any circumstances."

Hannah rolled her eyes. "You used to sing all the time. Your mom told me all about it."

I shrugged. "That was years ago, girl. Some things are better left . . . unsung."

"Or maybe it's just time for a new verse. I have a feeling you could come up with a doozy." Bella waggled her brows. "Give it some thought."

"Right now the only thing I'm giving thought to is getting someone to help. There's so much going on in my brain at one time." I lit into an emotional saga about all of the things still left undone, both at the shop and at the church. My dissertation included a passionate cry for help with the technical aspects of the fund-raiser.

"Oh, I've got the perfect person to help you." Bella clasped her hands together and grinned—a rather suspicious grin, actually. "With the fund-raiser, I mean." She crossed her arms at her chest, a smug look on her face. "My brother Armando."

"The one with the goatee?"

"He shaved that off. He's clean as a whistle now."

"And he does sound?" I asked.

She nodded. "And lights too. And all sorts of other things. He lives in Houston. Works at a . . ." A long pause followed. "Anyway, he's really good at what he does."

"What does he do for a living?"

"Well . . ." She paused and seemed to be thinking through her answer. "A little of everything. Sort of a jack-of-all-trades, I guess you'd say. He's great with technical things. He's worked as a deejay and a sound guy. And he's worked at a music store too. Oh, and he had a job once at a computer repair place, so he even knows how to program music for churches. Right now he's going from place to place running sound and working parties."

Hmm. A jack-of-all-trades. Just what we needed.

"I think you'll like him." She grinned. "He's pretty savvy. And churches these days are looking for people like that to run their sound and lights."

"I've been trying to get my dad into the twenty-first century." I sighed, thinking about how antiquated our little church was compared to others I'd visited. How stuck in the seventies we were. How I'd been dying to introduce my father to things like PowerPoint slides on the overhead screen and cool lighting during worship. So far he'd turned up his nose at every idea, though I had a feeling his real concerns had more to do with cost than moving into the twenty-first century.

"My brother will be perfect for you."

I gave Bella a look, and she put her hand up. "I—I mean for your church. For the fund-raiser. And we're always looking for an excuse to get him back on the island. Mama misses him."

"Ohhh, I remember Armando," Hannah said. "He's really . . . handsome." A concerned look passed over her face, a sure sign there was more to this guy than either of these two was willing to admit. Oh well. I needed an Italian heartthrob running sound at my dad's church about as much as I needed the calories from a bacon double cheeseburger.

My stomach rumbled at the thought of food. A bacon double cheeseburger did sound really good.

"Didn't I meet your brother at Hannah's Bing and Bob party last fall?" I asked.

Bella shrugged. "You met the rest of the family but not Armando. He was supposed to come but didn't show up at the last minute."

"Sounds like a great guy." I fought the eye roll that threatened to convey my real feelings. Seriously? A guy who makes promises and then doesn't keep them? No thank you.

Her nose wrinkled. "What he lacks in manners, he more than makes up for in talent. I think you'll like him, and I know he would be an asset."

"Oh, I'm sure."

"He's come a long way since I first met him," Hannah said.

Translation: He had a long way to come.

"God has really softened Armando's heart," Bella added. "And I'm so proud of him."

Well, that sounded a little better.

"He's a real heartthrob," Hannah added, then quirked a brow. "You're gonna flip when you see him. I—I did." Her cheeks turned pink.

Wait a minute. It was all coming back to me now. I seemed to remember some incident involving Hannah and Armando. Hadn't he hit on her once? Back before she started dating Drew? Then again, he had changed, or so they said. And apparently both of my friends were keen on playing matchmaker today. On and on they went, singing Armando's praises.

I groaned as their attempts to match me up with Bella's brother carried on. In the back of my mind, I tried to imagine Aunt Willy's response to all of this. No doubt she would send him packing. Or insist that I marry him at once, should he be clean-shaven and hardworking.

Regardless, I would keep my distance from the guy. From everything I'd heard, he was nothing but trouble.

4

Walking on Eggshells

A compromise is the art of dividing a cake in such a way that everyone believes he has the biggest piece.

Ludwig Erhard

I've always loved my assistant, Kenny. Well, not loved him in the "till death do us part" way, but I've adored his work ethic, his humor, and his amazing talent with cakes. I've especially admired his ability to keep me going when I felt like giving up.

Take opening day, for instance. For over seven hours, Kenny and I worked side by side, giving away free samples by the dozens. Thanks in part to his humorous sales pitches, we sold dozens of cookies, over seventeen cakes, and more sticky buns than should be allowed by law. We also sold éclairs, pinwheels, and several dozen cupcakes. I'd never seen so much sugar pass through my hands.

Finally, around 4:30 in the afternoon, the crowd thinned and we were left alone. I began a conversation about Hannah's upcoming wedding, and Kenny chatted incessantly, clearly enthused and fully on board. Just one more reason why I loved him—he always supported me, no matter what.

Why, then, couldn't I love him in the way he seemed to love me? And when would I have the courage to tell him face-to-face?

Staring into his baby blues, I shot a silent prayer heavenward, asking the Lord to provide just the right opportunity.

I'd tried to fall in love with Kenny—convinced myself I could if I worked at it. But those feelings never came. Brotherly love, sure. The romantic stuff . . . not so much. Our few dates outside of the bakery had been awkward at best. Surely he could see that. He was probably trying to work up the courage to break my heart. I hoped.

I paused to look at his shaggy hair and scruffy face. Okay, so maybe Bella was right. He did look a little like the guy from *Scooby-Doo*. Still, Kenny would make some lucky girl a wonderful husband. More than wonderful. His dedication and passion for life would surely make her the happiest woman in the world, and his steady, consistent faith would make her feel secure in every sense of the word.

Reliable.

Steady.

Kenny.

Except right now I didn't want his version of

reliable and steady. Felt more like boring. Predictable.

Right away, shame washed over me. How could I possibly hurt a guy who had everything going for him? One who adored me, no less?

I spent the next hour trying to fall in love with him. I tried as I watched him wash the pans, steam billowing up around him from the hot water. I tried as I watched him pull a tray of cake samples out of the freezer. I tried extra hard when his long, shaggy hair fell into his eyes while he talked to a customer.

Still, I could not love him. Not like that. And I had to tell him—soon. Before he planned our honeymoon and named our children.

When the crowd thinned, I finally worked up the courage.

"Kenny?"

He glanced up from the register. "Would you believe we've made over nine hundred dollars today?"

"No way. Aunt Willy will be happy." I paused. "Look, I've been wanting to talk to you about—"

"And I heard one lady say that she was coming back tomorrow with her Bible study group. They're going to do their weekly study here. Isn't that cool?" He beamed. "We'll be a bakery and a ministry. God is so good." He got wound up, talking about how blessed he felt to be working alongside me. How this bakery could change lives for the better, sweetening not just the tongue but the spirit as well.

I sighed, not because of anything to do with God's goodness but because I felt so ashamed. He was such an awesome guy. Why couldn't I love him?

Oh well. Maybe tomorrow would be a better day to tell him that I could not—would not—marry him. Then again, he'd never actually asked. But just in case he did . . . no way, no how could I spend the rest of my life with this precious, godly, amazing, talented man.

I really needed therapy.

I also needed to close up the shop. A couple of minutes before five, I headed toward the door to lock up. The front bell jingled, and I caught a glimpse of a staggeringly handsome man ascending the four steps into the bakery.

The guy could've come straight off the cover of a Hollywood magazine. From a distance, his cocoa-brown eyes appeared to sweep over me, lingering as they reached my backside, well within his view. *Dude? Are you checking out my sticky buns?* Those lips—those enviable, full lips —curled up in a seductive smile. His thick, dark hair tapered neatly to the collar of his shirt, and tendrils of hair curled on his forehead.

Wowza.

I didn't mean to stare, but looking away proved

impossible, and even more as I observed his muscular stride. I knew his type, of course. Not that I'd had a lot of experience with Latin heartthrobs, but I'd seen my fair share of *I Love Lucy* episodes. And wasn't Ricky Ricardo Latin? Didn't you have to watch out for guys who stared at you the way this fellow was staring at me right now?

The handsome stranger smiled as he drew near. "Are you Scarlet?"

"I am."

He extended his hand. "Armando Rossi, Bella's brother. She asked me to stop by to talk to you about a gig at your church." He glanced around the shop. "Great place. Smells amazing in here. And I love what you've done with the decor." He flashed a white-toothed smile. "It's strange, but I always notice how a place is laid out. Probably because our family's been in the restaurant business for so long. You've done a great job."

"Thanks." I gestured to the near-empty cases. "I wish you'd been here earlier. Those were full this morning."

"Wow. You've sold a lot, then."

"Yeah, we had an amazing first day. Just a few things left."

He walked over to the case and stared down at a tray of double chocolate walnut brownies. "Almost looks good enough to eat."

"Here, I'll get you one. On the house, I mean."

I scurried behind the case, came out with the largest brownie, and put it on a plate.

Armando took a bite, and a look of pure satisfaction came over him. He sank into a chair and gobbled down the rest, his eyes now closed.

"Mmm. Tastes great." His eyes popped open as he finished, and I took a seat next to him.

"Thanks. I love to bake."

"Well, keep it up. If that's any indicator, this place will be a hit."

"Aw. Thank you." I relaxed, suddenly wondering why I'd prejudged this guy. He seemed great.

Out of the corner of my eye, I watched as Kenny entered the room from the kitchen. He stood, shoulders squared, fists clenched, as if ready to take this fellow down. But why? Kenny certainly had nothing to worry about. This Italian heartthrob wasn't here to marry me, after all—just to talk about running sound at my dad's church.

Still, from the look on Kenny's face, Armando had better watch his back. The two might end up in a boxing match.

I did my best not to chuckle at the image that presented. After all, Armando was taller, buffer, and . . . well, pretty much everything-er. Poor Kenny wouldn't stand a chance should a scuffle ensue. He could always utilize his cell phone to call for backup, but by the time help arrived, Armando would've squashed him like a bug.

From the looks of things, anyway.

My thoughts gravitated to a particular *I Love Lucy* episode—the one where Lucy tried to make Ricky jealous. That hadn't ended well. I had a feeling this wouldn't either.

Pushing my errant thoughts aside, I took in the handsome stranger. As I leaned closer, his cologne—*Yum! What is that?*—grabbed me and held on like a cowboy on a bronco. He began a conversation about the upcoming fund-raiser, which morphed into a full-fledged chat about my church, which transitioned into a conversation about life on Galveston Island.

At about this point, I was convinced God had sent Armando to me as a gift not just for the church but for me personally. Gorgeous. Suave. Sexy. Pure perfection.

Or not.

Turned out he had a sarcastic side. As the conversation transitioned, I picked up on a lot of attitude, particularly when we got to talking about life on the island. He wasn't a fan of island living and enjoyed poking fun at those who were.

What's up with that? How can I marry you if you won't live here with me?

He began to share about how he preferred Houston to living on the Gulf coast. As he turned the conversation back to the fund-raiser, as he rolled his eyes and went on and on about how dreadful it would be to have to spend so much time in Galveston if he helped out, I pretty much decided I'd rather work with anyone *but* him.

So much for thinking I might be a good match for your brother, Bella. Forget it.

I shook my head, unable to make sense of his ramblings. With such sarcasm eking out of him, he suddenly looked ugly to me. Deep down ugly, I mean.

"Why don't you want to live on the island?" I asked after his lengthy tirade about the island. "Why Houston?"

He gave me a pensive look. "How long have you lived here?"

"Since my father took the church. About six years. We moved down from Lufkin."

"Lufkin?" He snorted.

"What about it?"

"Nothing. Kind of . . . in the woods, right?"

Are you calling me a hick?

"Lufkin is a great little town," I said. "But I'm happy to live on the island now. I find it very exciting."

He folded his arms at his chest and leaned back in the chair. "Sounds like something a typical tourist would say, which just confirms that you haven't been here long. Otherwise you'd be dying to get *off* the island, not on."

Okay, I felt like slapping him at that proclamation. Six years of living on the island did not a tourist make. And I certainly had no aspirations to leave. Still, I could see the determination etched in his brow. This guy wasn't going down without a fight. Fine. I'd give him a fight.

I opened my mouth to speak, but he interrupted me. "You'll see." He sighed and looked at the glass cases. "It gets old after a while."

I couldn't imagine it. How could hanging out at the beach ever get old? How could working on the Strand, the coolest historical street in the universe, get old? How could spending time with people like Bella and Hannah—doing the thing I loved, no less—get old?

"You've got to be kidding me," I argued. "The sound of the waves hitting the shore? The smell of the saltwater? The families gathered at Stewart Beach under beach umbrellas?" Those images had forever imprinted themselves on my mind, and I loved them.

"Whatever." He released another sigh, and his gaze traveled back to the glass cases. I could see him eyeing the cheesecake but pretended not to notice.

You don't deserve any cheesecake, mister. And if I could take that brownie back, I would.

I shifted the conversation to the fund-raiser, now all business. Out of the corner of my eye, I watched Kenny again. He was looking more handsome by the moment, shaggy or not. Good, solid, reliable Kenny. Marriage material.

My suddenly handsome assistant hovered closer than a helicopter coming in for a landing—and was about as subtle. At least two or three times I caught him, mop in hand, bumping into Armando's chair. Accident? I think not. And the huffing sound he made after Armando's dissertation about church life left little to the imagination as well.

Perfect.

"So." Armando stretched, showing off his biceps. I did my best to avoid looking. "Tell me why I should do this thing at your church? Talk me into it." He looked at the white chocolate raspberry cheesecake again. "Because, frankly, church stuff is not exactly high on my list of exciting things to do."

How could this guy be related to the Rossis? No way. They were kind. Fun-loving. Godly. Full of enthusiasm for life. Crazy about all things Galveston. He was . . . ugh. Not my type, for sure.

Time for a distraction. I dove into a lengthy discussion about the fund-raiser, doing my best to sing the praises of our little church—our precious, sweet church—but I seemed to lose him about halfway into it. He rose and walked over to the glass counter, now staring at the few remaining products inside.

You know that line in *Jerry McGuire* where the girl says, "You had me at hello"? Well, I'm pretty sure I had this guy at white chocolate raspberry cheesecake. The boy stared through the glass at the display of cakes I'd just set up and practically drooled all over himself. Fine. I knew his type. If I couldn't win him over with my charms, I'd get him with my sweets. Before the day ended, he would plan to run the sound at our event. A belly full of homemade cheesecake would do the trick. I hoped.

I rose and walked behind the counter. "You like cheesecake?" I asked.

"Yeah, my aunt Rosa—"

"Oh, I know all about your aunt Rosa's cheesecake. I've tasted it firsthand. She's great. Probably the best ever."

"Big of you to admit," Armando said.

I hated that he'd called me big. Probably just a slip on his part. Still, it didn't set well with me. "I come in a close second," I managed after a couple seconds. "If you don't mind my saying so. Want a piece?"

"At six dollars a slice?" He smirked. "Why would I pay that kind of money when I can go home and get Aunt Rosa's for free?"

I wasn't sure which struck me as odder—the fact that he assumed I'd charge him, or the idea that he still considered the Rossis' house his home. Biting back the words, "So, Galveston is your home after all?" I pulled out the cheesecake, cut a large slice, and plopped it onto a plate.

"I'll give this to you on one condition." Lifting

the plate, I held it just under his nose, close enough where he could drool all over it.

"Let me guess." He rolled his eyes. "You'll swap out the cheesecake for my work at the church?"

"Mm-hmm." I nodded, then pulled the plate away and set it on top of the glass case. "Your decision."

He stared at the plate for a moment and folded his arms at his chest. Seconds later he grabbed the slice and shoveled a big bite into his mouth, a dreamy expression on his face. "Mmm." He took another bite. Then another. About five bites in, he gave me a sheepish look. "This might very well turn out to be the most expensive piece of free cheesecake I ever ate."

"Yep." It might, at that. I planned to work him hard over the next few weeks. He would earn that piece of cheesecake, no doubt about it. And hopefully, somewhere along the way, I would find it in my heart to tolerate the guy.

5
Cream of the Crop

Inside some of us is a thin person struggling to get out, but they can usually be sedated with a few pieces of chocolate cake.

Author unknown

The following Saturday afternoon, I left Kenny—sweet, shaggy Kenny—in charge of the bakery so that I could slip away to meet Armando at the church. No point in delaying the inevitable. We had to put a plan into action, and I needed this guy's help.

We would put on a great talent show, fully decked out with lights, sound, and all other technical necessities. The community would be wowed. My dad would see the value of twenty-first-century living, and Armando . . . well, Armando would be forced to spend quality time with godly people who—I prayed—would do more than tolerate him. Perhaps if we handled ourselves in a proper manner, he could be won over, not just to church people but to a renewed faith.

If I could stand being around him.

As I drove to our little church, I spent time

praying. Surely the Lord would change my heart regarding this guy. How else could we do this if I couldn't tolerate spending time with him?

I pulled up in front of the church and saw a red sports car sitting there. Quite a contrast—that fancy, newer-model car in front of our tiny, worn-out building. As Armando climbed out and glanced my way, I could see the curious expression on his face.

"Not quite what you were expecting?" I asked as I walked in his direction.

He shook his head. "Nope. My parents go to the Methodist church. It's huge."

"Yeah. Lots of people are into those big churches. But we've always had a thing for smaller ones. Makes for a more intimate setting."

I regretted those words the minute his brows elevated.

"Well, more intimate in the spiritual sense," I added.

"Of course." He gave me a curious look. "But why would you want it to stay small? Doesn't that sort of defeat the whole 'get them in the door and lead them to the Lord' thing?"

"Oh, I'm not saying we want it to be small forever. Just saying that's how it's been. We're used to it. It's . . . comfortable." The word *comfortable* wasn't spoken as a death sentence, but it somehow felt that way.

"Is there something I should know?" he asked.

"Some reason why people don't like to come here?"

I did my best not to sigh. "Those who do come love it, and they love the close-knit community. I think more people would be interested if we updated a few things. We'll just leave it at that."

"Ah." He followed on my heels as I walked to the door leading to the side hall. I used my key, but as always, the lock gave me fits. After a couple moments of watching me struggle, Armando took the key and forced the lock to budge.

"I did a little stint as a locksmith," he explained.

"Oh." *Is there anything you haven't done?* I thought about Bella's description of him—how she'd called him a jack-of-all-trades—but quickly shut down my train of thought before it derailed the conversation.

"You ready to get to work?"

"Sure." He hesitated, and his gaze shifted to the ground. "But just one thing first."

"What's that?"

He glanced back up, a boyish smile on his face. "Did you bring any of those brownies with you?"

Now it was my time to quirk a brow. "Who wants to know?"

He shrugged. "I'm just saying . . . the way to a man's heart is through his stomach."

Yeah, and I want your heart about as much as I want a lobotomy.

Thank God I hadn't spoken the words aloud, though the temptation to do so gripped me like a vice. He stared at me with those dark brown puppy dog eyes, eyes so filled with love—for brownies, of course—that I had no choice but to come up with something kind to say.

When in doubt, employ a teaser.

"We'll just have to wait and see what I brought with me." I gave a little shrug. "Patience, my friend."

Not that he was really my friend.

"I can tell you one thing you've brought." He pointed at me. "You realize you're still wearing your apron from the bakery, right?"

"I took off from work in such a hurry that I didn't notice," I explained. "Sometimes I wear this apron home from work and forget I've got it on until time to get in the shower at night."

"At least you haven't showered in it."

"Yet."

That got a laugh out of him. He pointed at a brownish smudge on the right side of the apron. "What's this?"

I stared at it for a moment. "Chocolate filling for the éclairs."

"And this?" He pointed at a lime-green smudge.

"Four-year-old's birthday cake. Turtle theme. I went a little crazy with the lime-green shells, but it turned out okay. The mother liked it better than the son did, I think."

"That's probably a good thing, since she's the one who paid for it." He pointed at the pocket on my right side. "And this?"

I gasped as I noticed a bright blue stain oozing through. "Ugh." I reached inside my pocket and pulled out a bottle of fondant coloring gel. "Now how did that get in there?"

He shook his head. "I don't even want to know, but it's a great color on you. Matches your eyes."

Sure it does. My eyes are—Oh wait, they were blue. Just not that shade of blue. Still, if the guy was trying to flirt, he certainly knew how to go about it.

"Baby shower cake," I said after a moment's thought. "Little boy. Obviously."

"Ah." He stared into my face so intently that I felt the temperature in the room go up by two or three degrees. "You really love what you do, don't you?"

"Well, of course. Don't you?"

He laughed—not a "well, of course I do" sort of laugh, but more of a "you have no idea how far off base you are" kind.

I led the way into the church, half curious about his reaction to our worn-out building and half proud mama hen. My comments shifted from "This is the room where I teach the three-year-olds" to "This is our makeshift office" to "This is the fellowship hall. I know it's small, but it cleans up nice for weddings."

"Weddings?" That seemed to stop him cold. "You do weddings in a place this size?"

"Well, yeah." I paused to think it through. "I mean, obviously not the kind of weddings you guys do at Club Wed. These are really scaled down. A lot of people in our church are from low-income families. They couldn't afford a wedding at your place."

Oh, ouch. Talk about a slap in the face.

I backpedaled as quickly as I could, shame washing over me. "I'm sorry. I didn't mean anything by that."

"No offense taken." He looked around the room, and I could read the curiosity in his expression. "I wasn't saying there's anything wrong with having a wedding here. Just wondered how you managed to fit everyone inside. Seems a little smaller than I expected, that's all."

"It's bigger than it looks. We've easily had 150 in this room."

"I see." Armando nodded. "And you make the cakes for these weddings?"

"I do."

"If they're half as good as those brownies—the ones I hope you brought with you—the wedding guests are probably in heaven."

Flattery will get you nowhere, fella.

Okay, maybe it would. I reached into my purse and came out with the Ziploc baggie holding the brownies. He took one look and his eyes bugged.

"Th-thanks." Armando grabbed the bag from my hand and opened it. A couple moments later, the same look of pure delight that I'd seen at my shop earlier in the week crossed his face. Little did he know I was prepping him for the great reveal—the soundboard. No doubt he would need a double dose of chocolate once he saw how antiquated our system was.

"Mmm. These brownies are great." He smiled, and I took note of the chocolate on his teeth. "Have I mentioned that you're a great cook?"

A wave of embarrassment washed over me. "Thanks. I've always been at home in the kitchen. Did I mention that my aunt has a famous bakery in Houston and that she's the brains behind this venture?" Well, maybe not the brains, but certainly the pocketbook.

"Bella told me something about that. She mentioned that your aunt is a little scary."

"Yeah." I sighed. "But she's a great baker and taught me a lot as a kid. I've always loved making cakes and cookies. I also had lots of one-on-one time with my mama when I was growing up. She's pretty savvy in the kitchen too."

"You're an only child?"

"Yep."

"Lucky."

"I am?" Strange, I'd never considered myself lucky being an only child. In fact, I'd always longed for a sister, which was why I'd taken my friendship with Hannah so personally. "Why do you say that?" I asked after a moment.

He rolled his eyes. "Trust me, growing up in a houseful of brothers and sisters is highly overrated, especially in the Rossi family."

"What do you mean?"

He shrugged, then glanced my way. "Let's just say I never quite measured up to the others and leave it at that."

In that moment, I saw a hint of pain in his expression. I almost felt sorry for him but couldn't figure out why.

"In a family like mine, you are constantly compared to the others," he added. "Sibling rivalry is one thing, but favoritism is another."

"I see." Only, I didn't. Not really. *Did I mention I'm an only child?*

He carried on, passion lacing his words. "Trust me when I say that I wasn't good in sports, I couldn't cook like my older brother, I couldn't manage a business like Bella, et cetera, et cetera, et cetera. Do you want me to go on?"

I had a feeling he would anyway, so a response seemed futile.

His jaw tensed. "I'm not as good as the rest, at least as far as my parents are concerned." Those chocolate-brown eyes of his clouded over. Well, not literally, but I could definitely see the angst written there.

"They said that?"

"Not in so many words." He took another nibble of the brownie. "Don't know what started all that. That's not why you brought me here." He gave a little shrug, and I could read the embarrassment in his eyes. "I think we're supposed to be looking at the sound system, right?"

"Right. Are you ready?" I asked after he popped the final bite of brownie into his mouth.

"As ready as I'll ever be." He licked his fingers clean, then shifted the baggie from one hand to the other. I took it from him and carried it to the trash can, chattering all the way. For whatever reason—probably nerves—I said something about Lucille Ball. That led to a story about my favorite *I Love Lucy* episode, which in turn led to a conversation about my infatuation with all things Lucy.

"So, this fascination with Lucy . . . is that why you dye your hair red?"

"What do you mean, dye my hair red?" I batted my eyelashes and played innocent. "And it's auburn, thank you very much. But how did you know it wasn't my natural color?"

Armando quirked a brow. "I have sisters, remember?" He pointed to my part. "Besides, your roots are showing."

Okay, now I wanted to smack him with the back of my hand. How dare he point out my roots? I opted to keep the conversation going instead of punching the guy's lights out.

"For your information, Lucy had tenacity. Did you know that she was in dozens of movies before anyone even knew who she was? She was always the funny girl. The one in the background. But she was never really seen as a great beauty."

Armando looked duly shocked. "Then you clearly have nothing in common with her."

"I . . . I . . . well, anyway, she worked hard to become known as a professional in her industry, and I work hard too."

"I see that. In fact, you work harder than anyone I've ever met."

"Please. Have you met your own family? The Rossis are known across the state for their work ethic."

He mumbled, "Not all of the Rossis," then rolled his eyes again. Seemed like he'd been doing a lot of that today.

"What do you mean?"

"Nothing." He paused. "It's just that my parents don't really take my work seriously."

"What do you do?"

"I run sound at a club in Houston."

"Ah."

"See? You don't take me seriously either."

"I never said that. I have great respect for people who know how to do technical stuff like sound. My dad is always struggling to get people to work in the sound booth on Sunday mornings. Not a lot of people know how to run the

65

board, so I always admire someone who does."

"What kind of board?" he asked.

I shrugged. "I'm clueless. But I'd be happy to show you, if you're ready to see it."

"Sure."

He tagged along to the sanctuary. I pushed the door open and stepped inside my favorite place in the world. Though small, the sanctuary still made my heart sing. I particularly loved the colorful stained-glass windows from the 1970s. With the sunlight streaming through them, they captured my imagination every time. They seemed to captivate Armando too. He paused and stared in silence at the "Feed my lambs" window. For a good thirty seconds he said nothing, then finally managed a weak "Wow."

"Wow, as in 'Wow, that's amazing!' or 'Wow, that's really cheesy'?" I asked.

"Wow, that's pretty cool." He walked over to the window and touched it, a look of innocent wonder on his face. "I love the way the sunlight comes through. Pretty amazing, actually. Never saw colors like that before."

"I love it in here in the afternoons. Sometimes I come and sit in one of the pews when no one's around, just to get inspired."

"Inspired? For your cakes?"

"Yep. Well, for the colors I plan to use in the fondant or frosting. And I like to pray in here. It's quiet and . . ." I shrugged. "Holy."

"Holy." He repeated the word as if trying to make sense of it and then grew silent. So silent, in fact, that the same holiness I'd alluded to suddenly enveloped the room.

Must've been too much for him. Either that, or he didn't feel it like I did.

"So, where's this sound booth?" Armando glanced around.

I turned on my heels toward the back of the room. "Back here. Follow me." I led the way to the small sound area in the back of the sanctuary, bracing myself for the inevitable.

He glanced at the little table and then looked to his right and left as if expecting something more. "This is it?"

"Yeah." I sighed.

"Where's the projector?" He pointed up to the ceiling.

"Don't have one."

"Really?" This seemed to leave him more perplexed than ever. "Well, where's the light-board, then?"

"Don't have one of those either."

He slapped himself in the head and muttered something under his breath. "So, you're doing a show without any form of audiovisual except sound?"

When I nodded, he glanced down at the one thing we did have—the soundboard—and flinched. "*This* is your soundboard?"

"Uh-huh." Not much, but it was all I could come up with.

"So, this board . . ." He pointed and wrinkled his nose, a sure sign that he didn't approve. "How long have you had it?"

I shrugged. "It came with the church, and we've been here for six years."

"Obviously it's older than six years. Trust me, I've seen just about everything, and I've never seen anything like this. In my lifetime, anyway." He reached to brush some dust off of one of the levers. "How old is the church building?"

"I think it was built in '71."

"Mm-hmm." He shook his head and reached for a knob, which pulled off in his hand. "I'd say that's about how long this has been here. And I'd be willing to guess they bought it used."

"Seems to work okay. We hear my dad just fine on Sunday mornings." I paused to think about that, then realized I'd better admit the whole truth, not just part of it. "Well, except for that weird shrieking noise every now and again. But we've gotten used to it, to be honest. The microphone is kind of lousy. It's taped together."

"Yep. Noticed that." He rolled his eyes.

"Hey, don't blame me. I told my dad to get one of those wireless things, but he doesn't want to spend the money."

Armando continued to examine the soundboard.

"Sometimes you have to spend money to make money."

"Well, we're not in the moneymaking business," I argued. "So I guess that doesn't really apply in our case, right?"

"But you're trying to raise money to get these kids to Nicaragua, right?" He stared into my eyes. "That's the point? To raise funds to take them halfway across the world?"

"Well, Nicaragua isn't exactly halfway across the world," I said. "But yeah."

"And you're counting on this talent show—this show with no lights, no visuals, and lousy sound—to provide the money for a trip that will take food, clothing, and other essentials to poor children in another country. Isn't that what you said?"

"Glad you've got the whole picture. And yes. The answer is yes." I placed my fists on my ever-expanding hips and sighed. "I get it. We're in bad shape." For once I wasn't referring to my sticky buns, though all of this angst was certainly making me ache for something sweet to eat. A few cake bites would be good right about now. Wash away this problem. Right?

He gave me one of those "you're too stupid to get this, but I'm going to say it anyway" looks. "Okay, well, I'm telling you that this sound system won't cut it. You can't expect people to put on a show if they're not able to be heard. And it wouldn't make any difference if you had great wireless mics or not, with a board like this." He went to work flipping switches and yanking levers.

"Hey, be careful with that. You're going to break—" I didn't get to finish the sentence because one of the levers snapped off in his hand. Probably should've warned him it'd been loose for a while.

He rolled it around in his hand and shook his head. "I have a board I can bring in for the night, but you need to look at getting a new one for the church. This thing's on its last leg."

I did my best not to sigh.

One of the boys in our youth group, a kid named Devon, approached. I knew he'd come to help the other teens with fund-raiser materials, but I cringed as I introduced him to Armando. No telling who would be the worst influence here— Devon with his street smarts, or Armando, the self-proclaimed bad boy. Though twenty years apart in age, they probably had a lot in common, starting with attitude.

"Dude. Like your tat." Armando pointed to the serpent tattoo on the teen's upper arm.

"Thanks." Devon shrugged. "Got it after my sister was killed."

"Your sister was killed?" The concern in Armando's voice was palpable. "What happened?"

"Her boyfriend was driving."

"And?"

Devon shrugged. "Don't get me started, okay? Not sure you want to hear my version. Or anyone's version, for that matter. But the guy is out walking the streets, if that makes any difference to you."

"Wow." Armando looked perplexed but didn't say anything else.

"You here to update this system?" Devon pointed to the board.

Armando grimaced. "Not sure there's any hope of that, to be honest."

Devon rolled his eyes. "Ya think? I've been telling them that for months. They won't listen to me."

I watched as Armando and Devon locked eyes. Talk about two peas in a pod. Punky, know-it-all Devon was a younger version of the older, more puffed-up Armando. Yep. They were too much alike.

Suddenly I could hardly breathe. Too much testosterone in the room.

Devon dove into a lengthy conversation about the poor conditions at our church, and I felt like a shrinking violet. After five minutes of their conversation, Devon headed off to the office to help some of the other teens put together a brochure for the fund-raiser.

Armando's phone beeped. He glanced down at it for a moment and then looked my way.

"Everything okay?" I asked.

"Yeah. It's just Bella." He typed something into his phone "The family is meeting for lunch. She wants to know if we'll meet them at Casey's."

"We?"

"Yeah, we. As in you and me."

Now, I loved Casey's as much as the next girl, but I couldn't figure out why Bella Neeley would include me in a family dinner, unless perhaps she saw this as some way to match me up with her brother. Little did she know I couldn't stand the guy.

Forget it, girl. He's definitely not my type.

My stomach growled, and Armando stared at me as if waiting for an answer. "I'm not exactly dressed to go out. And besides, my aunt Willy is stopping by to pick up a key to the bakery." *So she can come and go as she pleases and pretty much control my life even more than she does now. But you probably don't need to know all of that.* I smiled.

"You look fine."

I paused to think it through. "Maybe Willy could swing by Casey's and get the key from me. She probably won't mind."

"Invite her too."

"Oh no." I shook my head—maybe a little too hard. "No way. You don't want her there, trust me."

He didn't look convinced. "The whole family is

going. What's one more? My parents won't mind a bit, I promise. They love it when lots of people show up."

"You don't understand. Aunt Willy is a piece of work."

"How so?"

I pondered my response. "Well, for one thing, she's pretty bossy."

"Sounds like my aunt Rosa."

"She's got some . . . issues."

"Like?"

"She wants to rule the world?" I offered a weak smile. "Honestly, she's not that bad. I guess you would say she's a little eccentric."

"Have you met my family?" His right eyebrow elevated.

"Yeah. But no one in your family has the same sorts of issues."

"I'm sure it'll be fine. Just call her on the way." He headed toward the door, clearly in a hurry to leave.

Tagging along behind him, I muttered, "I . . . I guess."

Wait. Had I just agreed to join them? Really?

"Want to ride with me?" he asked, glancing back over his shoulder at me.

"Sure."

Well, I thought I was sure until I got a closer look at his vehicle—a microscopic sports car barely big enough for one, let alone two.

Houston, we have a problem.

When the girl was bigger than the car, a few mathematical calculations had to take place so that said girl could enter said car. I mean, if x is larger than y, then y becomes, "Why me, Lord?"

Or not. Somehow I managed to squeeze into the metal contraption, though I felt like a whole dill pickle in a teensy-tiny jar meant to hold only those little hamburger slices. Thank goodness Armando put the top down. Otherwise I might've drowned in pickle juice.

Okay, slight exaggeration. The convertible did make for a fun drive along the seawall. After a few moments I found myself relaxing. *See, Scarlet? You might shop in the plus-size department, but you can have normal-size fun.*

Sort of. With my chubby thighs pulled up to accommodate the lack of legroom, my circulation got a little iffy. Oh well. There would be plenty of time to circulate later. I still had a call to make. A very important call.

Seconds later I had my auntie on the line.

"What's all that noise?" her high-pitched voice shrieked in my ear. "I can barely hear you."

"I'm in a convertible," I hollered back.

Armando shifted gears, and the car jolted forward at a faster speed. The wind caught my hair and whipped it into my face.

"Blasted convertibles," my aunt said. "Waste of money, if you ask me."

I didn't, but that's not the point.

"When you pay that much for a car, it should at least have a roof on it."

I quickly filled her in on my lunch plans, but she balked . . . until I mentioned the name of the restaurant. I had her at the word *Casey's*. Turned out it was her favorite place for stuffed crab. She agreed to stay for lunch, saying something that sounded like, "Well, a girl's gotta eat, I suppose. Might as well stop by. But don't expect me to be social."

I never do.

We ended the call, and I cringed as I thought about Willy joining the Rossi gang for a family lunch. No doubt she would have everyone's nerves on edge by the end of the meal.

"She's coming?" Armando asked as I shoved the phone back in my purse.

I nodded and wondered when—or if—the feeling would return to my legs.

We arrived at Casey's minutes later, and I faced the awkward challenge of getting out of the pickle jar without humiliating myself. Thank God Armando turned to face the seawall for a minute to watch a surfer. I somehow managed to ease my way out, though the lack of circulation proved to be problematic when I attempted to stand.

Oh. Help.

After a moment, the feeling in my legs returned,

and I offered a brave smile just as Armando turned to face me.

Slick move, Scarlet. Sneaking out before he could offer to help you.

Not that I was sure he would've helped me, but whatever. We headed to the door, and I smiled as I saw the whole Rossi clan seated just inside. They waved—a welcoming, loving wave—and I entered the restaurant, half excited and half terrified to see what the Lord had in store for me.

6

Suh-weet!

I tried to commit suicide by sticking my head in the oven, but there was a cake in it.

Lesley Boone

Only two words come to mind when I think of Casey's seafood on the seawall: yum and double-yum. It's one thing for a chubby girl to control her tendency to overeat while at a restaurant she barely tolerates; it's another thing altogether to control herself at a restaurant she absolutely adores. And with stuffed crab on the menu, who stood a chance? Not me. Oh well. I could diet another day. So what if Armando saw me enjoying my food? It wasn't like he noticed me.

We approached the Rossi family table together, which garnered a "well, what do we have here?" look from Armando's mother. She glanced at my apron—*Shoot! Did I really forget to take off my apron?*—and offered a confused smile. I pulled off the apron, and my gaze traveled around the table. Bella. D.J. Bella's parents. Aunt Rosa. Uncle Laz. Bella's older brother—what was his name again? His wife, Marcella, who ran the florist shop. Bella's younger sister with her newborn. The sister's husband.

Yep. I pretty much knew everyone in attendance.

Well, all but one. An older fellow seated next to D.J. threw me a little. He certainly didn't look like he fit into the group, but I couldn't avoid his genuine smile. It lit up the restaurant.

As I took a seat next to Bella, she made quick introductions. "Scarlet, this is D.J.'s uncle Donny from Splendora."

"Splendora?" Now that certainly got my attention. I faced him, unable to hide my enthusiasm. "We're practically neighbors. I used to live in Lufkin, just north of there by an hour or so."

"Been to Lufkin many a time!" The older fellow extended his hand. I hesitated to shake it, what with the oil under his fingernails, but did so anyway. He offered a boyish grin and lit into a conversation about life in Splendora, his thick Texas twang captivating me at once. Having lived in east Texas for years prior to my move to Galveston, I recognized a kindred spirit.

What Uncle Donny lacked in suave demeanor, he made up for in rustic good looks. The man had sort of a backwoods charm about him, and a muscular physique. Not bad for an older fellow. And he was certainly the laugh-a-minute sort.

Then I noticed an overwhelming scent. What

was that? After a moment, I recognized the smell—gasoline. Weird. Was the restaurant about to go up in flames? It took me a minute or two to realize the smell was coming from Uncle Donny. But I was too polite to ask about it.

About halfway into the lunch, the scent died down, and I found myself relaxing. Likely bored with the conversation about the upcoming wedding, Uncle Donny turned my way.

"What do you do for a living, Scarlet?" he asked.

"Oh, I'm a cake decorator."

"The best on the island," Bella chimed in. "She's making her best friend's wedding cake too." She began to share about the four-tiered wonder I planned to make for Hannah's big day. To be honest, I'd hardly had a minute to think about it, what with the new shop opening and all. But now that she mentioned it, the whole plan came flooding back over me again.

The waiter showed up to take our drink order, and Donny leaned my way, the overpowering scent of gasoline now taking my breath away. "I've always loved cake," he said. "I'll have to visit your place while I'm in town."

I lifted my napkin to my nose and pretended to dab it. "Do you enjoy shopping on the Strand?"

"Only been down it a couple a times." He ripped a piece of garlic bread in half and pressed a large piece in his mouth. "Don't get down to the island much, except to fish with D.J. Spend most of my time at my truck stop in Splendora."

Ah. Well, that certainly explained the gasoline scent.

"Ever heard of Donny's Digs & Dogs?" he asked.

I shook my head. "Donny's Digs & Dogs?"

"Yep. It's the best truck stop and hot dog stand south of Lufkin." He puffed out his chest and swallowed another piece of garlic bread. "Surprised you ain't heard of it, being from up north and all."

"Well, we've been on the island for six years," I explained. "Hardly ever get up that way anymore."

Off he went on a tangent, bragging about life in the piney woods of east Texas, his drawl now thicker than the scent of gasoline, which appeared to be diminishing the longer we were together. Or maybe I was just getting used to it. Who knew.

At that moment a familiar voice rang out. I did my best not to visibly cringe as Aunt Willy entered the room.

"Had a devil of a time finding a place to park out there." She swept the back of her hand through her wispy curls. "And with that wind blowing up such a storm, my hair must look a mess."

It did, but I would never tell her so.

"You look like a million bucks, kid. If my

opinion means anything." The words came from Uncle Donny, who rose as she came to the table and then gestured for me to move down a seat to accommodate my aunt. She looked perplexed but took my seat with a grunt. At this point he introduced himself to her, and she sneezed. Loudly.

I could only imagine what must be going through Aunt Willy's mind as she laid eyes—and nose—on Donny for the first time. I could tell from her upturned nostrils that she picked up on his scent. Then again, who wouldn't? You could smell the man coming from a mile away.

Aunt Willy didn't say anything, but the sneezing fit continued. Donny handed her a previously used tissue, which she rejected. She reached inside her Gucci bag and came out with a sterling silver tissue holder, one with her initials engraved on it.

"Nice tissue holder you've got there," Donny observed. "Where'd you get it?"

She looked down her nose at him as she said, "My assistant ordered it from Tiffany's, I believe."

"Cool." He tore off another piece of bread and shoved it in his mouth, talking around it. "Wonder if they're made in China."

"I sincerely doubt it." She turned her back to him, facing me. Her eyes widened, and I could read the disgust in them. "Scarlet, you and Bella haven't discussed Hannah's wedding without me, have you?"

"Oh no, ma'am," Bella said. "Happy to talk with you about it if you'd like, but I don't know about getting in a quiet conversation with the kids around." She gestured to Tres, her four-year-old, and Rosa-Earline, her toddler. Auntie apparently found the noise coming from the duo annoying, at least judging from the expression on her face.

"Perhaps this isn't the best time," she said. "But when you do meet, please involve me. I hate to be overlooked." She snapped her fingers to get the waiter's attention and muttered something under her breath about the poor service.

"Cain't imagine anyone could overlook you, even if they tried." The words came from Uncle Donny, who now dipped a fresh piece of bread into a mound of butter he'd created out of several previously foil-covered pats. "Just sayin'."

Auntie released a slow breath and stared him down. Though she was only half his size—give or take—I honestly feared for the man's safety. She couldn't do him any real harm, but one glance would likely scorch his soul for a lifetime.

Thank goodness D.J. turned the conversation to the upcoming wedding, which deterred Aunt Willy and turned us back to the reason for this visit in the first place—a fun family gathering with people who knew how to share love, albeit in a chaotic, crazy way. Kids fussing. Grown-ups arguing. Waiters delivering the wrong food items. Auntie complaining all the way.

Yep. Just another day in paradise.

All things considered, the meal went pretty well. Ironically, I spent most of it talking to D.J. and Armando about the church's sound issues. Aunt Willy jabbed me with her elbow a couple of times and whispered, "Get me away from this man," referring to Uncle Donny. He, on the other hand, looked like the cat that stole the cream every time he glanced Willy's way, which he did repeatedly. Go figure.

I managed to down a full plate of stuffed crabs. Armando glanced at me a couple of times as if intrigued by my willingness to shovel down so much food in front of a watching audience. Not that anyone was watching but him. And not that I cared. Okay, maybe I did.

Dude, why do you keep looking at me? Keep your eyes in your head.

After the meal ended, I passed off the spare bakery key to Aunt Willy, who bolted from the place like a woman possessed. Donny made a couple of comments about the engine in her BMW, then looked on, clearly intrigued, as she pulled out of the parking lot, driving faster than usual.

Bella and I said our goodbyes, promising to meet up again later in the week. When the crowd thinned, Armando and I were left standing in the parking lot staring at one another. For the first time it occurred to me that I'd ridden with him.

That meant I'd have to get back into the little red pickle jar and ride back to the bakery. Either that, or I'd have to jog all the way.

Nah, I'd ride in the pickle jar.

With a click of the remote, the locks popped open, and Armando opened the passenger-side door for me. With a belly full of stuffed crab, I could hardly ease my way down into the car. Had it shrunk while I was inside the restaurant? With my knees pulled up to my chest, it certainly felt smaller.

He closed my door and came around to the other side, then took his spot behind the wheel. With a squeal of tires, we headed out onto the seawall. Lovely.

Lord, surely this is not how you planned for me to go, right? I don't want them to have to send the Jaws of Life to pluck my chubby body from this tiny metal cracker box of a car. Please, Lord.

Armando turned on the radio, and a popular song blasted out. Before long I found myself humming along, more relaxed than before.

"So, what did you think of my aunt Willy?" I asked after the song ended.

He turned the radio down a little and gave me a wide-eyed look. "I'd say you were right to warn me. Kind of a scary old broad."

"Kind of." I sighed. "But it doesn't run in the family. That's good, I guess."

"Hey, we've all got weird relatives. Might as well admit it."

"Maybe, but your aunt Rosa is normal. My aunt is . . ." I bit back all of the words that tried to force their way out.

"Hold up a minute." Armando glanced in the rearview mirror and then eased into the next lane. "What makes you think for one minute that my aunt Rosa is 'normal,' as you call it?"

"She's sweet and kind and—"

He grunted. "Are you kidding me? She chases the neighbors with a broom. I thought we were going to end up in court once because of it. And she filed a lawsuit against the dry cleaner once because they messed up a blouse. The woman has a temper like you wouldn't believe. Scary." He pointed to his forehead. "See this spot right here? This is where she whacked me with a ladle night before last."

"No way."

"Definitely true. I went into the kitchen to get a soda and ended up sampling the garlic twists before they were done. She came after me and left a mark. Not the first time either. She used to chase me around the house as a kid."

"Huh?" That stopped me cold.

"Yep. And she and Laz used to have a huge argument going over Frank Sinatra and Dean Martin. The shouting matches lasted into the night."

"Arguing over Dino and Ol' Blue Eyes?" I

shuddered. "Is that a joke? Who would pick Frank Sinatra over Dean Martin?"

Armando's gaze narrowed. "Don't ever let my aunt hear you say that, okay? She'll take you down in a New York minute."

I swallowed hard. "O-okay." So maybe Rosa wasn't the soft, quaint old lady I'd pictured. Still, she was a sure sight better than my cranky old aunt, wasn't she?

Armando lit into a story about something Rosa had done in front of the camera crew during her most recent filming of her Food Network show, *The Italian Kitchen*, and I sighed. Maybe we had more in common than I knew. Maybe—just maybe—my family wasn't the only one with a token funny girl. Funny in a "gee, she's really something, isn't she?" sort of way, I mean.

My thoughts shifted back to Willy, and I almost missed Armando's next question. He caught me on the tail end of it.

"Did you grow up tied to the pew like my family?" he asked.

"Tied to the pew?" I looked his way, intrigued by the question.

"Yeah, you know—in church every time the doors were open. Forced to go to Sunday school. Sent away to church camp. You know what I mean." He gave me a knowing look, as if all of those things were something akin to serving time in prison.

"Well . . ." I paused to think through my answer. "I wouldn't say I was tied to the pew, but I did grow up in church. No one forced me to do any of those things you mentioned. I enjoyed them, actually."

"Oh." His mouth rounded in a perfect *O*. "You're one of *those* girls."

" '*Those* girls'?" I bit back the comment that threatened to erupt. "What do you mean by that?"

"A good girl." He spoke the words as if they were a curse, not a blessing.

My temper rose right away. Suddenly I didn't feel as holy as he'd implied. "Well, of course I'm a good girl. No one had to tie me to a pew to make me behave, though. For your information, I make my own decisions."

He turned off of the seawall onto Broadway, then glanced my way, obviously not believing me, if such a thing could be judged from the expression on his face. "Even though your dad's a preacher?"

"Yes. I chose to go to camp. I chose to show up on Sunday mornings. And FYI, I'm choosing to go on this missions trip to Managua. I'm looking forward to helping those kids in the orphanage."

"Of course you are." He rolled his eyes. "Say no more. I know your type."

"Fine." I turned my attention to the window, ready for this trip to come to its fateful end. We would find someone else to run sound. No problem. Maybe D.J. would do it. He seemed like a great guy. A Christian guy. Not the sort to make fun of us "good girls."

"Fine." Armando's voice trailed off behind me.

As we pulled up to the church, I thought about what he had said. Well, after the steam stopped pouring from my ears. Though I knew I should turn the other cheek—in theory, anyway—right now I just wanted to give him a piece of my mind. Instead, I somehow weaseled my way out of the pickle jar, offered him a forced smile, and took off marching toward the church.

7

Short and Sweet

Man cannot live on chocolate alone, but woman sure can.

Author unknown

Bella showed up at the bakery later that day to talk about Hannah's wedding. Well, in theory, anyway. She really wanted to grill me about my time with Armando. Go figure. Thank goodness Kenny was already gone for the day. I'd sent him off at four o'clock when he mentioned getting a haircut. Bella joined me in the back room as I put my baking pans away.

"You're being evasive, Scarlet." She crossed her arms and narrowed her gaze, as if trying to get me to open a vein and spill out every thought in my head.

"Evasive?" I shoved a stack of round cake pans in the cupboard and then focused on her. "How so?"

"You need to tell me how it went with my brother."

"He agreed to run sound for the event. He's even loaning us his soundboard. And he's talking about putting us in touch with someone who can rent out a lightboard really cheap. So I think we're good to go." I climbed down from the little step stool and offered a weak smile, knowing my words would likely not satisfy her.

"That's not what I'm talking about." She gave me a knowing look. "I'm glad he can help you with the fund-raiser, but I'm dying to know what you thought of him as a person."

Yeah, I knew, all right. She was asking, "When are you two going to get married and have a few kids?" Only, I didn't plan to ever marry him. Never in a billion years. In fact, I wasn't even sure I could make it through this fund-raiser event with him involved, though I certainly planned to try.

"As a person, he's . . ." I struggled to come up with the right words. "He's a guy."

"Well, of course he's a guy," she said. "And a handsome one at that, if you don't mind my saying so. Even more so now that he's shaved off that ridiculous goatee." She paused. "Of course, you didn't see him with the goatee, so I don't suppose you'd see the difference. But you'll have to trust me when I say you're seeing the cleaned-up version."

Hmm.

"Right. Well, Bella, I really don't think you need to try to set me up with—"

"Were there sparks?" Her eyes shimmered, and she appeared to slip away to a far-off place. "The

first time I met D.J., there were sparks. Big ones."
A girlish giggle followed. "Of course, when I met
D.J., there were all sorts of things happening at
once. We met over a misunderstanding." She dove
into the story of the day she'd met the love of her
life but lost me somewhere around the point
where she mentioned "the forever kind of love."

How could I tell her the truth without offending
her? The only sparks I'd felt around Armando
were the kind fueled by my irritation at the stupid
things he'd said just before dropping me off at
the church. Had he really called me "one of
those girls"? What was wrong with being a good
church girl, anyway? He spoke the words like
some sort of disease.

Ugh. Anger rose up inside me as I remembered
our conversation all over again. *Jerk.*

Bella continued rambling, clearly oblivious to
my true feelings. Then again, I hadn't managed to
get them out, had I?

When she paused for breath, I smiled weakly.
"I'm sorry to break this to you, Bella, but
Armando's really not my type."

Her smile faded. "What's your type?" she asked,
tiny frown lines now creasing her forehead. "Not
Kenny, right?"

I paused to think about that. "If you'd asked me
a few months ago, I might've said Kenny was my
type. He was raised in church. His parents are
good friends with my parents. We're like-minded

in every way that matters—spiritual, emotional, everything." *And certainly more suited than your brother and I will ever be.*

"Sounds like you two are a match made in heaven. Maybe I misjudged the situation." Bella shrugged. "But . . ."

"But we don't have a lot of chemistry." I paused again. "Well, as friends we do. He'll always be a close friend. And a great confidant. I know he cares about me. But there's got to be more to it than that."

"Do you mind if I tell you a story, Scarlet?" she asked. "It won't take very long."

When I shook my head, she lit into a lengthy tale about how different she and D.J. were, about how the Lord had taken their differences and used them to merge two completely opposite worlds. I didn't want to get pulled into her tale, but I found it impossible to resist. Sounded like something from a movie script.

"He's a cowboy from Splendora, and I'm an Italian girl originally from Jersey—transplanted on Galveston Island as a kid." Bella spoke with great animation. "We met by accident—at least, that's what most would say—but I truly believe it was a divine meeting." Her gaze narrowed, and she leaned forward as if to share this as a secret between the two of us.

"Wow."

"Yep. And we're as different as night and day.

Different ideas. Different denominations. Different styles. You name it. But instead of butting heads, we just learned to celebrate our differences."

"And your kids? How do you figure out which world to offer them?"

She shrugged. "They get the best of both. They have a daddy who loves NASCAR, hunting, fishing, and Texas two-steppin'. They have a mama who teaches them Italian and shares her love of great cooking. And speaking of food, they're pasta fanatics but love a good plate of barbecue too. It's really the best of both worlds."

"Lucky kids."

"*Blessed* kids. I sometimes think how boring it would be if I'd married someone my parents had chosen." She shivered. "You know I was practically engaged to someone else once upon a time, right? Tony."

"Your sister's husband? That handsome movie star lookalike with the thick, wavy hair?"

"Yep." Her nose wrinkled as if the whole idea disgusted her. "We dated for years before I met D.J. And I really, really tried to make it work. I'm not sure if I can convey just how hard I tried."

"Oh, I get it, trust me." *Kenny, I want to love you. You're such a great guy. But I just can't.*

Bella sighed. "I had a feeling you would get it. Like I said, I tried to love Tony, but in my heart I knew better. He wasn't the guy for me. I needed someone . . . different." The edges of her lips curled up in a delicious smile. "I needed D.J. He's the one I was waiting for, except I never knew it until he came into my life." She leaned in to whisper, "And by the way, I even had a chance to date Brock Benson once. Not a lot of people know that."

"W-what?" Was she serious? Brock hotter-than-the-sun Benson? Last season's *Dancing with the Stars* champion and my all-time favorite movie star? I felt faint at the very idea. Seeing him at last year's Dickens on the Strand parade had been the highlight of my life.

"It's true," she said. "I turned him down for D.J." A giggle followed. "Even the hottest guy in Hollywood couldn't compare to my backwoods hero."

Backwoods hero. For whatever reason, the words got me tickled. They also got me thinking about Uncle Donny. Though he was rustic and a little on the smelly side, there was something rather endearing about him. He was like that familiar, happy-go-lucky uncle that every family needed. The one who cracked the dumb jokes and made folks smile when they were having a bad day.

Well, not all folks. I couldn't imagine Aunt Willy smiling in his presence. Then again, I couldn't imagine Aunt Willy smiling at all.

Bella hung around another few minutes, then headed out to pick up her kids at her mom's place.

I'd just waited on my last customer at ten minutes after five when the bell at the front door jingled. I glanced across the room to see Armando entering the bakery. Ugh. He came up the stairs and crossed the room, a sheepish look on his face.

"Hey."

I kept my place behind the glass cases and muttered a bland "Hey" in response.

"Do you have a minute to talk?" He leaned against the glass, and I bit back the temptation to scold him, since I'd just cleaned it.

Instead, I put on my all-business face and kept busy. "I'm just closing up. Kind of busy right now."

He could take whatever he wanted from that phrase. I hoped he would take the hint and skedaddle.

"You here alone?" He looked around as if expecting Kenny to pop out of the back room at any moment.

"Yeah. You caught me locking up." *Take the hint, mister. Time to go.*

"I'm headed next door to help my brother out. I don't know if you heard, but Jenna's on an extended leave of absence."

"Jenna, Bella's best friend?" She'd worked at Parma John's for as long as I could remember. "Why?"

"Yeah." His brow wrinkled, and I could read the concern in his eyes. "I guess there's some sort of

95

complication with her pregnancy or something? Not sure I really understand it all, but the doctor told her she has to be on bed rest for the next two months. So I'm going to fill in while she's gone."

"Wait . . . you're working at Parma John's?" When he nodded, I said, "Meaning, you're back on the island for good?"

"Well, I'll be staying at my parents' place for a while until they don't need me. But I'll be working next door for the next couple months, at least." His gaze shifted to the ground and then back up at me. "Which is good, I guess, because I'm running low on sound gigs in Houston right now. And the lease is up on my apartment in a week, so I've been trying to figure out whether or not to stay there." He shrugged. "I usually move around a lot."

"I see." My gaze shifted to the sweets inside the refrigerated glass cases. So, the boy who hated Galveston Island was destined to return and to work next door at Parma John's. Weird.

"I don't have any gigs lined up for the next month. I . . ." He turned red in the face. "To be honest, I canceled the club gigs. I'm tired of that scene."

"You are?"

"Yeah. It gets really old. And I can't handle the smoke. Messes with my sinuses." He laughed. "I sound like an old man, don't I?"

"No. You sound like a guy who's ready for a

change of scenery." *And a change of lifestyle, from what I can gather.*

"Yeah." He flashed a dazzling smile, those sexy eyes of his sparkling. "Anyway, I wanted to stop in and say I'm sorry. I really do hope you'll forgive me."

My heart skipped a beat. I kept working but didn't look his way. Couldn't look his way. "For what?" I managed.

"For what I said earlier." He gave me a genuinely kind look. "It was really stupid, I know, but I really didn't mean anything by it. In fact, I'm not even sure why it slipped out in the first place. I hope you won't hold it against me."

"I don't hold grudges." *Unless your name is Aunt Willy, in which case I tend to hang on to my angst longer than I should. But I'm working on it.* I shrugged. "No biggie. Besides, you're entitled to your opinion. I'm entitled to mine. Let's just agree to disagree about whether good girls are a bad thing, okay?"

"They're not. I know they're not." He rested his weight against the case and groaned. "And I didn't mean to insult you. It's just that so many of the girls I've known . . ."

I put my hands up and looked him squarely in the eye. "Let's get this straight. I don't need to know anything about the girls you've known. Trust me. I can assure you I'm not like any of them, okay?"

He flinched, and I could read the pain in his eyes. "Hey, I don't know what sort of ideas you've got about me, but it's not like that. I might not've been the best Sunday school kid, but I'm not all bad. I'm really not." His injured expression left little doubt that I'd hurt his feelings.

Okay, now who was judging who?

Or would that be *whom?* I was never quite sure of that one.

"I've known a lot of girls who were . . ." He shrugged and appeared to be trying to find the right word. "Good."

"How can you make the word *good* sound so . . . bad?" I asked.

"I don't mean to. I'm honestly intrigued by people who can live right." He raked his fingers through his hair. "Anyway, I'm sorry I said it like that. Didn't mean to hurt your feelings. I'm really happy to help you with your fund-raiser. In spite of my stupid mouth, I'm not a bad guy, I promise. And not as insensitive as I come across. I like what you're doing at your church, especially when I see kids like Devon who could benefit. This whole Nicaragua trip sounds really impressive to me."

"It does?" That certainly caught me off guard.

"Well, yeah. Helping kids in a third world country? Providing meals for people? Taking eyeglasses and clothes? I like it. And I appreciate that guys like Devon are on board. He seems to be my kind of kid."

"I'm glad. He's been through a lot, so it's pretty miraculous that he's part of the group. To say he's from a rough background would be putting it mildly. From what I understand, anyway. I've never actually met his family."

"I see."

"Anyway, I'm glad you see that bigger picture. It's not just about sound and lights. It's not even just about the fund-raiser. It's about the lives that can be changed along the way."

"Right. I get that. I'm not a complete jerk." He gazed at me so intently that I broke out in a sweat. Then again, the temperature in the room had gone up a few degrees this afternoon, hadn't it? "What can I do to make it up to you, Scarlet? I'm really sorry."

I thought about his question for a moment before responding. "Actually, I do have an idea. Maybe you could help me out."

"Awesome." He looked relieved. "What?"

"Now that you're working at Parma John's again . . ."

"You want a lifetime supply of pizza?" He grinned. "Because I'm pretty sure I can arrange that. Any toppings you like. Any size."

"Well, that would be great, but I'm trying to watch my calories." *In theory, anyway.*

"Why?" He looked genuinely perplexed by this.

"I . . . I just am." *Are you completely blind or just oblivious? Dude, you've surely noticed my sticky buns.* "Anyway, I need your help." Pointing to the tray of cake samples, I smiled. "See these?"

His eyes lit up. "Yeah, I've been drooling over them since I walked in."

"Do you think your brother would mind setting them out to give to customers at the restaurant?"

"Give them away . . . for free?"

"Well, yeah. They're samples of the product. Just enough to tease potential customers and make them want more."

That seemed to worry him. "Pretty risky."

"What do you mean? They're not poisonous or anything." A nervous laugh wriggled its way out, though I tried to squelch it.

Armando reached for a sample and popped it into his mouth. "I mean, the customers probably won't get any if I'm working there. I happen to love your cake."

"You . . . you do?"

"Yeah." He gave me a playful wink. "But don't tell my aunt Rosa, okay? She's a diva cake baker, and she'd flip if she knew I actually preferred someone else's baking to hers."

"Well, it's because of your aunt Rosa that I'm nervous about asking. Your family might not be keen on helping me promote my business when she's better at baking than I am."

Armando drew so close I could smell his yummy cologne. "She's not better," he whispered into my ear. "Just so you know. You're the best. If someone held a competition today, I would vote for you."

His words sent a shiver down my spine. And judging from the "come hither" look in Armando's eyes as he backed away, he might've been talking about more than cake. Or was I just imagining that?

Obviously someone else was imagining it too. I heard the sound of someone clearing his throat. I looked up to see Kenny standing across the room, clean-shaven, with a fabulous new haircut. Wowza. *Boy, do you clean up nice, or what?*

Armando must have noticed too. He took a little step back and shoved his hands in his pockets while muttering "Hey" to Kenny, who just stared him down.

Yikes.

I looked back and forth between the two men: Kenny, the solid, stable, reliable, godly, currently unshaggy man I'd adored for years . . . and Armando, the jack-of-all-trades, the one who moved around a lot, the fellow I'd been so angry at just a few hours ago.

Strangely, I couldn't remember now why I'd been angry with him. And for whatever reason, I also couldn't seem to remember where I'd left my common sense. Back in the kitchen, maybe? Regardless, I'd better find it quick and put it to use. Without it, the layers of my proverbial cake were bound to crumble.

8

Sugar and Spice

We light the oven so that everyone may bake bread in it.

José Martí

The following Monday, Aunt Willy made another surprise visit to Galveston Island. Seeing her again so soon made me wonder who she'd left in charge of Crème de la Crème, her store in Houston. Then again, her employees jumped when she said jump, so no doubt they were doing a fine job running the place in her absence.

She entered the bakery, clearly a woman on a mission. This I could tell from the furrowed silvery brow and the look of determination in her overly made-up eyes. *Really, Aunt Willy? Liquid eyeliner? Didn't people stop using that in the eighties?*

I met her at the counter after waiting on a customer. No doubt she would appreciate my willingness to put the customer's needs ahead of her own, especially when said customer dropped eighty dollars as a deposit on a birthday cake.

I wiped my hands on my apron and offered,

"Hello, Aunt Wilhelmina. Glad to see you again."

She leaned my direction, her expression quite serious. "Scarlet."

Not exactly "Hey, I'm tickled to see you! Can we do lunch?" but it was something.

"Is everything okay?" I asked, my concern growing as I saw the frustration in her eyes.

"I need to talk to you. Is this a good time?"

I gestured for Kenny to wait on an incoming lady so I could focus. "It's fine. What's up?"

She pointed to the kitchen and then headed that way. *Am I supposed to follow you?* Apparently so. She kept going, so I chugged along on her heels, a sinking feeling coming over me. What had I done to upset her this time? Likely I'd find out. Soon.

We reached the kitchen, and she gestured for me to close the door leading to the shop, which I did. Auntie leaned her petite frame against the storage shelf and crossed her arms. "Scarlet, I need you to promise me something."

"What's that?" I asked, more than a little nervous.

I half expected her to give me instructions regarding her burial plot or something, but she went a completely different direction. "Promise me you will never marry a man."

"I—I beg your pardon?"

She shook her head. "I mean, promise you'll never marry a *typical* man. You don't need to end up tied to his checkbook, unable to go anywhere or do anything unless he gives you permission."

"Oh, well, I—"

She paced the kitchen, her thin wisps of hair bobbing up and down. "That's the last thing any woman needs, trust me."

Okay, now we weren't talking about me anymore, were we? But still, none of this made sense. If women never married and had kids, would the human race continue? Clearly not. Still, I'd better not argue the point. The way things were going in this conversation, I'd lose the argument on a technicality.

She waggled her finger in my direction. "I'm telling you this for your own good."

Personal observation: when someone says they're telling you something for your own good, they don't really mean it. They usually just need to get something off their chest.

Her expression grew even more serious. "You don't want some guy who sits around in his easy chair, chugging down beer after beer, talking about how the little woman needs to be kept in her place. A man like that will pull you into a prison you can't get out of."

"Actually, I don't know any men like that, Aunt Wil—"

"And those men who run around shirtless, trying to show off their . . . their . . . muscles." She shuddered. "They're the worst." She pointed a bony finger in my face. "Beware of any man who rides around the neighborhood in his golf cart with no shirt on."

Eew! "E-excuse me?" I managed. "Aunt Wilhelmina, I really don't think you have anything to worry about here. Most of the guys I know aren't very muscular, to be quite honest. And I don't even know any man who owns a golf cart. So your fears are in vain."

"That's not my point. And you know very well the type of man I'm talking about. You don't want that kind. So promise me you'll think long and hard before making a commitment."

"A commitment?" *Huh?* "To . . . ?"

She narrowed her gaze. "To anyone who resembles what I've just described."

I couldn't fathom who she meant. Kenny was none of those things. A far cry from it, in fact. And the only other man who'd ever paid me a bit of attention was . . . Hmm. I couldn't think of anyone.

She drew closer and lowered her voice. "Now, I don't want to stereotype, but there are some male chauvinist types out there who turn out just like the fellow I described. They might be handsome and charming as young men, but they grow into old fools. And trust me, they buy golf carts. And tackle boxes. And hunting licenses. They run around topless"—she shivered—"thinking they're muscular when they really just look ridiculous.

Trust me when I say that muscles don't look the same after sixty or seventy years of puffing them up."

She went off on a tangent, using the word *Casanova* approximately five times. Okay, six. Only when she spoke the words *Latin lover* did I really get nervous.

Casanova? Latin lover?

Oh. *Ack.*

In that moment, I realized who she'd been referring to all along. Armando Rossi. But why? What in the world had I ever done to give her the impression that I might be interested in someone like him? Crazy.

Okay, so he was a little Casanova-like. And yeah, he had great abs. That much was obvious, even with the guy fully dressed.

Not that running around shirtless was a crime, especially not on Galveston Island in the summertime. Still, he was nothing like the man she had just described. And I sincerely doubted his muscles would get saggy, even in sixty years. Okay, maybe in seventy. But I really didn't want to project that far ahead. Couldn't I just admire his physique now?

And what was up with all that male chauvinist talk? Sure, Armando had mentioned a couple of sarcastic things in passing about women working in the kitchen, but in his family, most of the women did, right? I mean, they owned a pizzeria, for Pete's sake. But what in the world had given her the idea that I might be interested in him?

Other than riding in his red sports car to lunch.

And sitting next to him at Casey's.

And working with him on the fund-raiser.

Hmm.

"Just mark my words, Scarlet," Aunt Willy said. "You don't want to grow old and bitter."

She was right about that. And if I'd ever wondered what that might look like, the example was standing directly in front of me. Only one question remained: What Casanova had jilted my aunt when she was my age? What saggy old man had once caught her eye with his shirtless muscles and arrogant charm?

Yes, someone had surely left his mark. A crazed hunter with a golf cart, apparently. Still, I had the strangest feeling she wasn't through with this lecture yet. Nope. From the look on her face, we still had a ways to go.

"And another thing," Willy continued, now pacing the tiny kitchen. "I am happy to see you develop a relationship with the Rossi family, but a kink has been added, one I had not anticipated. One that could derail my whole plan to endear your business to theirs."

"A kink?" I couldn't imagine what she meant. Had something gone wrong? Something I hadn't heard about yet? A thousand possibilities ran through my foggy brain, but none of them made sense.

"Yes." She stopped walking and looked me in the eye. "The addition of that awful . . . awful . . ."

"New pizza topping?" I tried.

"No."

"Tiramisu?" I offered. "Because I don't really see it as competition, since they're Italian and we're not."

"No." She grunted. "Scarlet, you're deliberately missing my point. I'm talking about that awful, awful man."

"Awful man?" Was she talking about Armando again? If so, why?

Auntie's expression tightened. So did her tone. "That horrid man from the country. The one who reeks of gasoline. He's the kink I'm referring to."

"Ah." So that was what we were really talking about here. "Uncle Donny."

"Yes." She rolled her eyes. "I know his type. He's a good old boy." She stressed the last three words, and her wrinkled brow shared her opinion.

"What's wrong with that?" I asked. "Good. Old. Boy. Three very positive words, I'd say."

"Not when they're strung together. You obviously don't know the type of man I'm referring to, Scarlet, which is why I felt the need to drive all the way to Galveston Island to fill you in. You need to be warned so you don't fall prey."

"Wait—fall prey? And . . . type?"

"Yes, Scarlet. Type. He's the kind of man who . . ." She shook her head. "Oh, never mind."

"No, tell me. I'm trying to understand."

She crossed her arms at her chest and stared at me. "A good old boy is anything but. He's usually a bad old boy."

"How so?"

"Scarlet, you're far too naïve."

"I am?" Was she saying that because I hadn't dated much? "It's really not my fault, Auntie. My sticky buns have been a deterrent. You've said so yourself. Besides, being naïve isn't a bad thing. May I live to be a hundred and still have some degree of naïveté. Hope I never lose it, in fact."

She'd just opened her mouth to respond when the front door jingled, and I heard a strangely familiar voice call out a twangy "Yoo-hoo! Anybody here?" from the bakery.

Aunt Willy's eyes widened, and she gasped. "Th-that's him."

Yep. It was him, all right. Uncle Donny in the flesh. The kink in our plans.

I heard Kenny greet him, and laughter rang out across the bakery as he called out for me to join them.

"See, Aunt Wil—Wilhelmina?" I said with a smile. "He's a great guy. He's a lot of fun."

She shook her head.

"Well, I can't keep him waiting. No point in being rude." I headed back out into the bakery, thinking she would follow me. She did not. Seconds later I stood in front of the glass cases with Uncle Donny's arms wrapped around me in a bear hug. He still reeked of gasoline, but in his Hawaiian shirt and khaki shorts, it wasn't as strong as before. Besides, I found myself so distracted by his tube socks and sandals that the gas smell no longer affected me.

"Scarlet, I was next door having lunch when Armando told me I needed to come by for some cheesecake. He swears it's the best on the island, even better than—" Donny grinned and pulled off his cap to run his fingers through thinning hair. "Shoot. Better not say it out loud. Rosa might find out."

"Oh? Armando told you my cheesecake was good?" I'd have to thank him later.

"Yep." Donny plopped his cap back into place, then leaned forward and stared through the glass cases. "He told me I needed to sample all of your wares and take some trays of goodies back to my place in Splendora. What do you think about them apples?"

"Really? You want to sell my baked goods in your gas station?"

He turned slowly and faced me. "Honey, Donny's Digs & Dogs ain't no gas station. Not a traditional one, anyway. It's a full-service rest stop for travelers. We've got great food, great service, and the cleanest restrooms for miles." His gaze traveled back to the glass cases. "And we're about to have the best baked goods too. If you'll make up a few trays for me to sell, that is. I think my customers are gonna love 'em!"

This managed to draw Auntie out of the kitchen. Nothing like a little business transaction to get the old gal past her fear of good old boys, even good old boys who wore funky socks and reeked of gasoline.

Funny how that smell went away after a while. I hardly noticed it anymore.

Uncle Donny took one look at my sour-faced aunt and his lips curled into a delightful smile. When she approached, he took her hand and gave it a little kiss. "Well now," he said. "This is a pleasant surprise. So very lovely to see you again, sweet lady."

"If we're talking business, I'm in." She pulled her hand back. "I'm the backbone behind Scarlet's business."

"I see." Donny waggled a brow in playful fashion. "You're the backbone. Well, ain't that the best news in the world, then."

Depends on who you ask, I guess.

Thank goodness I didn't speak the words aloud. Still, as Aunt Willy dove into a lengthy conversation with the man about my new role as provider of baked goods to the town of Splendora, I couldn't help but sigh. By the end of their little chat, she'd agreed—on my behalf, of course—on the number of trays, the content thereof, and the percentage Donny could keep from the proceeds. Go figure. All of this while I stood idly by, leaning against one of the glass cases and contemplating jumping off a pier into the Gulf of Mexico.

Before he left, Uncle Donny looked my way and offered a little wink. "Glad to be doing business with you, girlie."

Lovely. Looked like I had another new business partner. Just what I needed to pull the noose a little tighter around my neck.

Then again, I wasn't sure if Donny was talking to me or Aunt Willy. What did it matter, really? When you did business with one, you did business with the other, right?

Why that revelation suddenly left me feeling a hundred pounds heavier, I couldn't say. I suddenly had the desire to bake—and eat—a dozen sticky buns all by myself. And then, just for fun, I might have to chase them down with a slice of cheesecake.

9

A Lot on My Plate

Approach love and cooking with reckless abandon.

Dalai Lama

Less than an hour after Willy left, Kenny headed off to make a cake delivery. The afternoon crowd died down, and I found myself alone in the kitchen, doing what I loved best: baking. Something about mixing up the batter, pouring it into those freshly greased pans, watching it rise in the oven . . . made my heart sing. And all the more, since I planned to actually eat some of the sweets today. Who needed to diet, after all? Not me!

I practically danced across the kitchen, batter-covered spoon in hand. It became my microphone as I sang along with the worship music coming through the PA system overhead. No one could hear me anyway, right?

Right. Well, no one but God, and I had it on good authority he didn't care about the quality of my singing voice, as long as I spent time making a joyful noise in his presence. No one could argue the fact that I was doing that. For a few minutes, at least.

"Who's that lovely songbird I hear?" A familiar singsongy voice rang out from the bakery, and I stopped singing right away, a little horrified to be caught in action. How would I ever live this down?

"Sounds like an angel choir," another familiar voice said. It took me a minute to place them, but I finally realized why the voices sounded familiar.

My heart sailed to my throat, and I quickly called out, "Be right with you!" then dropped my spoon and headed out to the bakery. I couldn't help but smile as I saw three of my favorite ladies in the world standing there, drooling over my baked goods.

"Twila! Bonnie Sue! Jolene!" I ran to embrace the trio of buxom women, thrilled to see them. "What brings you to the island?"

"Girl, we've come all the way from Splendora on a mission." Twila messed with her beehive hairdo, staring at her reflection in the glass case. After a moment, she gasped and pointed to the case's contents. "Ooo, that's sugar!" she squealed. "You can smell it in the air."

"Nothing like the smell of sugar to get a girl excited," Jolene added. She ambled over, her wide hips swaying this way and that.

"Yes, I feel like I've died and gone to the

sweetest room heaven has to offer." Twila giggled. "If I have, this certainly answers any lingering questions about whether or not they have sweets in heaven."

This got a chuckle out of Jolene, who seemed overly giggly today.

The trio took several steps closer to the glass cases and peered inside. "Ooo, I'll have three of those." Bonnie Sue pointed to my sticky buns. The ones inside the case, of course.

"And five of those." Twila pointed to a tray of M&M cookies.

"I'm trying to cut back on calories and carbs." Jolene's nose wrinkled. "So I guess I'll take three of those brownies. They're low in carbs, right?"

Um, no. But thanks for asking.

Bonnie Sue looked around the shop, her brow wrinkling. "We heard that Donny was here today. Have you seen him?"

"D.J.'s uncle Donny?" I nodded, my curiosity aroused. "He was here an hour or so ago. Left to go next door to Parma John's to visit with Armando again, I think."

"Well, perfect! I'm hankerin' for some pizza." Bonnie Sue's face lit up, and in that moment, I saw the truth. She had the hots for Uncle Donny. But surely these ladies hadn't come all the way to Galveston to chase down a gasoline-scented good old boy. Right? Of course, they did say they were on a mission, but no one had been specific.

Could it be they were avoiding the topic, fearful about my reaction?

Deep breath, Scarlet. Don't wear your emotions on your sleeve. Just makes for a messy sleeve.

I waited on a couple more customers, then joined the ladies at a table, where they nibbled on sweets, expressions of pure joy on each face. I wanted to stop their conversation and share a piece of turtle cheesecake with them.

Twila spoke around the bites of sugary goodness. "Scarlet, as I said, we've come on a mission. We're here to offer our services."

"Services?"

"We heard about your little fund-raiser and we love the idea. We've always had a heart for missions work, so this is right up our alley."

"Oh?"

"Yes." She grinned. "And I think we can help."

"Really?" This certainly got my attention.

"Yes, Armando told us all about it." Jolene took a teensy-tiny nibble of the brownie, then set it back down. "He said you might be able to use us."

"We're singers, you know." Bonnie Sue beamed as she brushed the cookie crumbs onto a napkin. "Maybe you recall us singing at the Bing and Bob party several months back?"

"Ah yes." I remembered it well. They were really good. Tight harmonies and everything. But why in the world would they want to join us for a fund-raiser?

"We've come up with the most delicious idea," Twila said. Her gaze shifted to the glass cases. "A trade of sorts."

"A trade?"

"Yes." She practically drooled. "You see, I'm hosting a ladies' luncheon at my church in Splendora next month and need some baked goods."

"I see." Suddenly it all made sense.

"You have a talent for baking," she said.

"And we have a talent for singing!" Jolene threw in.

As if to emphasize their point, the three of them struck a chord and dove into "On the Good Ship Lollipop." A customer entered the store at that very moment and stood at the bottom of the steps, obviously mesmerized as the women continued their song. On and on they went, singing in rich harmony and basically filling the bakery with joy. I loved every minute.

Apparently so did the customers. By the time the tightly wound trio ended, seven more people had entered the shop. They broke into spontaneous applause, and the Splendora ladies took a bow.

"Thank you!" Twila grinned, then turned to me, her expression serious.

"Thank you very much!" Bonnie Sue added in an admirable Elvis impersonation.

"So, what do you say, honey?" Jolene gripped my hand.

"Yes, make my day." Twila clasped her hands together as if in prayer. "Tell me we can swap services—cake for songs."

"Cake for songs." I nodded. Never thought I'd see the day when I'd trade one for the other, but it seemed like a logical choice. They needed cake. I needed entertainers, and these ladies certainly fit the bill. Everyone on the island knew who they were. They'd been a big hit at Dickens on the Strand during the Christmas season. If they sang at our little fund-raiser, I might be able to involve local media. Why, sure. Someone from the paper could come and write about it: "Splendora trio lends support to small church missions team." I could almost read the headline now.

"You've got it, ladies!" I said.

This, of course, got a round of applause from everyone in attendance. I waited on my customers, who seemed as excited about the possibilities as I did. A couple of them agreed to take fund-raiser flyers, and one even offered to do a little write-up in her church's newsletter about it. Sweet!

About five minutes into an animated discussion about the fund-raiser—suggestions now flowing from all in attendance—Kenny entered. He greeted the ladies with a broad smile but quickly excused himself once they started ranting over his new do. Twila loved offering suggestions about hair products, which apparently made Kenny nervous. Well, that, and the fact that she kept touching his hair. He took off in a hurry, disappearing into the kitchen to finish the projects I'd started.

The ladies turned their attention back to me, all giggles and smiles. "Such a lovely boy," Twila said.

"Godly young man, isn't he?" Bonnie Sue gave me a wink.

Could you be any more obvious, ladies?

"Now, speaking of wonderful young men, Armando says your baked goods are the yummiest on the island." Twila was all business now. "And now that I've tasted them for myself, I have to agree. These are the best."

"Yes, the very best," Bonnie Sue agreed.

"Now, we really must settle on what to serve at the tea." Twila rose and walked to the glass cases. "Several of our ladies are on a diet, you see, so we'll have to be careful." She pointed at a tray to her right. "What about those little éclairs? They're lower in calories, right?"

"Well, the whipped cream is light and fluffy," I said. "But I'd hardly call them low-cal." Far from it, in fact.

"Still, we can bill them as low-fat if you use light whipped cream. Okay?"

"O-okay." I shrugged. Whatever it took to make them happy.

"Not that the rest of us are dieting." Bonnie

Sue rubbed her ample midsection and smiled. "Slimming down isn't high on my agenda." Her nose wrinkled. "Well, not high enough, I guess."

Twila sighed. "I'm just so addicted to sugar." She gazed down at the cheesecakes, a dreamy expression on her face.

From the look of pure delight on these three faces—and the earlier conversation with D.J.'s uncle Donny—I'd apparently won over the whole town of Splendora, Texas, with my sweets. And speaking of sweet . . . how sweet was it that Armando had suggested these precious ladies sing at my church's fund-raiser? That spoke volumes to me. And the fact that he'd bragged about my baked goods? Well, that was just the icing on the cake. Suddenly I could hardly wait to see him to say thank you.

I didn't have to wait long. Just a few seconds into the oohing and aahing, the front bell jingled and Armando raced inside. We all looked his way as he scrambled up the steps into the bakery, his face tight with worry.

"What's wrong?" I set down the tray of goods I was holding and faced him, my heart racing.

"It's Laz."

The Splendora ladies gasped in unison. I could read the concern in their eyes. And in Armando's, for that matter.

"Your uncle?" I asked.

"Yes. He and Rosa were in the middle of taping

an episode of their television show when he doubled over." Armando's eyes flooded. "He . . . he had a heart attack."

"Oh no." My breath caught in my throat.

I could barely make out Armando's next words. "The producers . . . called 911. They . . . they've taken him to the hospital in an ambulance."

"Oh, that poor man." Twila paced the room.

"That precious man of God." Bonnie Sue looked as if she might faint. "He needs our intervention."

"We've got to pray, folks." Jolene grabbed my hand and, without even so much as a "let's bow our heads," engaged the Almighty in a passionate one-on-one, pleading for Laz's health. When she ended, everyone in the shop—including a couple of incoming customers—ushered up a resounding "Amen!"

When we finished, Armando looked my way, his brow furrowed. "Scarlet, I hate to ask, but is there any way you could help out next door? The whole family is headed up to the hospital, and I want to go too. But we can't close up shop just yet because there are customers eating right now. The lunch crowd will be gone soon. I just thought that maybe . . ." His eyes pleaded his case. "You're so good with customers and I know you'll do a great job, but I hate to put you out."

"Say no more." I reached to untie my apron and passed it off to Twila, who lobbed it over the glass cases.

"You sure?" Armando's brow wrinkled.

"Yeah. Kenny!" I hollered his name, and he appeared from the back room, covered in flour.

"Yeah?"

"Can you keep an eye on things here for a while? I have to go next door."

Kenny looked back and forth between Armando and me as if he wanted to punch Armando's lights out. Better blow out that spark before it fanned into flame.

"Armando's uncle Laz just had a heart attack," I explained.

"They took him by ambulance, and I need to meet the family at the hospital," Armando added.

Kenny nodded, a look of chagrin on his face. "Say no more." With a wave of his hand he gestured for me to leave. "Go."

"You sure?" I asked him.

"Yeah. Go on." He headed to the glass cases to wait on a customer, and I took off out the front door on Armando's heels. The three Splendora ladies tagged along behind me, chattering all the way. Twila offered her services as chief cook and dishwasher, and Bonnie Sue went on and on about how great she was waiting tables. Jolene didn't seem as enthused, but as the three headed into Parma John's, I knew they would join me in taking care of the restaurant.

Armando headed for his car but turned back to give me a winsome smile. "Scarlet, thank you. I'll call the restaurant as soon as I can to let you know how he's doing. Just see us through the end of the lunch crowd and then put up the 'Closed' sign."

"Is this really what you want me to do? I don't mind staying longer."

"I'm sure."

I could see the tears in his eyes and, for the first time, really felt sorry for him.

"Thank you so much. I really mean that. And please . . ." He seemed to hesitate. "Pray."

"I will. I promise. And if it's okay with you, I'll call my mama. She heads up a team of ladies who know how to pray the house down. They won't stop until they've heard that your uncle is in perfect health."

That brought a smile to his face. "I'm cool with that."

"Go." I gestured for him to leave. "Don't worry about anything here. Just take care of your family. I'm sure these ladies are going to be all the help I could ever need."

As he sprinted away, I thought about what I'd just said. Really, in a moment of crisis like this, family was the only thing that mattered. I paused to consider what I'd do if the shoe were on the other foot—if Aunt Willy were lying in a hospital bed.

I cringed just thinking about it. In spite of any angst I felt toward her, she was still my auntie, and I loved her. And in that moment, I felt led to pray for her as never before. In between frantic prayers for Armando's uncle, of course. Then, with a heavy heart, I headed into Parma John's to help hold things together.

As I stepped inside, I realized I'd never had a chance to actually eat anything today—sweet or otherwise. Maybe when things settled down, I'd have a piece of pizza. Until then, I'd better do what I did best—take care of customers.

10

Well-Baked

I don't exactly know what it means to be ready. A cake when the oven timer goes off? Am I fully baked, or only half-baked?

Jessica Savitch

I spent the next few hours bouncing back and forth between Parma John's and the bakery, where Kenny took care of a steady stream of customers. We would've shut the pizzeria down for the day after the lunch crowd left, but the Splendora ladies wouldn't hear of it. Turned out they were pretty good in the kitchen. No, not just pretty good—they actually came up with a new kind of pizza, one they labeled "chipped beef on toast." Only, it wasn't on toast. But I had to admit, it tasted mighty good. The patrons enjoyed it too. Before day's end, the ladies had added the new pizza to Parma John's menu board. Go figure. Hopefully the Rossis wouldn't mind.

By 5:30 I was worn to a thread, but I was determined to check in on the Rossi family at the hospital. After several back-and-forth text messages, I located Bella and her kids in the surgical waiting room, her parents nearby. I could tell from her red-rimmed eyes and puffy nose that she'd been crying. She also seemed exasperated with her children, who made their presence known with tears and arguments. Little Tres was in full-out terror mode, and the toddler, Rosa-Earline, seemed more tearful than usual. And exhausted. The poor kid looked frazzled. For that matter, the whole family looked worn down and frightened.

I took several steps in Bella's direction and offered what I hoped would be an encouraging smile. D.J. entered the room, his hands filled with items from vending machines. Uncle Donny entered behind him, hands equally as full. Why hadn't I offered to bring dinner from the restaurant? Ugh! I should have done that.

As they drew near, I noticed the familiar smell of gasoline emanating from Uncle Donny. That, coupled with the worry lines on the fella's fore-head, proved to be a momentary distraction.

"Has he come out of surgery yet?" Donny handed Bella a Diet Coke and a bag of chips.

Bella shoved the chips into the empty spot on her chair, then shook her head as she opened the soda. "No, but I'm trying not to worry. Just stepped away from Aunt Rosa for a few minutes to give her some space."

I knew there was more to it than that. She didn't want to let Rosa see her in tears. I didn't blame her. From what I'd just witnessed, the whole family was pretty shook up. No doubt. Though I hadn't known the Rossis long, they clearly stuck together.

Well, all but one. I still found it weird that Armando didn't quite fit into the family puzzle like the others. The resident bad boy seemed determined to hang on the outer perimeter.

Or maybe not. Minutes later he appeared, worry lines etched on his brow. Rosa entered the room seconds later, and Armando went straight to her and wrapped her in his arms, mumbling something in Italian. I tried to make it out, but my Scottish heritage did me no good there.

Armando glanced up. His concern seemed to vanish when he saw me. He stepped toward me. "Scarlet." His eyes brimmed. "I'm glad you're here. How did it go at the restaurant?"

"Perfect. Nothing to worry about."

"I knew you'd do great." He flashed an encouraging smile.

"Actually, Twila, Bonnie Sue, and Jolene did great. I just helped. Hey, and speaking of the Splendora ladies, they're going to be up here in a few minutes. I think they wanted to stop at the store to pick up a little gift for Rosa or something."

"They're so sweet." Bella sighed and took a swig of her drink, then ripped open her bag of chips. "Everyone is."

I settled into the empty seat next to her and

leaned closer, lowering my voice as I asked the first question on my mind. "How is he?"

She sighed. "They took him in to do some sort of procedure." She blinked back tears. "I honestly had no idea he was even sick. No one knew. He acted . . . fine." Now the tears flowed.

I slipped my arm over her shoulder. "He looked great at the restaurant yesterday."

"Yeah, that's just it. And he was right in the middle of filming an episode of their show." She paused. "I guess I should be thanking God that he's okay and that we live so close to a great hospital."

"Of course. But I totally understand why you're nervous. I would be." A shiver ran down my spine as I thought about how I might react should something like this happen to one of my parents.

"You want to take a walk?" She gestured to the hallway, and I rose to follow on her heels. When we rounded the corner, she looked at me and shrugged. "Just needed to get away for a minute."

"I understand."

"Did you know your dad came by earlier?" A hint of a smile turned up the edges of her lips.

"No." *I love you, Dad. Thank you for being such an amazing man.*

"He's great, Scarlet. I'll bet he's an awesome pastor."

"We're very proud of him. And yes, he's an awesome pastor. Everyone thinks so. Not your usual contemporary type, but solid as a rock."

"That was obvious. He prayed with Rosa. Really seemed to calm her down." Bella glanced her aunt's way. "It's been such a hard day for her. If you had any idea what she's been through to get to this point with Laz . . ." Bella's frown lifted for a moment, and she appeared to be deep in thought. "They were enemies for years, you know. Couldn't stand each other."

"No way."

"Yeah. Talk about opposites. And Uncle Laz was a pain, let me tell you. But I knew in my heart they were a perfect couple. That's what all the angst was about—unrequited love." She sighed.

I felt like sighing as well.

"The past few years, since they figured it out, have been great." Bella lowered her voice. "Though they still fight like cats and dogs, which is why people love their show so much. They don't hold back."

"Yeah, I've seen their show. It's one of my favorites. Love all the sparring."

"Well, that sparring is what has Rosa feeling so guilty right now. She's convinced the bickering somehow played into Laz's heart attack. Like maybe he got all worked up and it triggered this reaction or something."

"What do the doctors say?"

"He's had some sort of blockage for a while, I guess. No one knew. But Rosa also feels bad because their diet has been, well . . ." Bella shrugged. "We're Italian. You know? Lots of cheese. And carbs. And tiramisu." She sighed. "Looks like that's going to have to change. From now on the Rossis will be on a high-fiber, low-fat diet."

"Then whatever you do, don't order the new item that Twila, Bonnie Sue, and Jolene put on the menu at Parma John's."

"Oh?"

I shook my head. "Just trust me on this, okay?" I paused for a moment, thinking through what she'd said about Rosa and Laz's television show.

"I'm just wondering how this will affect their show," Bella said. "Viewers expect to see them make the foods they actually eat at home, and they assume that'll be traditional Italian fare. You know?"

"Yes, but they're also compassionate and they've fallen in love with your aunt and uncle, which means the viewers will want what's best for them. So I'm sure everyone will understand if there's a necessary change in the show's format. They'll appreciate it, even. Most people these days are working hard to get in shape."

Okay, not me, exactly. But most people.

"The viewers . . ." Bella sighed. "That's another thing. My aunt and uncle still have shows to record. Thank goodness Aunt Rosa has friends to call on." Bella reached to squeeze my hand. "Like you! You could take over one episode for her. I know that would be a huge relief."

"I . . . I could?"

"Sure. And speaking of which, Rosa wants to talk to you about something pretty important. Do you have a few minutes?"

"Right now?" I couldn't imagine she wanted to chat now.

"Yeah. I think she would feel better if she could get this behind her."

My curiosity was aroused, for sure. Bella led the way back to the waiting room, and I walked up to her aunt, who looked my way and then offered a weak smile. "Scarlet. I'm glad you're here."

"I'm just sorry it's under these circumstances." I took her extended hand and gave it a squeeze, then pulled her into an embrace. "I've been praying all day, by the way."

"Thank you." She gave a little sniffle and reached for a tissue. "Please don't stop."

"I won't. And my mama's got half our church praying too."

"Thank you. I feel sure he's going to be fine. No doubt about it." Her wrinkled brow clued me in to the fact that she wasn't completely sure, but I offered an encouraging nod. She gazed into my eyes with greater intensity than before. "In the meantime, I need to ask a favor, honey."

"A favor?"

"Yes. I really have no choice, you see."

She gestured for me to take the seat next to her, so I did. "No choice?" I echoed.

"Yes. You're the only one I could think of who might be able to help me. I have quite the dilemma on my hands."

"I see." Only, I didn't. Not yet, anyway.

A lingering pause followed on her end. "Laz and I are scheduled to be on a cake competition in a few weeks. It's being filmed in Los Angeles. The network set it up months ago, and we've been looking forward to it for ages."

My heart skipped a beat at the very idea. To lose such an amazing opportunity would be awful. "And now you have to cancel it?" I asked.

She shook her head. "No, we can't cancel. You don't understand. It's for charity. All of the contestants are Food Network hosts, and the winner gets a twenty-five-thousand-dollar check for their charity of choice. My charity . . ." She dissolved in tears. "*Our* charity is the American Heart Association."

"Oh. Wow."

"Until today, I wouldn't have considered it a coincidence, but now I see that it's more than a coincidence." She gripped my hand. "Scarlet, you have to do it for me."

"I—I beg your pardon?"

"The competition. You have to do it for me. I'm sure I can work it out with the network executives for you to appear in my place. As I said, you're the only person who came to mind, and I would be thrilled and honored to have you represent me. Would you consider it?"

I swallowed hard and begged my heart to slow down. "A-are you sure?"

"Yes." She gave me a pensive look. "I think your cakes are wonderful, honey. I always have. In fact, I think some of your recipes are better than my own."

"Oh, no way, Rosa."

"Yes, honey. Accept the compliment, because it's true. And you're great with stacking and decorating, which is key in a competition such as this. We're very much alike, you know, only you're younger. And faster." She gave me a little wink. "And faster is better when the competition is timed."

"What a kind thing to say. Thank you."

"You're welcome. That's why I've encouraged you to take on some of the cakes I can't do myself for Club Wed, because I trust you. And because I trust you, I'm comfortable telling the network that you will appear in my place."

"But . . . television?" I had one of those weird out-of-body moments where I thought I might very well be dreaming. The idea of appearing on camera made me feel nauseous, and all the more when I contemplated everyone in the nation seeing my overly plump self.

Doesn't the camera add ten pounds?

Ugh.

"You might be a little nervous at first," Rosa said, "but that feeling goes away." She sat up a little straighter in her chair. "Now, let me tell you about the event." She forged ahead as if I'd agreed to do this. Which I hadn't.

Are you going to do this, Scarlet?

I couldn't imagine my sticky buns appearing on television. No way, no how. And yet here sat a woman who not only believed it was possible but was making it so.

"It's a themed competition," Rosa said, her voice now carrying a lilt. "Wedding cakes from various cultures. We were chosen to do an Italian cake, so I'll have to share my vision." With a wave of her hand, she appeared to dismiss that idea. "Or, if you like, you can research that yourself. I trust you, as I said."

"Oh, but Rosa . . ." I stood and paced the tiny waiting room. "I—I can't even imagine being on television. I'm so . . ." The word *fat* almost slipped out, but I stopped it. How could I convince this precious woman that I feared going in front of the camera because I felt sure people would judge me due to my size?

"You're afraid of being in front of people?" she asked.

"Oh." Hmm. "Well, not really. I used to sing in front of people all the time when I was a kid, so it's not that."

"Good. Then it's all set. Your assistant will have to join you. Do you think he would mind? You definitely can't do this on your own, and who better to join you than someone you trust?"

"Kenny?" I chuckled. "He'll think he's died and gone to heaven." Immediately I slapped my hand over my mouth. How dare I blurt out the line about dying while standing in a hospital waiting room? And in front of a woman whose husband was currently in surgery?

Rosa didn't seem to notice. "Yes, Kenny can help you. This would be the big break you've been waiting for. Unless you think your aunt would prefer to do it with you."

At the mere mention of the idea, I felt a little faint. Surely not. Aunt Willy's hand wasn't as steady as it had once been. And these days her managerial skills took up most of her time. She left the baking and decorating to others.

"I think Kenny will do fine," I said.

"Oh, I'm so glad you're willing. I can't tell you what a relief this is." Rosa's eyes misted over as she offered a faint smile.

Had I really just agreed to do this? If so, why? And . . . how? I mean, when I thought about appearing on television, I felt nauseous. Then again, the nausea might have something to do with the smell of the hospital.

"I'll pray about it, Rosa. I promise."

"Oh, I already have." She offered me another

weak smile. "The Lord and I are very close, and I'm sure he's already given me his answer. I knew the minute you showed up that you were the one."

"I'm the one." I spoke the words aloud but didn't believe them.

Well, until I glanced across the room into Armando's eyes. The confidence they exuded convinced me, if only for a moment, that I was indeed the one. And I would do the Rossi family proud when I appeared on national television in Rosa's place to bake, stack, and decorate a cake that represented their precious Italian culture.

If I could just drop ten or twenty pounds between now and then.

11

Driving Me Bananas

Stressed spelled backwards is *desserts.*
Coincidence? I think not!

Author unknown

I decided to spend several days cutting back on calories and carbs so that I wouldn't humiliate myself on the upcoming television gig. Though I knew better than to skip breakfast, I did so anyway, convincing myself I needed to jump-start the day by basically starving myself to death.

By lunchtime on Tuesday I felt sick, but an apple made things better. Not that eating an apple for lunch was the best plan of action, but whatever. Dinner was a small salad. By the fourth day of my diet, I'd lost three pounds. By the fifth, I'd lost another half pound. Still, I had a lot more to lose, and very little time to lose it.

How did one marathon diet? I scoured the internet, looking for ideas. That left me more confused than ever. Should I stop eating meat? Give up sodas? Take supplements? Drink protein shakes? Live on vegetable juice?

That last one would be tough, considering I

didn't own a juicer. And I didn't exactly feel up to buying one, to be perfectly honest. I liked my carrots whole, thank you very much. And preferably in cake. With frosting. And lots of nuts.

How could I lose another twenty pounds or so from my sticky buns before the big day? I thought about that *I Love Lucy* episode where Lucy went on a diet so she could fit into a costume for one of Ricky's shows. How had she lost the weight again?

The sauna.

Yes, the sauna had done the trick.

And so I joined a gym the following Monday evening. Went twice on Tuesday—once before going to the bakery in the morning and once at night. Same on Wednesday. Kenny thought I'd lost my mind—at first. Then he decided to join me and even played the role of personal trainer. His first bit of advice to me, his client? Eat more. Specifically, protein. Sure, easy for him to say. The guy didn't need to lose a pound. Still, I pretended to eat so he would leave me alone.

I also sought out the advice and encouragement of others, telling them about my television gig. My parents were all over the idea. So was my aunt, who apparently saw dollar signs every time she thought about it. By the time Wednesday night rolled around, I'd almost convinced myself this plan was doable. I could go on national television and represent the Rossis. But just as quickly, fear overcame me, and I wondered if I could function with the lights and cameras in my face.

Oh. Lord. Help.

After my workout I headed to the church, arriving before anyone else, and went to the youth room, where I paced back and forth, asking the Lord's opinion on all of this. Rosa's words kept replaying in my mind: "You can do this, Scarlet. I wouldn't have asked you otherwise." And Armando's vote of confidence helped, for some strange reason. Still, I felt sick every time I thought about it, so I continued to pray.

At some point well into my pleading with the Almighty, Devon came bounding into the room, eyes wide. "Is it true?"

"What?" I stopped praying and looked his way.

"You're going to be on television?" Three teenage girls spoke in tandem as they entered.

I groaned. "Who told you that?"

"Armando." Devon flung himself into a chair. "I saw him at Parma John's today, and he told me you were going to do some sort of cake challenge on television. Is it true?"

"Well, I don't know yet. I—"

"Can we go too?" one of the girls asked.

"Yeah, I want to be in the studio audience," another chimed in.

I put my hand up. "First of all, I haven't decided to go yet."

"Of course you have." Armando's strong voice

139

resonated from the doorway. I glanced over at him and saw the confidence in his expression.

Dude, what are you doing at church on a Wednesday night?

Oh, right. To talk to my dad about possibly renting a new lightboard for the fund-raiser. I remembered now. Still, it felt odd to see him standing there in the doorway of the youth room.

"You're going to go, and it's going to be great. And with all of these guys cheering you on, how can we lose?"

"Yeah, Scarlet," the oldest of the three girls said. "You're always telling us to be brave, right? Isn't that what you said when I told you that I didn't want to perform in the talent show?"

"And isn't that what you told me when I said I didn't think I could leave my family and go to a third world country?" a younger one added.

"Remember when I thought I couldn't eat a whole cheesecake by myself?" Armando said with a sly smile. "You talked me into it."

"I did no such thing."

"You've got this in you, Scarlet," he said. "I know you do."

"Well, maybe, but—" How did he know, anyway? The guy barely knew me.

"No buts." Armando gave me a stern look, and I sighed, trying not to think about my sticky buns and their national debut in front of millions.

"This will go down in history as one of the

greatest opportunities of your life," he said. "And think of the business it'll bring in. People all over the nation will hear about Let Them Eat Cake. It's going to up your business like crazy."

"Yeah, we're gonna have to build you a website." Devon dove into a discussion about the importance of having a web presence, and before long everyone was chiming in, including my dad, who appeared in the doorway to see what all the ruckus was about.

"I'm trying to get them to see reason, Dad," I argued. "This is too much, don't you think? I'm already running a new business, making a cake for my best friend's wedding, and planning this trip to Nicaragua. It's just too much. Don't you think?" Surely he would agree. My father was a reasonable man.

He shrugged. "I only know that God won't give us more than we can handle, honey. That's been my experience, anyway. So he must think you're capable."

I groaned and fought the temptation to slap myself in the head. "He expects a lot from me." *You all do.*

"He trusts you, Scarlet," my dad said. "And think of the opportunity to tell others about not just the bakery but the church and this trip. If you put the word out to the viewers, they will be praying for the kids as they go."

"Yeah. They can pray for us." One of the girls

141

looked at me with that puppy dog look I found so hard to resist.

She wasn't the only puppy dog in the room. Armando's expression tugged at my heart too.

In fact, a thousand things tugged at my heart over the next several days as I prayed about whether or not to go. On Saturday morning I learned that Laz's at-home recovery seemed to be going well, in spite of his insistence that he could still eat tiramisu—this according to Bella, who phoned daily with updates. Hearing about his progress relieved me, of course, but didn't solve the problem. He still couldn't appear on television, so I had no choice but to take his place.

Kenny, for some reason, was the lone holdout. He didn't care much for the idea. I tried not to stress over that and figured I could talk him into it. With enough time. And prayer.

I broached the subject with him again, more frustrated and confused than ever. "Kenny, I really need an answer. Can you come on the show with me or not?"

He paced the shop, appearing just as agitated as the first time I'd asked him. "What does your aunt say?"

"She's all for it, of course. But she's a little worried about leaving the shop unmanned while I'm gone. I'll be in Los Angeles three days total."

"That worries me a little too. And I don't want to appear ungrateful, but I'm not really the go-to-

Hollywood type." He shrugged. "Don't have any aspirations of getting on the Food Network, to be honest."

"Me either. Not really."

"Then opt out. Just tell Rosa you're not interested."

"I would be doing it for Laz," I countered. "For his charity. You know? It's really about that. And it's great advertisement for Let Them Eat Cake."

"Yeah, I know. And I guess we could use the promotion."

"Tell me you'll do it. I don't think I could handle going without you."

He paced a bit and finally muttered, "I hate to let you down, so if you really feel like you need me, like you can't do it without me. . ."

"Great." I couldn't help but sigh as relief settled over me. "Rosa's coming this afternoon to tell me all about it. She's got the details on the kind of cake, the specifications, everything. We need to take good notes."

"I thought you wanted me to work on getting the kitchen organized this afternoon."

"Oh, right." I'd given him such a hard time about not having room for everything. The sweetheart had built some shelves up high to hold the larger mixing bowls.

"All for my girl," he said with a wink.

I sighed, wondering if—or when—I'd have the courage to tell him I couldn't be his girl. Today probably wasn't the best day for that, all things considered. But I would tell him. Soon.

Rosa arrived at a quarter to five, struggling a bit as she ascended the steps leading into the bakery. A little huffing and puffing and she finally landed at a table, where she took a seat and gave me an admiring look. "Scarlet, there's something different about you. Are you wearing your hair a different way?"

"No." I sucked in my belly, hoping she'd notice my six-pound weight loss. She didn't.

Instead, she scrunched her nose and examined my hair again. "Hmm. It's something. Maybe you're wearing a different color lipstick?"

"No, it's the same as always."

Look down! It's my hips! They're disappearing before your very eyes!

"Odd." She looked perplexed. "I could've sworn there was something different about you today."

I did my best not to sigh. Perhaps in time people would notice. In the meantime, I'd better cut back a little more on my calories and up my workout at the gym. Otherwise what was the point?

Aunt Willy entered on Rosa's heels. No doubt she wanted to be a part of this opportunity, being my chief investor and all. Again I tried not to sigh at the idea that she involved herself in every area of my life these days. Unlike Rosa, she didn't seem to notice any change in my appearance whatsoever, though I'd dressed in black, hoping to make the weight loss more obvious.

Nothing.

Nada.

And again I ask, why, Lord? Why?

So I focused on Rosa, who seemed a little distracted by all the noise Kenny was making in the kitchen.

"He's putting up new shelves," I explained.

"Should've waited to do that after closing up shop," Willy argued. "It's distracting."

"Oh, I know, but he's got a big night tonight. There's a summer sports thing planned with the kids in the youth group. He's such a big part of that, and we're working on the fund-raiser—"

"Better get this show on the road," Willy interrupted, and I sighed.

I turned to Rosa and smiled gently. "Before we do, how is Laz? I've been praying for him."

"He's better." A smile turned up the edges of her lips. "Stubborn old mule, if you want my opinion, but a recovering one, so that makes me happy."

Aunt Willy rolled her eyes. "If he's a stubborn old mule, then he's a typical man."

Rosa looked stunned. "Well, I wouldn't say that," she responded. "He's a very special man who's been through a lot over the past couple of weeks. I didn't mean to imply that he's anything but wonderful. He's just—"

"A man." Willy crossed her arms. "And we all

know what they're like, don't we, ladies?" Before we could respond, she forged ahead, all business. "Okay now, tell us about this competition. What do we need to do to get ready?"

We?

Did she for one minute think that I would take her on the show with me? My mind flashed back to that day in the hospital when Rosa had asked about having Auntie join me. It hadn't seemed like a good idea at the time, but now I wondered if she felt left out somehow. Perhaps she wanted to be involved.

So I asked her.

"I would sooner die a thousand deaths than appear on national television in a competition." Auntie looked disgusted by the very idea, as if I'd asked her to drink poison or something. "If you think I might enjoy something like that, then you don't know me at all."

Okay, then. I hear ya. And I'm right there with ya.

Still, with Rosa gazing at me so intently, I could hardly back out now, could I? And so I listened as she explained the plan of action. She pulled out a piece of paper. I joined her at the table and glanced at it.

"It's heritage day on *Cakes Galore*," Rosa explained. "Four teams—one Hispanic, one Italian, one Scotch-Irish, and one African."

Ah. Suddenly I wished I could play on the

Scotch-Irish team. A thousand ideas ran through my head about what sort of cake I would come up with for that.

"Most are new to the network," Rosa explained. "All but the Alvarez family. They have a great show called *Latina Lifestyle*, featuring all sorts of tasty Mexican foods."

"Yum."

"They're the competition." Rosa narrowed her gaze. "Now, you'll be making the Italian cake, of course, and even though it's a wedding cake, we thought the Coliseum would make a nice design."

"The Coliseum?" Auntie's brow wrinkled. "Not very romantic."

"Ooo, but it is." Rosa unfolded a paper with the most exquisite and beautiful rendition of the Roman Coliseum I'd ever seen.

I gasped. "Oh, I love it." The arches might prove to be problematic, though. How many were there, anyway? Dozens and dozens. They would have to be molded out of white chocolate, but I could probably handle that. And Kenny's carving skills were great, so shaping the Coliseum would fall to him.

"I love it too." Rosa grinned. "And it's the perfect representation of our family. We've been to Rome more times than I can count, and the Coliseum is one of our favorite places. It might help you to know that Laz and I started out like two gladiators in the middle of the ring, but we finally gave up our quarreling to come together." Her cheeks turned pink.

"I heard a little something about that," I said, then grinned.

"Well, it means the world to us that you're willing to help us share our love story with others, Scarlet."

"Of course."

"But watch out for the Alvarez family," she whispered in my ear. "They've got a great recipe for tres leches cake, from what I understand. And I think they're going to try to whip up something to compete with ours, so be prepared for that. But don't worry, sweet girl. I plan to give you a recipe for the best Italian cream cake you ever tasted, complete with cream cheese frosting."

Ack. Decorating with cream cheese was tough, for sure. But I loved the idea of merging Italian cream cake with the Coliseum design. Perfecto!

"Everyone says my recipe is the best in the state." Rosa beamed. "And I hate to brag, but I must agree. It's so yummy I could almost eat a whole cake by myself."

"I doubt it's *that* good," Aunt Willy muttered under her breath. "Seriously?"

Rosa gave her a curious look but didn't say anything. I could almost see the wheels turning in her head.

"I don't wish to stir up trouble, but if Scarlet appears on the show, I would prefer she use my recipe." Aunt Willy placed her hands on her tiny hips. "I insist."

"But she represents *me,*" Rosa said, her expression hardening. "So I must insist otherwise. She will use the Rossi family recipe."

Oy vey.

On and on they went, debating their various points. Auntie insisted that my appearance on the show was really more about the bakery. Rosa argued that I was there to fill in for her—to represent her. She was right, of course, but my aunt refused to budge an inch. Either I use her recipe or I could not appear on the show.

The bell on the front door jingled, and Armando walked in just in time to see this exciting showdown of wills. He looked back and forth between the two women as the argument continued.

After a couple of minutes of head bobbing, Armando put up his hand. "Ladies, ladies. Here's my suggestion: compare recipes."

"No." Willy shook her head, looking aghast. "Mine is a secret."

"Mine as well." Rosa crossed her arms at her chest.

Armando managed to distract Rosa, but Willy seemed intent on keeping my attention. "I'll email you the recipe." She spoke through clenched teeth. "But don't you dare let that woman see it."

"But Aunt Wil—"

Willy glanced back at Rosa and grunted. "I don't care if she's a national television star. Do not let her see my recipe for Italian cream cake. Promise?"

"Oh, I'm sure she can be trusted, Aunt Wilhelmina. Besides, her poor husband is still recovering, so—"

"Don't do it."

"Yes, ma'am." I bit back a laugh as I tried to imagine Rosa stealing Willy's family recipe. Still, Aunt Willy seemed to be taking this seriously. Very seriously.

My aunt marched out of the bakery, head held high. Rosa walked over to me, looking a little intimidated. "She's something else, isn't she?"

"You have no idea."

"Well, I'm glad she's gone, to be honest. I can give you what I came to give you—the family recipe." She reached into her oversized purse and came out with a slip of paper, covered in dried cake batter and barely readable. My eyes scanned it, and I smiled, realizing what a great cake this would make.

Another customer entered the store, and Rosa pulled me to the side to whisper something in my ear. "Scarlet, promise me something." Her words were strained.

"Sure." I glanced at the customer, relieved to see that Armando had slipped behind the glass cases to wait on her.

"This is an old family recipe," Rosa said. "It's been in the Rossi family for generations. It's an honest and true Italian cream cake, one that goes back hundreds of years. I can't risk the recipe getting out, so promise me you'll guard this with your life."

I couldn't help but think of Willy's admonition.

"I won't let anyone see it except Kenny," I said. "He has to."

"Of course. I meant—well, you know who I'm referring to."

"My aunt will never see this," I promised.

Willy would never know the difference, after all. The only people who would taste this cake would be the judges at the competition, and they didn't care whose recipe I used, as long as it tasted great.

"Thank you, sweet girl." Rosa reached up to give me a little kiss on the cheek. "You're saving my life. Literally. And I know you're going to win with this recipe if you follow the directions exactly. I've never had anything but rave reviews with it."

I offered what I hoped was a confident smile and nodded. Rosa turned on her heels, gave Armando a wink, and walked out of the bakery. He finished waiting on my customer—even managing to talk her into buying an extra dozen sticky buns—and then looked my way.

"Everything okay?"

"I guess so." My phone beeped, and I pulled it

from my pocket, noticing I had an email from Aunt Willy. How she'd managed to send the recipe that quickly, I couldn't say, but there it was.

I stared at the recipes, looking first at the one on the phone and then the one on the slip of paper Rosa had given me—back and forth, back and forth. Laughter bubbled up inside of me as the realization set in.

"What's so funny?" Armando asked as he drew near.

"You're not going to believe it, but they're identical."

"No way. Rosa's recipe has been top secret for as long as I can remember."

"Willy's too. But I'm telling you they're exactly the same. Well, with the exception of how many walnuts to add, but I can play that part by ear. I tend to run a little on the nutty side."

"Tell me about it." Armando chuckled, lifting my spirits.

Suddenly my confidence level rose too. I took this recipe as a sign that everything would be fine. I would go on the show, bake up the perfect Italian cream cake, shape it in a romantic version of the Coliseum, and possibly even win the whole thing. With Kenny at my side, of course.

Thank you, God, for giving me the confidence I need to see this thing through.

I heard a crash from inside the kitchen, and then a loud cry. My heart sailed to my throat. I ran to see what had happened, and Armando followed on my heels. We found Kenny sprawled on the floor, a ladder lying next to him. Nausea gripped me when I saw the pained expression on his face.

"Kenny?"

He shook his head but didn't say anything.

"Kenny? Are you okay?"

He looked the other way, and for the first time I noticed the weird position of his left arm, sort of twisted behind him. Oh. Ouch.

"Your arm!" I went to him at once and began to fuss over him in a mother hen sort of way. "Kenny, I'm calling 911."

"Over. My. Dead. Body." He spoke through clenched teeth.

"But your arm is . . ." *Broken* seemed too simplistic a word. I'd never seen an arm in this position before. Hoped I never would again. Another wave of nausea washed over me, so I looked away. I tried not to be obvious about it, but what could I do?

"I know." He attempted to stand, but his knees buckled and he paled. "But I'm not going out of here in an ambulance. Understood?"

"O-okay."

"You have to drive me." He winced. "And there's no point going to a doctor's office. I think the ER is the only option, unless you happen to know an orthopedist who works out of his home."

"I'll drive him." From behind me, Armando's

voice rang out. I turned, relief flooding over me as I realized he could help. "I don't think Scarlet's in any shape to be driving right now."

As much as I hated the chauvinistic comment, I didn't argue. Truthfully, I probably would've driven the car off the road with my nerves in such a frazzled state.

Armando knelt next to Kenny and analyzed the situation, then blew out a breath. "Man."

"Yeah." Just one word from Kenny, but it resonated like ten or twenty.

"What were you doing?"

Kenny gestured with his head to the shelf above us, the one I'd asked him to fill with oversized mixing bowls. I bit back the sigh that tried to weasel its way out. I'd caused this. If I hadn't been so concerned about climbing the ladder myself, this never would have happened. Look at where my fear had landed me.

Or, rather, where it had landed him. I leaned down but did my best not to focus on his arm for fear I might get sick. Instead, I looked at Armando.

"Here's what we're going to do." Armando proceeded to give me instructions for how we would get Kenny to a standing position and then out the door. "Our family's pizza delivery van is just outside," he added. "We'll slip you into the back of the truck like we're heading out to make a delivery or something. I'll lead the way."

He took charge, getting us out of the door, closing up shop, and even deterring an incoming customer—all without raising any red flags. My stomach felt nauseous, and all the more as we settled into the Parma John's van and I got a closer look at Kenny's arm.

At this point I could only think of one thing— well, short of feeling sorry for Kenny, of course.

My assistant was now out of the cake competition.

Kaput. Over. Finished.

And if he was out of the game . . . so was I.

12

Too Many Cooks

Keep calm. There's nothing a cupcake can't solve.

Anonymous

A couple of days after Kenny's accident, I found myself working alone in the kitchen. I'd spent the better part of the last two days praying for his recovery, especially after learning that he would require surgery once the swelling went down. Every time I thought about it, I felt like crying— not because of my situation with the cake challenge but because I'd caused all of this in the first place. Why oh why had I asked him to build the shelves in the kitchen? Carpentry wasn't his forte. Baking was.

I expected too much from Kenny. I always had.

That only made me feel guiltier by the minute. I had taken advantage of Kenny a thousand times over, knowing he cared enough about me to do what I asked regardless. And now look at the consequences. I'd caused him pain not just emotionally but physically. Yes, he would recover, but the guilt I carried left me sad and tired. And alone. Very, very alone.

Still, the show must go on—at least that's what Kenny said every time he called, and he called approximately seven or eight times a day to see how things were going at the shop without him. I didn't have the courage to explain that my tears had frightened away a potential customer or that I'd burned an entire tray of brownies. I also didn't tell him about the late delivery of the birthday cake, or the disappointed mother of the bride who'd stopped by hoping to see my design of her daughter's cake, only to learn I hadn't started it yet.

No, I couldn't seem to get anything right today, but that certainly didn't stop me from trying. And it definitely didn't keep me from pretending like everything was fine when Kenny called for the eighth time. When I finally shared a few concerns about the upcoming competition, he just chuckled and said, "I have confidence in you. You can do this, girl. I know you can."

But I couldn't. I knew it in my gut. Not without him, anyway.

Or could I?

Only one way to know for sure. Just after closing up shop for the day, I decided to try my hand at Aunt Rosa's Italian cream cake recipe. I'd thought through her plan of building the Coliseum and wondered how in the world I could accomplish it alone, without Kenny to do the lifting and lugging. Looked like I would have no choice but to ask Auntie to join me on the show, whether she wanted to or not. The idea didn't set well, but what else could I do? If anyone knew how to bake a great cake, she did. Yes, we would make a fine team—me with my steady hand, and her with her lopsided liquid eyeliner. As long as the camera didn't zoom in on her face. Or my hips.

First, however, I had to conquer this recipe. Mixing it proved to be problematic, now that Kenny had put the mixing bowls up out of reach. In spite of his fall, they remained high above on the shelf. I pulled out the ladder and scaled it, praying all the way. I accidentally measured out double the flour and had to start over.

"Why, Lord?" I shook my batter-covered spoon at the ceiling. Then again, God wasn't up in heaven shaking a spoon at me, now was he? No doubt he wasn't keen on me doing it to him. A quick repentance followed on my end. In fact, I needed to repent for quite a few things, including my bad attitude regarding my aunt.

I somehow managed to get the batter going and greased and floured the sample-size pans. Fighting the temptation to lick the spoon, I dumped the batter into the pans and shoved them into the oven.

Now, I'd been tempted before. I worked with sweets all day, after all. But I'd never known temptation like I did during the half hour those cakes were in the oven. I wanted to eat every last bite when they came out.

But I couldn't. I had to remember my sticky buns. They would make their appearance on camera in just a week or so. If I wanted to make a name for myself—for something other than the vast expanse of my backside—I needed to stay focused on my diet. Rumbling stomach or not. Weakness or not. It would be worth every bit of effort when I took the prize for Rosa. When I showed the world what I was made of.

And now, ladies and gentlemen . . . we present to you the winner of Cakes Galore, *Scarlet Lindsey! Scarlet hopes you will look beyond her chubby physique to see the fun-loving girl on the inside, the one who plans to wow you with her baking abilities and her willingness to try new things. Join Scarlet as she proves once and for all that big girls really do have more fun . . . in the kitchen.*

I found myself daydreaming about the upcoming competition. Referring to Rosa's design of the Coliseum, I let my thoughts drift. Until I smelled the familiar scent of burning cake.

I reached for a hot pad and yanked the cake pan from the oven, groaning as I saw the burnt edges. "Why?" I hollered to the ceiling. Why today, of all days? And why the test cake for the show? Probably some sort of punishment for my internal desire to eat, eat, eat. The Lord knew I wouldn't possibly cheat with a burnt cake. Still, what could I do with it, if not eat it? Forge ahead and decorate? To start over now meant washing bowls and pans, mixing up a new batch, and allowing time for baking. I'd be here all night!

Still, what other choice did I have? I needed to get this right at least once before attempting it on national television in front of millions of viewers. How else would I know if I could do this?

Oh. Help.

I scaled the ladder to grab a clean mixing bowl. As much as I hated to do it, I needed to start over. Thank goodness I managed to grab a bowl with little problem.

My back ached and my heart felt even more twisted, but I forged ahead, thinking of Lucille Ball and that crazy episode where she tried to make money bottling and selling her aunt Martha's salad dressing. The workload involved nearly destroyed her psyche, but she pushed on. I would take my cues from Lucy-girl and go for the gusto, no matter how difficult things got.

The next couple minutes were spent slamming pans around as I regrouped and searched for enough ingredients to begin the mixing process again. Doing so relieved some of the tension that wound my neck and shoulders into knots.

A voice sounded behind me, and I turned, gasping as I saw Armando standing there. I could read the concern in his eyes as he watched me slam-banging the pots and pans into submission.

"Scarlet. You okay?"

"Yes." I nodded, then sighed. "Okay, no. I'm not okay." I fought the tears that threatened to tumble down my cheeks. "I ruined the cake."

"Which cake?" He had a good point. The place was filled with cakes.

"The test cake for the competition," I explained. "I ruined it. 'Destroyed it' might be a better description. This whole thing is a . . . challenge." The last word slithered out, taking my energy with it.

"Ah." He reached for an apron and slipped it over his head. "Good thing I'm up for a challenge, then." His eyes twinkled as if he knew some great cosmic secret, and then he pointed toward the work at hand. "Where do we start, boss?"

"W-what?" Was he kidding? If so, I found no humor in his joke.

"I'm a whiz in the kitchen." He gave a dramatic bow. "You've tasted my pizza, no doubt. Extra crispy on the edge, nice and soft in the middle. So I'm asking where we start. I'm your guy."

Those words sounded mighty good, but I was pretty sure he didn't mean them that way. He was my pizza guy—and I'd been avoiding pizza for days. *Good grief, a thin pepperoni with extra cheese sounds really good right about now.*

"But pizza and cake are two different things,"

I argued after fighting off the temptation to head next door for a gooey slice.

"Not so different. Both have yeast." He grabbed the empty bowl.

"Well, yeah."

"Both have to bake to the perfect golden color."

"True."

"Both require great timing and skill, which I happen to have." He sniffed the air. "No offense, but one of us missed the mark on the timing of that last cake. Unless you happen to like your Italian cream cake well done. Personally, I like mine light and fluffy with cream cheese frosting on top."

"I know, I know. Me too." I bit back the groan that threatened to erupt. "But I still say cakes and pizzas are totally different."

"Look, Scarlet . . ." He drew so close that his yummy aftershave captured my imagination and made me a little weak in the knees. "I'm all you've got. Take it or leave it."

As much as I wanted to bite back with, "I'll leave it, thank you," the boy had a point. I really did need someone to help. And he was, after all, quite muscular. Not in a "driving the golf cart shirtless" sort of way, but more in a "he could probably help me stack the cakes on national television" sort of way.

How could I argue with that?

He continued to sing his own praises, looking

and sounding a little more like that shirtless golf cart man every minute. If Auntie had been here to witness this, she would have encouraged me to send him packing. Still, I couldn't afford to do that. Not when I needed his help.

Well, not his help, necessarily, but someone's help. *Anyone's* help.

"Scarlet, I grew up in the kitchen, remember? I know what I'm doing because I learned from the masters. Aunt Rosa and Uncle Laz are both chefs and bakers. And I worked at Parma John's for years. What else do you need to hear before you're convinced I'm the right person to help you?"

"I'm just saying that pizzas and cakes are worlds apart. For one thing, this cake requires decoration. You guys don't decorate your pizzas."

"I beg to differ." He looked offended. "I use pepperoni, Canadian bacon, and lots and lots of cheese. It's an art form, and you have to admit, our pizzas are truly as beautiful as they are tasty." A half smile cracked his serious façade, and I could see that he was still teasing me. "Might not be fondant and froufrou flowers and such, but we get the job done."

I started to argue the whole "decorate the pizza" idea but decided he was probably right. Parma John's did put out some beautiful pizzas. Everyone on the island agreed.

Mmm. Just thinking about them made me

hungrier than ever. A Mambo Italiano special would taste great right now. How long had it been since I'd eaten a real meal? From my growling stomach, I'd have to say too long.

He clapped his hands together, observed my messy kitchen, and then looked at me. "Now, where do we start?"

"At the very beginning, I guess." I offered a weak smile. "It's a very good place to start." I pointed to Rosa's recipe card, and he smiled.

"I recognize this."

"You do?"

"Yeah." He picked it up and gave it a closer look. "She's notorious for writing things down and then covering them with batter. Half of her recipes aren't readable because they're covered in the batters of cakes or cookies from years gone by."

"That makes them even better to me."

"Me too." He went to work measuring out the ingredients on her list, and before long we were busy mixing them up. As we worked, we found ourselves enmeshed in a deep conversation about what his life was like as a kid. He had no problem telling me about the many times he got sent to the principal's office for acting up in school. I couldn't relate, since I was always a teacher's pet. Still, I remember the sort of "bad boy" he referred to. I'd known many as a child.

Did they all grow up to be "good old boys," as Aunt Willy called them?

Lord, is Armando a good old boy?

Listening to him pour out his heart about his childhood just made me feel sorry for him, especially his stories about how he had struggled in school. Man.

"Sounds like you got bored easily," I observed as I poured the batter into the greased pans.

"Still do, I guess," he said. "I start one job, then get bored and jump to the next. So I start something else and end up bored there too. I guess you could say I've tried a lot of things."

"Like?"

He shrugged. "Well, I've worked as a deejay. And a sound tech. Got tired of the club scene for a while, so I worked with a locksmith. Oh, and I did this multilevel marketing thing once. And sales. Worked for a mortgage company doing sales. But you know what happened with mortgages."

Actually, I didn't, but I wouldn't bother him with my ignorance. I knew nothing about mortgages. I barely remembered to pay my parents the little rent check we'd agreed on every month. Not that they cared.

Armando kept going, oblivious to my thoughts. "And I worked at Parma John's most of my teen years and well into my early twenties before I moved to Houston. That's where I acquired my excellent cooking skills. But I hate to brag. That would just be wrong."

"I see."

"I know, I know . . . I've jumped around. Aunt Rosa says I don't have stick-to-itiveness. Her word, I think."

"No, trust me, I've heard Aunt Willy use it too. But it sounds like you're multifaceted." I checked the temperature on the oven and popped in the largest pan.

"Guess so." He shrugged. "I've always been this way, even as a kid. I'd get bored and act up. Kept everybody worked up most of the time."

"Did anyone ever test you for ADD?" I asked. "Sounds like you're a classic case to me."

"Nah." He grinned. "They just whopped me upside the head and told me to shut up and sit down. Or to stop burning the kitchen down. That sort of thing."

"Ooo." Visions of flames lapping up my bakery flashed through my mind. "I still think you must have ADD tendencies. Either that, or you're a genius."

"A genius?" He didn't look convinced. At first. Then a little smile crept up. "You really think that's possible?"

"Sure. I heard a story once about a guy—maybe Einstein?—who was labeled a slow learner as a kid because he was so bored in class. Turned out it was because he was so far above the others." I put the next pan in the oven, determined to stay on top of things so we could get this job done.

Armando flashed a jubilant smile, drawing my attention away from the cakes. "Thank you."

"For what?"

"For thinking for one minute that I might be anything other than a total failure. I'm not sure anyone ever saw potential in me before. If we win this competition, maybe they'll see I have value."

"Surely they already do."

"Trust me when I say they just don't get me. Mama says when God made me, he broke the mold."

"How so?"

"I guess they think I'm a bum because I can't hold down a job."

"A bum?"

"Okay, so they haven't exactly come out and said it, but that's the way they make me feel." He squared his shoulders. "But it's not true. I have an entrepreneurial spirit. I was born to be the boss."

"Of what?" I asked as I finished putting the remaining pans in the oven.

He paused, his gaze shifting to the ground, then finally looked my way. "The world?" A chuckle followed. "Kidding. But if you'd asked me when I was a kid, that would've been my answer. Problem was, in my house there were so many of us that no one even asked that question. I think everyone just assumed we'd all go to work for the pizzeria. Or the wedding facility. Anything else seemed outside the realm of possibility. You know?"

Actually, I did know. From the time I came out of the womb, my parents had been grooming me for church work. Or missions. I'd known it all along, especially as an only child. Heaven forbid I decide to become a brain surgeon or anything shameful like that. My mother would probably crawl into a hole and avoid all of the other church ladies should it come to that. Her heart would certainly be gripped with pain if I opted out of my designated calling.

But cakes were my calling. Right? I peeked through the glass into the oven. So far, so good on this batch.

Not that cake baking would keep me from going on missions trips. No sir. I'd felt the tug to do missions work at an early age and couldn't wait to hit the tarmac running. Once we raised the funds, anyway.

Armando kept talking, but my thoughts had shifted. If anyone understood this sort of pressure from parents, I did, though my mom and dad were subtle. They didn't come out and say, "You're going to marry a pastor," but they had mentioned in passing—maybe ten or twenty thousand times—that my future would be brighter than a copper penny should I marry such a man. Never once in the history of my upbringing did I remember them saying, "Hey, Scarlet, why don't you marry a no-account bum who jumps from job to job because he gets bored easily? And while you're at it, ask him to help you stack cakes into the shape of the Coliseum, because we're pretty sure your life will be grand if you do."

I cringed, in part because I couldn't imagine my mother saying that last part, and in part because I couldn't figure out why I was suddenly thinking of marrying Armando.

I'm marrying Armando?

I shook off that bizarre idea in a hurry. A girl couldn't very well marry someone she hardly knew, especially someone as unsuited for her. No, I'd better stick with Kenny. Good, solid, reliable Kenny, who was in church every time the doors were open. Who gave of himself to the poor. Who smiled in spite of the pain in his arm. Who called to check on me even when the attention should be on him. Who baked a mean chocolate cake and built some amazing lopsided shelves in my kitchen.

Yes, Kenny was looking better all the time. If only I could fall in love with him. Wouldn't that be grand?

But as I gazed at Armando, as I pretended to listen while he carried on about the Rossi family, I realized he too was looking better all the time. In fact, as I stared into those cocoa-brown eyes—eyes that held me spellbound—it occurred to me that this shirtless, no-account bum driving his proverbial golf cart straight through the heart of my kitchen had never looked so good.

13

A Piece of Cake

Let's face it, a nice creamy chocolate cake does a lot for a lot of people; it does for me.

Audrey Hepburn

Very few things in life intimidate me. Short of Aunt Willy, of course. But I have to admit that walking onto the set of *Cakes Galore* at the Food Network studios terrified me on every level. We were given one hour to bring in our supplies and get them set up, but I spent much of that time trying to calm my nerves.

I made my way across the studio, my gaze shifting to the large camera above. It loomed in ghostlike fashion as if taunting me. I would have to remember never to reveal my backside. Aunt Willy would probably come up with some kind of wisecrack about my sticky buns looking even bigger on television.

Behind me, Armando let out a whistle. "Man. This is something else."

"I know, right?" I turned to face him, noticing what looked like a hint of fear in his eyes. Really? He'd been on television before, on his aunt's show.

Seconds later he looked completely relaxed and gazed at the camera with a boyish smile. Likely this was all no big deal to him. It was a huge deal to me, though. Probably the hugest thing that would ever happen to me. What other girl from Lufkin, Texas, had the opportunity to fly to Los Angeles to appear on national television on a cake show?

I worked alongside Armando setting up our station. He paused periodically to comment on the various cameras and microphones hovering above us. Seemed he was more fascinated by all of that than the cake we would be baking in less than an hour.

Stay focused, boy! Stay focused!

I tried to reel him in but found it nearly impossible. Maybe his distraction was a good sign. If he didn't get too worked up now, maybe he'd stay relaxed throughout. Then at least one of us wouldn't be freaked out.

At nine o'clock a.m., the television audience entered the studio, along with the judges. I'd met them earlier, but seeing them face-to-face terrified me. One of them—an older woman with a fascinating updo—wore a stern look on her face, even when offering bits of encouragement.

A producer introduced us to the other contestants, all network regulars. I was particularly taken with the Alvarez family and could hardly wait to see what they would come up with. The

171

Scotch-Irish clan was keeping their lips sealed about their plan of action, but the African contingent dressed in colorful aprons, clueing me in to the fact that we had a whopper of a cake to anticipate from their team.

As we settled into place, I heard cheers from the audience members. Glancing out, I saw Bella. She gave me a little wave and I waved back. Our two aunties flanked her, one on each side. To Willy's right, my mother cheered, and my father—God bless him—leaned forward, elbows on knees, as if ready to spring to the stage to my defense if I should need him.

I might.

And then there were the Splendora sisters and Uncle Donny. How they'd managed to get tickets, I couldn't say. Rosa must've arranged it. Still, I couldn't have asked for a better cheering section. Twila, Bonnie Sue, and Jolene whooped and hollered, almost to the point of causing embarrassment. Oh well. Better too much confidence than too little, right? And it didn't hurt that so many cheered us on. Bolstered my faith, for sure. I knew those Splendora ladies were praying, which also helped.

Glancing at Armando, I offered a bold smile. "We can do this," I said.

He nodded and whacked me on the back, good-old-boy style. "Yep. We'll get 'er done."

I cringed and hoped Aunt Willy hadn't overheard. She was probably envisioning him on a golf cart now. Without a shirt, of course.

A tiny giggle escaped me as I remembered the advice my theater director had given me in high school: "Picture the audience members in their underwear, Scarlet. It'll help you overcome your nerves."

Somehow envisioning my aunt Willy in her granny panties only made me more nervous, so I shifted my attention back to the cakes. There would be plenty of time to imagine everyone in their tighty-whities later.

Not that we had time for such nonsense. The announcer gave the audience some instructions and pointed to the clock. Before I knew it, the "get to it!" buzzer sounded, and we were off to the races. The director snapped the scene board, and I tried to focus on the cake but found it difficult with a cameraman in my face.

Step away, mister! You're not ruining this for me!

Releasing a slow breath, I did my best to look relaxed.

Fat chance.

Armando, on the other hand, looked perfectly natural in front of the camera. No doubt. He definitely had the upper hand, thanks to his family's years in the industry. The cameraman shifted the camera in Armando's direction just in time to see him hefting three of our largest cakes

173

from the fridge. Thank goodness he had muscular arms. I found myself mesmerized by them, in fact.

As I stared at Armando's biceps, my breath caught in my throat and I couldn't remember what to do. I'd rehearsed it dozens of times before, but with my mind in a blank state, I stood frozen. The world continued to spin. At least, I think it did, but I couldn't seem to move.

"We can do this." Armando leaned my way. "Trust me, Scarlet," he whispered in my ear. "I'm not going to let you down." His words gave me the courage I needed to get this show on the road.

In that moment, as I gazed into those gorgeous chocolate-brown eyes, as 250 audience members looked on . . . I believed him. Trusted him. Saw in him what others had apparently not seen over the years. Talent. Skill. Dependability. All of this was wrapped up in a strong, handsome physique, which certainly didn't hurt.

For a second I focused solely on the previously baked cakes in my station—cakes I'd worked hard to prepare—then I looked at Armando. He brushed a loose hair off of his forehead and grinned. "Take us there, captain. Just tell me what to do. I'm all yours."

"We should probably . . ." I glanced at the cakes. "You start stacking and cutting. I'll get to work on the frosting."

"You got it." He started working on the largest

of the cakes, which would make up the base of the Coliseum.

I still couldn't quite picture how we would accomplish the details of this monstrosity once the whole thing was put together. Sure, I'd brought molds to make the arches, but with nearly a hundred of them needed, would we have time? And would they harden in this heat?

I glanced up at the overhead lights and groaned as a tiny bead of sweat trickled down my forehead. Brushing it away, I kept working.

Stay focused, Scarlet. Stay focused.

Still, the whole thing seemed overwhelming. Out of the corner of my eye, I watched the clock as the first hour ticked down. *Really? An hour? Didn't we just start?*

And who came up with this idea for the Coliseum, anyway? I second-guessed myself a dozen times as Armando stacked and cut, stacked and cut. What made me think we could build such a monstrosity in only six hours? And using an Italian cream cake recipe, to boot? Ugh! This recipe was heavy. Bulky. Kind of like my thighs.

But now my thighs weren't quite as large as they'd once been, were they? No. Thanks to three weeks of crash dieting, I'd trimmed off seventeen pounds. Likely some sort of world record was due me, but there was no time to think about that now. I had far more important things to tend to.

Like the gladiators.

I ran to the back shelves and pulled out the mold to start making the little fondant gladiators. We needed a handful of them. Not many. But their placement in the center of the Coliseum would make the whole thing believable and would convey the symbolism that Rosa had asked for.

Why, Scarlet? What sort of crazy plan have you agreed to? Who puts gladiators in a wedding cake? How unromantic is that?

Of course, the beautiful arches would add the element of romance. Once I reminded myself of that, I felt a little better about the situation. For a minute, anyway.

Arches! I needed hundreds of them! Better get busy on those. Molding and shaping hundreds of them would take most of the day. And if we missed those, the whole plan would crumble.

But first I would finish the cream cheese frosting. I needed buckets of the stuff, and only homemade would do. We had to get through the taste test in order to impress the judges, and what better way than with superior, homemade frosting? The yummy stuff offered more temptation than everything else put together. I could eat it by the bucketful, in fact. If I could just remember how to make it.

Is it getting hotter in here, or is it just me?

Okay, it's definitely getting hotter.

And what's up with the squishy feeling in my stomach? Why, Lord? Why now?

Ribbons of liquid weaseled their way down the center of my back. The dampness cooled me down a bit but didn't serve to calm my nerves—or my stomach. It continued to roll like the waves in the Pacific, churning, churning, churning.

Chocolate. Chocolate. Where's the white chocolate for the arches?

I'd brought tons of it. But where was it?

Oh, right. On the shelf.

As I stared at the shelf, I thought about Kenny and his arm. What a sweet guy to put up new shelves for me. And what a price he'd paid. His poor arm. I whispered a quick prayer for him, then tried to regroup.

Shelves.

What was I supposed to be doing again?

Oh yes, chocolate.

I saw it, but a wave of nausea prevented me from grabbing it. Ugh.

"Scarlet, are you okay?" Armando paused from his cutting to glance my way.

I gave him what probably looked like a wild-eyed nod and kept going. "I need chocolate."

"There's no time to eat right now, honey." He gave me a wink.

"Not. To. Eat." Though I definitely needed something to eat. Skipping breakfast probably hadn't been my smartest move, but who had time for breakfast? With my sticky buns being so large and all . . .

No, I couldn't think about my sticky buns right now. I had other things to do.

What was I doing again?

Oh yes, the chocolate.

I groaned, then located the missing white chocolate pieces and went to work melting them in the double boiler. Though I watched over them like a hawk, something seemed wrong.

No way.

The first batch hardened on me just as the overhead camera swung close. I threw out the batch just as we passed the two-hour mark. Off in the distance, Bella cheered, but when I glanced her way, the concern in my aunt's eyes sent a shiver down my spine.

Not that shivering was a bad thing. Not in this heat. I needed to cool down. Needed to think.

Think, Scarlet. Think. You've melted chocolate a thousand times before and it's never hardened on you. Do. It. Again. This. Time. Do. It. Right.

Probably sensing my terror, Armando paused from his cutting to help me. He whispered words of encouragement in my ear and managed to get me calmed down, though the weird out-of-body experience continued. For a minute, I envisioned this all as some sort of hazy dream. I would wake up and laugh, then tell Mama about my wacky television debut.

It's not a dream.

Armando began to hum a happy tune. I couldn't

quite make it out, but it calmed my nerves. Sort of.

I went to work on the arches, ribbons of sweat trickling down my back. I'd prepared myself psychologically for so many things but hadn't given any thought to the heat. The room had to be at least ninety degrees. Likely the frosting would cause the cakes to go slip-sliding off of each other. Why oh why had I gone with the cream cheese frosting idea? Fondant would've been so much neater, especially with this heat.

Oh. Help.

And why wouldn't these little molds cooperate? I'd used them back home and they didn't give me fits. Why here?

Oh, right. The heat. It caused the chocolate to stick to the molds.

Refrigerator. Put them in the refrigerator.

Brilliant idea, Scarlet.

I'd put the frosting in there for a few minutes to stay cool until we needed it. Then again, cream cheese frosting hardened in the fridge, didn't it? Maybe that wasn't such a great idea after all.

Only if you leave it in there too long, Scarlet. You can do this.

I stood in front of the open fridge for a moment, trying to cool down, but it didn't seem to help. The camera swung behind me, and I could almost envision the voice-over: "Crazed baker cools buns in fridge."

I checked on the frosting and found it to be in

decent shape. Not too runny. A few more minutes in the fridge wouldn't hurt.

Armando didn't seem terribly concerned about the heat, but he wouldn't be. What did he know about cakes, really? I could count on him to lift and lug, to stack and cut, but decorating? I'd have to do that on my own, slippery frosting or not.

"You okay over there?" Armando spoke with a forced smile as the camera swung back my way. I could read the fear in his eyes as he took in my haggard appearance.

I nodded, but I could feel the river of sweat now flowing down the small of my back.

As the camera moved on to the next duo, he drew near. "You look kind of . . . sick."

"Is it hot in here?" I whispered through clenched teeth.

"It's warm, but nothing unbearable."

"I just feel a little . . . weird."

"Hope you're not coming down with some-thing." Armando looked alarmed. "Do you need to sit down?"

I drew in a couple of deep breaths and whispered, "What would Lucy do?"

"Lucy?" Armando looked perplexed by that question. "I don't know anyone named Lucy."

"Well, I do. She had Lady Clairol red hair just like me."

"Ah. That Lucy."

"Yes, that Lucy. And she would keep going. No.

Matter. What." I raised my frosting-covered spoon in the air triumphantly, but doing so upped my wooziness. Oops. Closing my eyes, I sucked in a couple of deep breaths and willed myself to stay calm.

At this point, the show's emcee stopped by to ask why we'd chosen to go with the Coliseum cake. The camera swung around in a close-up of my sweaty face. Great. I knew I should explain the role the Coliseum had played in Rosa and Laz's love story, but how? With the room spinning, I could barely collect my thoughts.

"Oh, it's, um . . ." I blinked several times and tried to focus.

Thank God for Armando. He jumped in and, with a twinkle in his eye, shared the whole tale, even growing misty as he mentioned his aunt and uncle overcoming their sparring to fall in love.

I continued to work as he shared, but the heat was really getting to me. I paused to take a few breaths as the camera shifted to the next group of contestants.

After several deep breaths, I remembered the *I Love Lucy* episode that took place in the chocolate factory—the one with the out-of-control conveyor belt. If Lucy could handle the stress, so could I.

Armando gave me a curious look, then went back to work, now carving the Coliseum into shape. Within minutes he'd created a form so breathtaking, so perfect in structure, that the cameraman headed back our way for another shot. I gave him an admiring nod and whispered, "Thank you."

"You're welcome." He took a step back to examine it. "Now what?"

I directed him to the fridge to get the first tray of hardened chocolate arches. He pulled it out and his nose wrinkled. "Those are the arches?" he asked.

"Yeah. The first batch, anyway."

"They look more like the windows on the *Titanic*. Shouldn't they be rounded on top?"

"I . . . I guess." I stared at the printout of the real Coliseum, the room now spinning. Had someone turned up the heat again?

I heard Bella holler out another encouraging cheer. I squinted to see her, but with the lights in my face, I couldn't quite make her out. Then again, I couldn't quite make out anything. Weird. They must've done something with the lights.

"Scarlet?" Armando flashed me a concerned look. "Are you all right?"

"Huh?" Was it just my imagination, or was the room spinning? I pinched my eyes shut and took a few deep breaths. Probably nerves. Or the heat. I tugged at my collar and prayed for a cool breeze to float by.

It didn't.

I could feel Armando's stare, even with my

eyes closed, so I opened them and peeked at him.

"Again I ask . . . are you all right?" He took hold of my arm. "Your face is really red."

I put my hands on my cheeks and could feel them burning. "It's just so hot in here. It's hot to you too, right?"

"Yeah, it's warm, but not the kind of hot you're describing." He gestured to a chair in the back of our little area. "I think you need to sit down, Scarlet."

In spite of the spinning room, I could not— would not—sit. Not with a wedding cake to bake in front of millions of people.

Wedding cake.

We are baking a wedding cake, right? Not a birthday cake?

Wait. I think we're baking a turtle cake for a little boy, right?

No. A baby shower cake. That's why I have blue fondant gel in my pocket.

But I couldn't find the bottle of fondant gel in my pocket. Forcing myself back to the task at hand, I made a conscious decision to keep going with this Italian-themed wedding cake. No matter what.

Only one problem—the little white stars. I saw them every time I blinked. When I looked at the cake, there they were. And when I shifted my gaze to Mama's face in the television audience, I still saw them.

After a minute or two, I felt sick. Really, really sick. My stomach did the hula, and the stars morphed into magnificent, shiny orbs floating in front of my eyes. Before long they consumed me. A surge of nausea gripped me just as the camera swung round to get a close-up of our cake. Panicked, I tried to decide what to do. If I bolted, everyone would know I was sick.

Okay, no way could I bolt. My vision—blurry as it was—had now nearly disappeared completely.

But my stomach—oh, my stomach! The cameraman, likely sensing my problem, swung the camera around to the Alvarez family just in time for me to grab a mixing bowl—an empty one, thank God—and empty the contents of my stomach, feeble as they were, in front of everyone in attendance.

A gasp went up from the audience. Not that it mattered. By now my vision was nothing but stars.

Stars, stars, and more stars.

I gave myself over to them, floating away on a cloud of white.

14

Humble Pie

When you share a cupcake, you share love.
Author unknown

There's something rather disconcerting about
waking up on a soundstage with cameras hovering
over you. The room shifted in and out, in and out,
and I thought—through the haze—that perhaps
I'd died. The sweet, sugary smell of cake lingered
in the air, and I drew in a breath, blissful. Happy.
Relaxed.

*Oh! There's really cake in heaven! I knew it! So
much for all those years of fretting.*

Just as quickly, I faded back out again. In that
foggy place, I had the strangest dream. I dreamed
a handsome Italian man hovered over me, calling
me back to earth once again, back to a place of
torment and pain, bright lights and fiery ovens,
filled with temptation.

*Oh, what handsome angels you've created,
Lord! Fabulous surprise!*

"Scarlet! Scarlet!"

The angel's face faded from view, along with
his broad shoulders and muscular arms.

185

"No!" I would not go. I would not! Earth was a place of slippery frosting and cranky bosses. A place of deadlines and broken arms, chocolate arches and lopsidcd wedding cakes. A place where single women with broad backsides made total fools of themselves in very public fashion.

I will not go there, Sam I Am! I will not bake it in a pan!

Through the fog, I thought I saw the bony finger of Aunt Willy waggling in my face and her voice calling out, "Sticky Buns! Look what you've done! You've humiliated me in front of millions!"

Millions?

Yes, in heaven there were certainly millions. They hovered around me, singing at the top of their lungs. Certainly not the heavenly choir I'd imagined, but they were loud. My head began to swim as I tried to make sense of everything.

Lord, heaven isn't quite what I pictured. Not at all, in fact. It's very . . . loud.

And hot. Goodness, was it ever hot here. I'd envisioned heaven to be cooler. And not so bright. Stars, yes. Angels, yes. But overhead cameras and lights?

Really, Lord, that's a little much.

My aching head proved problematic, and the fog began to lift. I realized I couldn't possibly be in heaven. Wasn't there some Scripture about no more pain or something like that? And that cameraman—the one swinging in low to catch a close-up of my face—was definitely no angel.

No, I hadn't died. I only wished I had.

I attempted to sit up, but the stars reappeared. *Ooo, pretty! Look at that one.* I reached out to grab it, but nothing materialized in my hand, so I tried again. Darn! "Come here, little star! I want you! You belong to me now!"

"Scarlet, lie down."

I turned to smile at the handsome Italian angel next to me. "Armando." I gripped his hand. It did materialize. It also held me steady as I rested my head on the floor once again.

What pretty overhead lights. They're so shiny. I giggled, wishing I could float away on bright, glistening clouds. Maybe if I kept my eyes closed, I could.

An unfamiliar voice rang out. A fellow I didn't recognize leaned over me and patted me on the shoulder. "Stay calm, Scarlet. We're calling the medics in to look at you. Then we're sending you to the hospital to be examined."

"Medics?" I echoed the word. It tripped across my tongue like a little song. "What are medics?"

"People who help you."

"Help me?" Why did I need help with so many angels afoot?

The fellows with all of the equipment swept in around me, asking a thousand questions at once and forcing me back to reality.

My head took a little swimming trip over

Niagara Falls, one bizarre rush of pain followed by another on its tail. In that moment, it all came back to me in a flash. The television studio. The cakes. The heat. The fainting spell. All of it.

I sat up quickly—okay, too quickly—the world now spinning faster than before. Not that I cared. I had to get up. Get busy. Build a Coliseum. Put gladiators in the center. Find a way to make my family proud. Redeem the time. Lose twenty pounds. Undo this mess!

Oh, Lord . . . help!

"Nooo!" I didn't mean to holler the word, but there it was for all to hear.

"Calm down, honey," one of the judges said. "Take a deep breath. You're ill."

"No I'm not. You don't understand." My mind reeled as I tried again to make sense of things. "I know what's wrong. Why I fainted, I mean."

"Why?" This voice came from my mother, who had somehow worked her way down from the studio audience to my side. "Are you sick, honey?"

"No. I didn't eat this morning." I sighed as the faces of both my parents came into focus. "I, well . . . I didn't eat yesterday either."

"Are you serious?" Armando rose and sprinted across the room. He returned moments later with a thick hoagie sandwich. "There's a whole tray of these in the back. Why didn't you help yourself? The producer told us to."

"I would have, but . . ." A groan escaped my lips. "You don't understand, Armando." I now spoke through clenched teeth.

"Understand what? You're hungry, you eat. That's how it's done in my house." He shoved the sandwich into my hand, and I stared at it, drooling. *How do I love thee? Let me count the ways!*

Still, I couldn't eat it, not in front of a television audience. And with a camera hovering over me.

I pressed the sandwich back into his hand. "How can I eat a sandwich when I look like this?" I gestured to my hips, which sprawled across the floor, looking wider than ever. The cameraman zoomed in on them. Lovely.

"Like what?" Armando looked perplexed.

"Like *this*." I gestured to my sticky buns, thinking perhaps he needed his vision checked.

"Are you trying to tell me that you haven't been eating because you don't like the way you look?" He switched the sandwich to his other hand and shook his head.

The medics continued to examine me, one listening to my heart with a stethoscope and the other pumping up the blood pressure machine. One of them, a thin fellow with a long face, handed me a glass of orange juice. "Drink up, sister."

I fought the urge to say, "I'm not your sister," and instead opted for, "Do you know how many calories are in this juice?"

He stared at me like I'd lost my mind. "Drink it anyway."

Okay, now his stern voice reminded me of my first grade teacher, Mrs. Morgan.

I swallowed the juice, and the stars dissipated a little. Armando tried once again to feed me, and this time—likely because twenty-five people now hovered around me with terrified expressions on their faces—I took the hoagie in my hands and sighed. I even took a little bite.

Oh. Yum.

Tasted good. Really, really good. I'd forgotten just how yummy food could be. Especially carbs.

I took another bite. Then another. Before long I'd eaten the whole thing and was asking for another. The cameraman captured the whole embarrassing thing—every frame, every nuance —right down to the mustard on my left cheek, which Armando dabbed away using a napkin. He didn't look at all embarrassed, which raised my opinion of him even more.

My mother continued to scold me for getting myself into this predicament—*Thanks, Mama. No place like a soundstage to be chastened*—and her tears flowed. My father—godly man that he was—knelt down and prayed over me. The Splendora sisters got involved, and before long we were having a full-fledged prayer meeting on the floor of the Food Network soundstage. With cameras hovering over us. And the producers looking on.

Turned out the Alvarez family members knew how to pray too. They got involved, apparently unconcerned with the outcome of the contest. The other contestants looked on, intrigued, but kept working on their cakes. Who could blame them? This was a competition, after all.

Cake!

I looked at our Coliseum cake, realizing just how much work we still had to do on it.

"Armando." I tried to stand, and he stopped me.

"What are you doing?"

"We're going to get this done. Help me up. Hurry."

"Scarlet, you can't possibly—"

"Miss, you really need to stay seated." The paramedic kept up his first-grade-teacher voice, though it was now grating on my last nerve.

Okay, I didn't actually have any nerves left, but whatever.

I shook my head and offered a confident "I feel fine."

I did, actually. Funny what a little food could do for a girl who hadn't eaten in a couple of days.

"Honey, you can't very well get up off the floor and dive right back into the competition." My mother's words likely sounded like the voice of reason in her ears, but they didn't ring true to me. "You'll pass out again."

I looked at my mother and asked the one question that I knew would sway her. "What would Lucy do?"

Seconds later Mama's frown reversed itself. "She would get back up, dry her tears, and put on a show. She would prove to Ricky that she had the goods."

"And that's just what I'm going to do." With Mama's help I rose. I saw my aunt still seated in the television audience. She looked horrified. No doubt. Her niece had just humiliated her publicly. But I would make good on this. Not for her sake, necessarily, but for mine. I had to redeem the time. If the gladiators could do it, I could too.

Somehow I managed to regroup. No, *regroup* was too tame a word. I came back with a redheaded, fiery, belly-full-of-sandwich-and-feeling-all-right roar. With the stars now gone and my strength intact—not to mention adequate calories to fuel me for the task—I saw the Coliseum through new eyes. I would not be fed to the lions. I would win this thing.

I kept a watchful eye on Armando, who seemed more concerned about me than the cake. At least three times he asked how I was feeling. My "fine" response didn't seem to convince him.

So he hovered.

Not that I minded. No, something about his nearness gave me the courage to keep going, even when the decorative pieces didn't turn out quite as I'd hoped. He put together the cream cheese frosting, and I began the arduous task of lopping it on, then smoothing it out, layer upon layer, layer upon layer. For whatever reason, the process got me giggly. I started laughing, which really got the cameraman intrigued. He drew near and caught the whole thing on film. Still my laughter persisted. Had I really just fallen flat on the soundstage in front of millions of viewers? Why that made me laugh, I couldn't say.

I finally got my giggles under control, at which point Armando drew close and whispered, "How are you, really?" in my ear.

I responded, "As great as a person who's just humiliated herself in front of a television audience could be."

"Trust me, if you want to talk to someone who knows what it's like to bounce back after making a fool of himself, I'm your guy." He gave a winsome smile. "I happen to have a lot of experience in that arca."

That got a chuckle out of me once again. For a moment, anyway. Things took a serious turn after that. As we worked to decorate the Coliseum, Armando told me about his humiliations—the ones he'd confessed to family members and the ones he hadn't. He spoke from his heart, completely calming my nerves and helping me focus without freaking out at the task at hand. In other words, I got so lost in his story—his amazing, heartfelt story—that I almost forgot I was on television. Until the cameras swung in my face, I mean. But even then he shooed them away and kept me sighing over his woeful tale.

It's funny. You can learn a lot about a person working with them—him—under stressful conditions. Some of your preconceived ideas fly right out of the window. Or, in our case, right out of the arches.

Arches!

We somehow put together over a hundred perfect little arches. As we worked to ease them into place on the exterior of the now-frosted Coliseum, the whole thing began to take shape. I could hear the cheers of encouragement from the audience members. Invigorated by their enthusiastic reception of our work, Armando and I kept going. What really kept me going, however, was the distraction of his chatter. I guess his voice had a calming effect. Or maybe it was his ability to tell a great story. Either way, he held me spellbound and even got me laughing at one point.

Half an hour before the clock ran down, I looked at what we'd done and tried to analyze our plan of action. The outside of the cake looked dreamy. Romantic. But something was still lacking. Oh yes. The gladiators. Warriors. Fighters.

Like me.

I did my best to reshape the new half-melted little guys into the image I'd seen in my head, but it just wasn't working. Thank goodness Armando's sculpting skills turned out to be pretty good. No, not pretty good. Amazing. He'd even crafted slightly larger bride and groom gladiators, complete with swords in their hands, that he placed in the center. Was there anything this guy couldn't do?

Suddenly it occurred to me why people called him a jack-of-all-trades. He really was good at a lot of things. When one excelled in multiple areas, he apparently had trouble making up his mind what he wanted to be when he grew up.

I got it. It all made sense now.

But I was only good at one thing—baking. Well, baking and decorating. And singing.

Okay, where the singing thing came from, I had no idea. Sure, I'd sung a melody or two in days gone by, but those days were behind me now.

Or not. I found myself humming a merry little tune as the cake came together. And by the time the buzzer went off, signifying the end of the event, I was in full-out songbird mode. Armando wiped his hands on his apron, high-fived me, and joined me in a rousing chorus of "Oh Happy Day."

I glanced down the line at the other cakes. Though I couldn't figure out what a soccer field had to do with weddings, the Scotch-Irish cake really took my breath away. So did the colorful African extravaganza, so bright it lit up the room. What really messed with my head, though, was the Alvarez family's rendition of the beaches of Cancun. The sand was so real I wanted to take my shoes off and run through it. And the water! How did they get the colors just right? I'd never been able to create that perfect shade of aqua-blue with my fondant gels. Looked like the perfect honeymoon getaway.

Oh well. I turned to face Armando, who slipped his arm around my shoulder and gave me a big hug.

"Whatever happens," I said, "I owe you. Big-time."

"You owe me nothing," he responded. "Except one thing."

"What's that?"

"You can't deny the singing thing any longer. You're going to have to perform at the fund-raiser."

"Oh . . ." Ugh. Should've left "Oh Happy Day" off my repertoire. Now the boy knew I could sing.

I can sing?

The show cut to a commercial break, and the producer ushered all of the contestants into a back room. As we left the sound studio, I could hear Bella and the others cheering. I thought I saw Aunt Willy crack a smile—*Heaven help me! Am I seeing things?*—as she looked at the Coliseum wedding cake. Or maybe she just had gas or something. Either way, I felt proud of my work.

Obviously, so did Armando. He chatted up a storm all the way back to the holding room. Once we arrived, I was surrounded by the other contestants, all asking how I felt.

"Fine, fine," I said with a wave of my hand. "Just needed a little food." Hopefully the confidence in my voice would dismiss any concerns they might have.

"Oh, let me feed you." Mrs. Alvarez walked to the food table and returned with an apple and a bag of chips. "You need to keep up your strength."

I chuckled and opened the bag of chips. No point in going without any longer. I'd already proven that the crash diet plan ended with a crash landing on the floor.

"Why did you feel like you needed to go without food, anyway?" Armando whispered. "I don't get it."

I shook my head. "Are you blind or something?"

"No. My vision is twenty-twenty. Always has been."

"Then you have to see that I'm a big girl."

"Big?" He seemed to mull over the word. "You're perfect," he said. "In my family we would call that a healthy weight." A chuckle chased his words.

"Healthy?" I laughed. "So healthy that I ended up on the floor."

"That was your own doing." He grew serious. "And I hope I never have to watch you go through anything like that again, Scarlet. It really scared me. I thought maybe you were . . ." He raked his fingers through his hair. "Anyway, I was worried."

"Aw, thank you."

"So don't mess with that whole diet thing, okay? You're perfect just the way you are. And like I said, our family loves a healthy eater."

Did I need to remind him that his family was in the process of undergoing a radical change of diet, thanks to Uncle Laz's heart attack? Maybe I could save that for another day. Right now I needed to eat my chips. My not-so-good-for-me-but-how-can-I-keep-from-eating-them chips.

By the time they called us back out to the stage, I felt stronger than ever. Armando gripped my hand as the names were called. In fourth place, the Scotch-Irish team. Obviously their soccer stadium cake didn't impress the judges. I had to admit, it didn't seem very romantic. Then again, a Coliseum didn't either.

In third place, the African team with their royalty-inspired cake. That left only two teams—the Alvarez family and us. Armando's grip on my hand grew painful, but I didn't let go. Didn't dare.

There are those moments in life when you wonder if maybe you're dreaming. As the announcer called our names, proclaiming our Coliseum cake to be the best in show—er, best in competition—I had that weird out-of-body experience. Not like the one I'd had earlier, where I landed on the floor, but close. Only when they put the ribbon in my hand—along with a twenty-five-thousand-dollar check made out to the American Heart Association—did it all seem real.

I stared at the cake, giving the little gladiators a knowing glance. They'd fought the good fight . . . and so had I. And thank goodness I'd fought it alongside a warrior who knew how to keep a girl on her feet, even when she made a complete goober of herself in front of a television audience.

15

A Sweet Tooth

Vegetables are a must on a diet. I suggest
carrot cake, zucchini bread, and pumpkin
pie.

Jim Davis

When the competition came to an end and the
celebration drew to a close, I found myself alone
on the soundstage, clearing up our space. Though
exhaustion overwhelmed me, I still had a lot to
do before I could pack it in for the day and head
back to the hotel.

After a couple of minutes of alone time,
Armando joined me, beaming ear to ear. "Our
families are now best friends, FYI."

"Oh?" I looked up from my work into his
smiling face. "What do you mean?"

He began to dry my largest mixing bowl.
"They've all gone out to dinner at some steak-
house a couple of blocks from here. We're
supposed to meet them there when we're done
cleaning up. Bella says it's within walking
distance. She also said one of the judges told her
it's the best place in town for cheesecake."

I gestured to the mess and sighed. "As much as

I'd love a great steak—and don't even get me started on the cheesecake—it's going to take me hours to get my stuff packed up." I yawned.

"Nah, this won't take long. I'll help." He went to work alongside me, chattering merrily about the competition, which served to revive me once again. Strange how Armando always seemed to have that effect on me.

As he talked, I found myself completely invigorated. And relaxed. Gone were all anxieties. Now, with the twenty-five-thousand-dollar check in hand, I felt like a victor. With my partner's help, I'd brought honor to two families at once —my own and the Rossis'. If potential viewers could overlook that one little faux pas where I fainted dead away on the floor.

Maybe the producers will edit that part out.

If they didn't, maybe I could use the incident to publicize my business. Yes, people would definitely want to stop by Let Them Eat Cake to see me standing on both feet. Or, better yet, maybe I could stage a faint-in. People could come to watch me lie around on the floor like a goober. For some reason—probably exhaustion—that idea got me tickled. A faint-in. What would that look like? Dozens of people strung out across my bakery floor?

Now I couldn't stop the giggles. They bubbled up like carbonation in a diet soda. Skip that— make it a real soda, one loaded with sugar.

"You okay?" Armando looked up from another mixing bowl.

"Yeah." I bit back a laugh. "Just thinking."

"Obviously thinking about something funny." He wiped the bowl dry with a dish towel, smiling all the while. "By the way, I love your laugh."

"You do?"

"Yeah, it's priceless. Almost as great as your singing voice."

That got a groan out of me. Why oh why had I sung in front of the boy? I'd never live it down.

The lights went down on the far side of the stage as the Alvarez family left. They waved their goodbyes, leaving Armando and me alone to finish up.

A couple of minutes later he stepped into the spot in front of me. "Hey."

I glanced up from my packing and smiled. "Hey."

"You have a little frosting right . . . there." He reached to touch my lip, and I felt a tingle run through me. "And a little more right . . . here." With the back of his fingertip, he brushed my cheek, and in spite of the heat in the room, I shivered. His hand lingered against my cheek, and I found myself giving in to the temptation to stand close. Very, very close.

"I . . . I can't thank you enough for what you did for me today," I whispered. "You were the best possible person to help me."

"I was about to say the same thing about you." His soft words tickled my ear.

"Me? How did I help you?"

Armando pulled me into his arms and gave me a tender kiss on the cheek. I fought the temptation to pull away as I thought about what Hannah had told me about him. How many other girls had he pulled into his arms over the years? Dozens? Still, I melted into his embrace, even sighing as my knees grew wobbly. Good grief. Must be the exhaustion.

Or not.

Armando brushed his fingertip down my cheek again. "You are a romantic soul, aren't you?" he whispered in my ear.

"For a church girl?" I asked.

His cheeks turned red. "I'm sorry I called you that. There's nothing wrong with going to church." He shrugged. "I plan to marry a girl like that."

I looked him straight in the eye as I took a step back. "So, let me get this straight. You don't necessarily date girls like that, but you plan to marry one like that?"

He looked as if I'd slapped him. "W-what?"

"You date a different sort of girl?" The words came out more as an accusation than a question.

"What are you talking about? Or, rather, who's been talking about me?"

"No one." An embarrassing pause followed my words. "I just thought . . . Oh, never mind."

"No." He took a step in my direction. "Someone told you I'm a player."

Ack. Now what? I couldn't very well deny it, now could I? Still, to speak the words aloud seemed so . . . rude. And presumptuous.

"Well, they're wrong. I might come across as a bad boy, but it's really more of an image I've put out there than anything. Inside . . ." He pointed to his chest—his muscular, golf-cart-friendly chest—and said, "I'm as good as gold."

I wasn't so sure about all that, but he had me at the word *image.* If anyone understood putting forth an image—*Hello? Did I not just lose seventeen pounds in three weeks?*—I did.

His hand lingered along the edges of my messy hair, and I felt a little tingle run down my spine at his touch.

"You've helped me more than you know, Scarlet. I'm not sure there are words enough to explain how or why, but I'm grateful."

The tip of his index finger traced my lips. As I gave myself over to the moment, the overhead lights flashed on, startling me back to reality.

I pulled away from Armando, horrified to be caught in such a compromising position, and all the more when I realized one of the judges had joined us.

Quick! What would Lucy do?

She would . . . she would . . . act like nothing was up.

So that's what I did. I got back to work cleaning my station. So did Armando, who now stacked pans to my right.

The judge with the interesting hairdo looked my way and quirked a brow. "Well, now. Celebrating, I see." She gave us a funny "I didn't know you two were a couple" look.

"Y-yes, ma'am." I kept working and tried to steady my breathing. "We're celebrating."

"Well, I'm glad I caught you two . . . together." A sly grin turned up the edges of her lips. "I came back specifically to ask you for something."

I stopped working to gaze at her. "What's that?"

She eyed the cake, and I could see the interest in her eyes. "I want the recipe for that Italian cream cake. That sample you gave us was divine. Truly. Never tasted anything like it in my baking career." She lit into a story about how long she'd been in the business—*Wow! Forty years? Really?*—and how she'd never tasted anything sweeter. Still, I could hardly focus.

I could see Armando visibly flinch as she asked for the recipe once again. I pretty much reacted the same way. To turn her down would be unthinkable. But to give her Rosa's—er, Willy's—recipe? Even more so. They would kill me. Both of them.

"I . . . I might have to get back to you on that," I managed after a moment's pause.

Armando and I spoke our next words in unison: "It's an old family recipe."

The judge looked back and forth between us. "Which family?"

"Well, both," I said. "His and mine."

"You're saying you merged recipes?"

"Sort of." I chuckled. "It's kind of a long story. But I don't think we're supposed to share it publicly. You understand."

She put a hand up and smiled. "Okay, okay, never mind. Say no more. Trust me, there are dozens of recipes I refuse to share too. I get it." Her gaze narrowed. "Besides, if I know your aunt Willy . . ." She pointed at me. "And I do. I went to culinary school with her, you know. She was a spitfire back then, and from what I've gathered, not much has changed. So, if I know her, she won't budge an inch on this recipe, especially if she knows I'm the one asking."

I gasped at that, in part because I hadn't realized my aunt knew any of the judges, and in part because the judge's words were so accurate.

The judge took off across the soundstage, muttering something about how sweet vengeance would be right about now. She stopped in front of our cake and cut another slice—this one pretty large—and pressed a bite into her mouth, a contented look on her face. Oh well. At least she left the little chocolate gladiators in place. They would live to fight another day. Hopefully we would too.

Armando kissed the tip of my nose and then laughed. "Can't believe we turned her down. She's the top dog on this show. And she seems pretty intimidating."

"No kidding. But I'm used to intimidating people. And speaking of which, how weird is it that she used to know my aunt?"

"Still, it looks like we won her over," Armando said.

"With a recipe that goes back several generations." I chuckled.

"Yeah, well . . . about that." He used his index finger to brush a loose hair out of my eye.

"What?"

"Just FYI, I have it on good authority—Bella— that Rosa got that recipe from the internet a few months back. Just found out this morning before we started taping the show. Didn't have time to tell you."

"No way."

"Yeah. The 'old family recipe' she once used didn't even come close to this one. Bella reminded me that she used to make the original years ago and no one cared much for it."

I laughed. "Maybe Aunt Willy did the same. Maybe that's why she was so reluctant for your aunt to see the recipe, because she was afraid she might google it and find out the truth." Yep, suddenly it all made sense. No wonder she didn't want Rosa to see it. She knew the truth would come out.

"I wouldn't doubt it," he said. "But can you believe they did that to us?"

"Nope. But let's let them think we believe the recipe is theirs. What would it hurt? I thought it was really good, regardless."

"It is special," he said. "It brought both of us together."

"O-oh?" I gazed into his eyes, and he slipped his arms around my waist. Thank God, they fit all the way around. That one thing alone gave me hope. Of course, I'd have to watch myself from now on. I'd probably put on at least two pounds this afternoon alone—a hoagie, chips, and an apple? What had happened to my self-control?

As I gazed into Armando's gorgeous eyes—as I envisioned the two of us riding down the street in his golf cart with his muscular, shirtless arm wrapped around me—I decided that self-control was highly overrated.

"I don't care whose recipe it is, as long as it served to make us a team." He placed another kiss on my cheek—so soft, so tender that it took my breath away.

In that moment, I secretly thanked Aunt Willy for stealing that recipe from the internet. Didn't matter what ingredients we'd added. The end result was this moment—this precious, God-ordained moment. And from where I stood, life suddenly seemed awfully sweet.

My stomach grumbled, and I realized how desperately I needed a meal. A real meal. Armando must've heard it too.

"We're getting out of here," he said. "I'm taking you out for a big, juicy steak and baked potato."

"But . . ." I thought about the calories in the steak and did my best not to groan.

"It's protein, Scarlet. You need protein, trust me. It'll keep you strong."

Protein wasn't all I needed to make me strong. I needed the strength and protection that Armando's arms gave me. I needed his smile, his wacky sense of humor, and his goofball charm. Most of all, I needed his encouragement, for he always seemed to know just what to say and how to say it.

He might not be a good old boy in the traditional sense, but right now, he looked really, really good to me.

16

Hard to Swallow

If you can't stand the heat, get out of the kitchen.

Anonymous

If anyone deserved a break after that television filming, I did. But I never got it. Arriving back in Galveston, I had less than two weeks to prepare for my BFF's wedding. That meant pulling together a shower cake, a wedding cake, and a groom's cake all while running a bakery. Oh, and putting on a talent show. A life-altering, "take this team to Nicaragua so that lives can be changed for the better and children can be fed" talent show.

I truly had no time to spare, not even a minute, and needed every bit of help I could get. Unfortunately, my assistant still had a bum arm. But the bum arm didn't stop Kenny. No sir. I'd never seen anyone work so hard with one good arm.

And talk about a crowd to feed. Even though the cake challenge hadn't aired yet, our local newspaper had picked up on the fact that I'd participated and splashed my name across the front page, along with a headline that read "Local baker hits the ground running. Literally."

I cringed but decided to use the PR to my advantage. Why not draw people in with that little teaser, then strike up a conversation about what had really happened? Garner interest in the products as they stood and gabbed? Yes, that would surely work. And I'd do everything I could to spread the word about the fund-raiser while I was at it. Posting flyers in the windows was the first order of business.

The bakery filled with customers early on Saturday morning. I could hardly believe how many people showed up hoping to meet me. Even Armando made an appearance, buying a whole tray of cookies.

"For the restaurant," he said.

Sure, sure.

More likely, he and his brother were eating them on the sly. As if the guy had any weight issues. He could swallow down as many calories and carbs as he liked, and they would turn into pure muscle—buff arms, a six-pack, and solid shoulder mass.

Not that I was paying attention or anything. That would just be wrong. Or right, depending on how you looked at him. Er, it.

The customers who flooded my shop were all

anxious to hear my story, and Armando was happy to oblige, giving them all of the gory details about how I'd hit the floor, scaring him to death.

Really, Armando? You had to tell them everything?

The whole thing seemed like a fuzzy dream now, a dream that kept growing exponentially as the story was repeatedly told. Of course, most wanted to know the reason for my fainting spell. A couple speculated that I might be pregnant, so I squelched that rumor like a bug. Then I shared my weight-loss story with anyone who would listen. They hung on my every word, especially when I explained how I'd gone without food for so long.

Let this be a lesson unto thee. Eat!

Three nurses, two dietitians, and one doctor chimed in, giving me dieting advice. One woman even tried to sell me some sort of miracle weight-loss product. I declined but took her brochure, then later tossed it in the trash.

Still, the idea of a commonsense plan to lose weight sounded good. I did need to lose a few pounds. Okay, more than a few. But I needed to do it the old-fashioned way—by eating right and exercising. No more crash diets. No more starving myself. No more self-imposed deadlines.

Not that any of the fellas in my life seemed to care about my weight. Sure, Kenny helped me out at the gym, but only because I insisted. And

Armando had looked downright confused by my confession that I'd been dieting.

No, I didn't need to lose weight to impress a guy—any guy. I would do it in sensible fashion for myself. In my own timing too. Even Aunt Willy would be impressed.

Then again, she was already thrilled with my performance on the cake competition. Well, all but the fainting part. Strangely, she had never mentioned that little incident. Every time she spoke of the competition, she bragged about the recipe she'd given me and how it had won the judges' hearts. Not one word about my time on the floor or the embarrassment it had caused the bakery. Hopefully it would never come up.

Still, when she made her way into my shop on the following Monday morning, I had to wonder why she'd showed up without calling me first. Turned out she just popped in to make sure I had enough supplies and to see how things were going. Go figure. She gave Armando a funny little look when she saw him seated at one of the tables eating a cookie. No point in saying anything to her about his ongoing presence just yet. Likely it would just trigger concerns on her end.

"I read the article in the paper, kiddo." She offered a genuine smile, and my heart nearly burst into song. "Nicely done."

I couldn't be sure if she meant the article was nicely done, or my ability to get publicity was nicely done. Either way, I'd take the compliment and go with it.

Is it possible, Lord? My aunt really loves me? Not just my business . . . but me?

"Have you seen more customers as a result?" she asked. "Thought I'd come down to the island and see for myself."

Ah. The truth comes out.

I nodded, hoping to keep her enthusiasm level high. "Oh, you have no idea. We've sold out of almost everything. I'm baking like crazy. People are buying everything, even those double chocolate chunk cookies."

"I love 'em." Armando held one up and then took a bite.

She glanced his way, her eyes narrowing to slits. "As I said, I've never seen much value in a cookie." She paused and looked at the near-empty glass cases. "On the other hand, anything that brings in money is a good thing, I suppose."

It always worried me when she brought up finances. Was she concerned about her investment, perhaps? I didn't blame her. She'd opened her wallet pretty wide to make my dream come true.

Our dream come true.

Suddenly I felt like a traitor for the strain I'd always felt in our relationship. She never would have invested in me if she didn't believe in me. And I'd proven myself to be a goober on more than one occasion, so the poor woman had reason to be concerned about whether or not I'd embarrass her, publicly or otherwise.

I would prove myself worthy. And I would do my best to enter into a relationship with her—not one where I just tolerated our time together but where we genuinely got along. We would be chums. Girlfriends. And I would start now by broaching a topic, one girlfriend to another.

I looked her way, observing as she touched up her hot-pink lipstick with a shaky hand. "Aunt Wilhelmina, can I ask a question?"

"Make it quick, Scarlet. I'm in a hurry." She snapped the lipstick closed and shoved it into a little Clinique makeup bag, then pressed the bag into her oversized Gucci purse.

"It's about Uncle Donny."

I couldn't help but notice Armando glance my way as I mentioned Donny's name.

Aunt Willy turned slowly and grimaced, setting her purse on a chair. "What about him?"

"I remember everything you said a few weeks ago—the whole bare-chested, golf-cart-riding story. The good-old-boy story."

Like I could ever forget that.

"What about it?" She huffed out a breath.

"Obviously, you think he's like that. And I'm assuming you don't get along with the man."

"Who could get along with a man like that?" She dove into a lengthy explanation about

215

how men like him thought they were God's gift to women. She completely lost me, in part because she'd never confessed a belief in God before.

"Don't you think he's nice, though?" I asked. "I mean, if you can get past the smell? And the way he dresses?"

"Nice?" She spoke the word more as a curse than a real possibility. "Certainly not."

"Oh."

She mumbled something about needing to talk to Kenny and then headed into the kitchen. I had a feeling she'd had enough of this conversation.

Apparently I wasn't the only one who picked up on that.

"Methinks she protests too much." Armando took several steps in my direction and whispered in my ear, his breath warm against my face. "If you ask me, she's smitten."

"Smitten?" I'd never heard a guy use that word before and couldn't help but smile.

"Well, yeah." Armando grinned. "She's opposed to everything about him, but that usually means there's some sort of denial going on."

Denial.

Yes, I understood denial. Lived in that state much of the time, if I was being honest with myself. I understood it every time I looked into Armando's handsome face. Understood it when I begged my heart to slow down every time he glanced my way. Totally understood it when I realized that any potential relationship with him —should either of us desire it—would have to wait until I knew for sure where he stood with the Lord. And whether or not his golf cart days were behind him.

Not that I judged him any longer, regardless of what I might've heard about him from family members or otherwise. No, the only ideas I had about him were the ones I'd formulated, based on getting to know him personally. And the man I'd gotten to know impressed me on nearly every level.

I understood something else too. No matter how difficult, I must tell Kenny that we could no longer consider our relationship as anything other than friends. He would understand. I hoped. In fact, he had probably figured it out for himself by now.

With Auntie in the back room and Armando staring intently in my eyes, I attempted to focus on the biggest task at hand—Hannah's wedding. There were recipes to test.

Focus. Focus. On Hannah's wedding. Not on Armando. Not on those beautiful eyes. Who has eyes like that? And the curve of his smile . . . Oy! And the broad shoulders. My goodness, our children will be gorgeous. A little Italian, a little I Love Lucy . . . but gorgeous. Okay, maybe not, if they end up with my hips, but surely no one will notice the hips if they have their daddy's eyes. Breathtaking!

"Stop it, Scarlet."

I didn't realize I'd spoken the words aloud until Armando's brow wrinkled. "Stop what?" he asked.

"Oh. Nothing," I managed.

Kenny came out of the kitchen with Auntie, and they both looked my way. I snapped to attention and offered a weak smile.

"We need to get busy on Hannah's cake design, Scarlet," Kenny said.

"Right, right." Only, I couldn't seem to think about anyone—or anything—but Armando right now.

Kenny leaned against the wall and gave me a concerned look.

"I'm fine, Kenny. Really."

"Sure you are." His rolled eyes clued me in to his take on all of this. "Fine."

Armando took a few steps toward the door and said something about how he needed to get back to work. I knew the incoming lunch crowd at Parma John's would keep him busy, but I could tell he didn't want to leave. I didn't want him to either. Even Aunt Willy seemed a little disappointed when he announced his departure. She paused to thank him for his help with the competition, and he smiled in response. Before long he had talked her into stopping next door for a slice of pizza. Go figure.

They walked out together, the bell above the door jingling as they went.

Kenny turned my way. "Well, I'm glad to have you to myself."

"Oh?"

"Yeah." He looked around the empty room, then drew near. "I've been thinking about something."

Me too. I've been thinking that I need to tell you I can't marry you. Or date you. Or lead you on one moment longer.

"Kenny, I really think we should—"

"Spend some quality time together." He stood a little closer. "I'm thinking about the new venue on the seawall. Pleasure Pier."

Not exactly what I expected him to say. "What about it?"

"Thought it might be a fun place to hang out one afternoon."

"Ah. As in, me and you?"

"Well, yeah." He flashed a boyish smile. "And I thought maybe we should take some cake samples up there. Now that everyone knows who you are, it would be fun to do more external promotion."

"External promotion?" This coming from a guy who enjoyed working in the kitchen, away from the crowd? Clearly someone had gotten to him. And I had an idea who. No wonder that little stinker of an aunt had sneaked into the kitchen to have a one-on-one with him. She'd had ulterior motives.

I did my best not to sigh as I thought about how she'd almost won me over. I moved away from Kenny, understanding the motive behind this little chat. "Did Aunt Willy put you up to this?"

"Well . . ." He glanced at the floor. "She mentioned it in passing."

"I see."

"But I like the idea. Besides, after we get rid of the cake samples, we can ride the Ferris wheel and eat some cotton candy."

"I can't eat cotton candy, Kenny. You know that."

"Still . . ."

"Let me think about it. I love the idea of hanging out at Pleasure Pier, but I'm not keen on marketing in this heat. Besides, this is a terrible week to bring it up. We have our first rehearsal for the talent show, and then Hannah's wedding is just on the heels of that."

"Speaking of the talent show, did you hear that Devon is talking about dropping out of the trip? He called me last night."

"No way." My heart felt like lead at this news. "Why?"

"Not sure. Something to do with his family, maybe? I talked to him for fifteen minutes, but he wouldn't come clean with me. Just kept dancing around the issue." Kenny paused. "If you want the truth, I think he's worried about leaving his mom alone. She's not doing well. He's not giving me specifics, but I have a feeling she's in pretty bad shape and he's the only one she's got."

"Ah." I didn't know what to do about that, other than pray. Still, I hated the idea that her issues might cause him to miss the trip. Maybe I could visit with his mom. See if I could encourage her in some way.

Yes, that's exactly what I'd do. I'd take her some brownies too. In the meantime, I'd agreed to meet Hannah to talk through her wedding plans, and she was partial to pizza. Meeting at Parma John's made sense on multiple levels, though I wondered how I'd stick to my new healthy eating plan with the smell of pepperoni in the air.

Okay, I really wanted to see Armando again. Wanted to watch how his cockeyed grin lit the room. Wanted to imagine what he'd look like driving a golf cart without a shirt on. I wanted to relive that special moment after the cake challenge when he'd traced my cheek with his finger and gazed into my eyes with so much interest that I thought about marrying him on the spot. I wanted to feel that tingle run down my spine as I heard the sound of his voice and the joy of his boyish laugh. Wanted to feel his kiss on my brow.

Ah, that kiss!

I headed next door at noon, ready to experience all of that once more. Well, all of that, and help my BFF wrap up loose ends for her wedding. Not that Armando would necessarily sweep me into his arms in front of his family members in the middle of the workday . . . but a girl could hope. Right?

Focus, Scarlet. Your best friend needs you. Her wedding is in a few days!

I would be there for her, no matter how much I longed to stare at Armando and dream about his kisses.

I found Parma John's loaded with customers. More so than usual. Maybe Armando had his own following after his stint on the cake show. That had never occurred to me until now, but a vast number of pretty young things watched him, giggling, as he worked. But he didn't appear to be paying much attention. No, as he shifted from table to table, taking orders, he was all business.

I watched from a distance as he waited on customers. Observed the way he talked to them —how his smile lit up the room. How he stopped to tease a little boy with a freckled face. How he paused at the table with the Splendora sisters to give them each a hug and a funny story. How he hollered orders back to the kitchen with a lilt in his voice—the kind of lilt that said, "I'm happy to be working here! Look at me—how happy I am!"

I wanted to celebrate that fact. All of his running had landed him right here. Where he belonged. He might argue the fact, but the argument wouldn't hold water.

From across the room he looked my way, and a smile as bright as sunshine lit his face. He headed my direction. "Scarlet."

"Armando." I gestured to the crowd. "You guys are busier than usual today. This is nuts."

"No kidding. Between the bakery and Parma John's, everybody and their brother want to be on Galveston Island today."

I knew I did, and all the more as he gazed into my eyes.

Oh! Kiss me now!

"Not that I'm complaining," he said. "This is great for business, and I'm ready for them." Armando slung a cloth napkin over his arm, à la fancy waiter, and grabbed a menu from the counter. "What's your pleasure, miss? We've got a great pizza special going on today. Your aunt even complimented me on it."

"My aunt?"

He pointed to a table in the corner, and I caught a glimpse of Aunt Willy seated next to D.J.'s uncle Donny, whose laughter rang out across the room.

What?

Convinced my eyes were deceiving me, I took another look. Sure enough, there they sat side by side, eating pizza. I pinched my eyes shut and reopened them, just to make sure it wasn't a mirage. Nope. No mirage.

Armando leaned close to whisper his thoughts on the duo. "I'm not sure she's keen on the idea that Uncle Donny showed up, but she's being gracious. He asked if he could sit with her, and she agreed, but I could tell her heart wasn't really in it."

Fascinating. From the looks of things, her heart was in it now. I was pretty sure I even saw her crack a smile. Or two. Or three.

"Gracious. Hmm."

I took a couple of steps in their direction but then stopped. I did have plans to meet with Hannah, after all.

"So, what kind of pizza do you want?" Armando asked. "I'll get it started."

"Can't have pizza. You know I'm supposed to be dieting, right?"

"Ah." Armando pulled the napkin off of his arm. He looked pensive as he led me to an empty seat at the counter. "I still have no idea why, but whatever." He gestured for me to sit, then opened the menu and pointed at a section I'd never seen before. "You'll be happy to know that we've added a new lighter-fare line."

"Lighter-fare . . . Italian food?" I chuckled.

"Hey, don't laugh. It was my idea. After what happened with Uncle Laz . . . well, I just thought it was a good idea. I've spent the last few days working on it. Even talked to a dietitian to make sure we've got the right balance of calories and carbs."

"Oh? Wow." Talk about impressive!

"Yep, look." He pointed at a new line of salads and sandwich combos, everything under five hundred calories. "I talked to a guy at my gym to get his recommendations for healthy, high-protein foods too. So you can eat at Parma John's every day and still lose weight."

The way he said "every day" gave me reason to think he might very well be here every day. Did he plan to stay on the island after Jenna came back to work, perhaps?

That would be a question for another day. Seconds later Hannah arrived in a dither. I could tell from her knotted brow that we needed some privacy, so I led the way to a table near the back of the restaurant, where we could talk through her wedding plans. I couldn't help but notice that Armando hovered near our table, offering refills on water, soda, salad, bread . . . everything. He even offered me a fresh cloth napkin when mine slid off my lap.

Yep, you're paying close attention, aren't you, boy?

Hannah must've noticed too. She gave me a "hey, what's up with you two?" look, not just once, but approximately half a dozen times. I just smiled and kept eating. And talking. The conversation shifted to her wedding cake— *Finally! A subject I know well!*—and we set the plan in motion. Though we'd talked about it a dozen times before, Hannah just couldn't make up her mind. She was torn between carrot cake and Italian cream cake.

Leave it to Armando to convince her that Italian cream cake would be the best option. *You go, Armando!* That new recipe happened to be one of my faves now. Okay, it was heavy on the calories, but I'd probably dance the night away at my BFF's wedding. I'd burn off those calories yet.

Hmm. As I thought it through, I realized my former dancing partner—Kenny—wasn't exactly in shape to dance right now. Oh well. The Texas two-step was highly overrated. I could cut back on the Italian cream cake and be a wallflower.

Or not.

As I gazed into Armando's eyes, as I picked up on the interest written there, I envisioned the two of us taking a twirl around the room. Hey, stranger things have happened. A good church girl. A rough-and-tumble bad boy come home to roost. Surely even the Lord would smile on the two of us taking a spin around the dance floor. Right? Of course, our families would figure out our little secret, but I didn't mind. Soon enough my parents would see the great guy I'd come to know.

"Scarlet, you still with us?"

I shook off my ponderings and gazed at Hannah. She looked worried. Frankly, I didn't blame her. How long had I checked out, anyway? Long enough to picture myself married with a couple of kids.

"You're off in another world." Her gaze narrowed. "I have a sneaking suspicion why. But before you do anything crazy, just ask yourself, what would Lucy do?"

I knew what Lucy would do, of course. She'd married her Latin heartthrob, and they'd made a life together in front of millions of people, earning millions in the process.

Okay, so he'd left her heartbroken in the end, but I didn't really want to go there. Not yet, anyway. Right now, as I looked up to see the handsomest waiter on Galveston Island headed my way with a pitcher of tea in his hands, I could only conclude one thing: Lucy would dive in headfirst. And she wouldn't look back, no matter what anyone else told her to do.

17

Take It with a Pinch of Salt

I've always thought with relationships, that it's more about what you bring to the table than what you're going to get from it. It's very nice if you sit down and the cake appears. But if you go to the table expecting cake, then it's not so good.

Anjelica Huston

The following day Armando agreed to meet me at the church. He surprised me by bringing a new lightboard, one he'd borrowed from a friend.

"Nicky said we can use this until he needs it again," Armando said as he settled the board into place on the back table. "He knows we're doing the fund-raiser, so he's cool with that. In fact, I have a feeling he might be willing to sell it to us after that. Your dad is on board. I talked to him about it already."

"If we can just figure out a way to pay for it." I felt like bursting into song as I looked at the lightboard, and all the more as I watched Armando plug it in and set the knobs in their various positions. "How can I ever thank you? You've been great."

He shrugged and kept working. "No biggie. Just thought it might help to do a real light show during the fund-raiser. People respond well to lights."

Yes. They. Do.

And right now, with ribbons of light coming through the stained-glass windows, playing off the color of his hair, I found myself responding more and more.

Focus, Scarlet.

"So, let me get this straight." He picked up the paper I'd given him with the list of performances. "Our first rehearsal is Thursday night."

"Yes." My heart quickened. I must've been nuts to schedule it one night before Hannah's wedding rehearsal, but I couldn't back out now.

"Sounds like we're gonna be busy this weekend," he said. "Bella asked me to run sound at Hannah's rehearsal on Friday night because D.J. can't be there. Pretty sure he's going to be at the wedding, though, so I'll come as a guest and watch you in action as a flower girl."

A groan framed my words. "I'm not a flower girl. I'm the maid of honor."

"I know." He chuckled and reached to brush a loose tendril of hair from the side of my face. "Just teasing. Wanted to see your reaction."

Tease me all you like.

"I'm also the cake baker," I added, "so this weekend is going to be nuts. I have no idea why I scheduled a talent show rehearsal for Thursday night. Don't know what I was thinking. I guess I just couldn't imagine putting it off until the next week because we really need the practice."

"Do you need to cancel?"

"No. Our show is in a week and a half." My nerves kicked in as I spoke the words aloud. A week and a half? Really? How would we manage? "This is really the only night that works for a lot of our participants. And besides, the Splendora ladies are going to be in town for some sort of event at the seawall, and we need to take advantage of the fact that they'll be on the island."

"Oh, right. That motorcycle ministry thing that D.J.'s parents head up." He began to tell me all about it—how Dwayne and Earline Neeley rode their Harleys from one end of the island to the other to win souls for the kingdom.

"Yeah." Though I couldn't envision any of them on motorcycles if I tried all day. "It just makes sense to hold the rehearsal when the ladies are here."

"Gotcha. They are your headline act, after all."

"Right. So we're working around their schedule, not mine."

Still, I couldn't imagine how—or when—I'd bake my BFF's wedding cake. No doubt I'd be baking through the night. "It's crazy, I know. I think I'll need a shrink when this is all over."

"Nah." He gave me a sympathetic look. "Just pray. God'll get you through it."

Okay, well, that answered my question about where he stood with the Lord. Mostly, anyway. At least he saw leaning on the Lord as a good thing. That was half the battle, right?

Armando glanced back at the list and ran his finger down the page. "I don't know most of these people, so bring me up to speed. What are they doing, exactly?"

I took the paper from him and looked over it. "Well, for one thing, the teens are going to do a human video."

"Human video?" He looked perplexed. "What's that?"

"They act out a song. In this case, it's a song about a man overcoming addiction." I went on to explain the depth of the piece and even got tears in my eyes as I described how powerful it was.

"Interesting." His eyes took on a faraway look for a moment, then he snapped back to attention. "What else?"

I scanned the page. "There's a really cute little girl in our church who does a great job with 'Happy Birthday, Jesus.' She sings it every Christmas."

"You do know it's June, right?"

"Yeah." I did my best not to sigh. "But desperate times call for desperate measures."

"I didn't realize we were that desperate." He

chuckled and glanced back down at the list. "Okay, what else?"

"Don't laugh, but D.J.'s uncle Donny offered to perform."

"Uncle Donny? The mind reels." Armando's eyes narrowed to slits. "What's his talent, or do I dare ask?"

"Apparently he plays the saw."

"The saw?" The edges of Armando's lips curled up in a quirky smile. "Seriously?"

"Yeah, and according to D.J., he's all the rage in Splendora. Even the trio of Splendora sisters agrees. Oh, and speaking of which, they volunteered their services for three Gershwin tunes. Their harmonies are amazing. I'm so relieved they're able to help us with this fund-raiser. You have no idea how blessed I feel."

"You can thank me for that." He patted himself on the chest. "I sent them to you."

"Yeah. They told me." I gazed at him, wanting to thank him, but got hung up on his broad shoulders. "I just found out from Bella that D.J.'s brother, Bubba, is going to sing some sort of opera thing. Something from his last show at the Grand Opera Society. Bella's mom says he got a standing ovation at the last show."

"Yeah, he's great. I just hope he doesn't show up in tights like the last time I saw him."

I tried not to panic at that idea. "You don't really think he would do that, do you?"

Armando laughed and shook his head. "No, trust me. He hates that part of it. That's the last thing he'd do."

"Good. Well, I'm sure he'll be pretty amazing." Not that I was into opera, but whatever. Surely he would win me over with an aria or two. I glanced back down at the list. "Oh, and our seniors' ministry is going to do a song. A hymn. They're not the greatest, but we love them and give them every opportunity to perform."

"Okay. Want me to do some sort of wild light show as they sing?" Armando waggled his brows in playful fashion.

"Um, no. Pretty sure my dad would kill you. But thanks for offering."

"That's a shame. I think I really could've dressed up their hymn. Added a lot to it."

As I thought about the hymn they would be singing, I started humming it. We dove back into our work at the board, but I must've started singing at some point, because Armando stopped working and looked my way.

"What?" I asked.

"Nothing. It's just . . . you have a great voice."

I winced. "What?"

"You're singing again. You do that a lot."

"I . . . I'm sorry."

"No, don't be. Like I said, you've got a great voice. I love it."

"Oh." I hardly knew what to say in response. "I . . . well, I used to sing a little."

"Why did you stop?"

Ack. I had two options here. I could tell him the truth—that Aunt Willy had ridiculed my singing voice as a kid—or I could lie and tell him there were more important things in life than lifting one's voice in song.

Then again, there were more important things. Like opening a bakery. Prepping for my BFF's wedding. Keeping everyone in the family happy.

He continued to stare at me until I finally spoke up. "I still sing."

"Good." He smiled. "Because you're really good. I think your solo will bring in a lot of money for the fund-raiser. I'm sure the others will agree, once I've told them."

"My . . . solo?"

"Well, yeah. At the talent show? I'm assuming that's what you meant when you said you still sing. What song are you doing?"

"Oh no, no, no, no, no." I put my hand up. "I sing in the shower. I sing in the car with the radio. But I do not—will not—sing in front of people." Never again. Not after what happened in third grade when my precious auntie ridiculed me in front of my fellow students and teacher. A shiver ran down my spine.

"What would Lucy do?" He stared into my eyes more intently than before.

"That's not fair."

"It's completely fair. And it's how you come to at least half of the decisions you make in life, from what I can tell. So, what would Lucy do, if offered an opportunity to perform?"

I sighed. "She would make her way to the Copa Cabana and do some ridiculous performance that would potentially ruin Ricky's career. But then Ethel and Fred would come to her rescue with some great a cappella vaudeville number to save the day, and Lucy would be bummed that they got the accolades but not her. She would tuck her tail between her legs and go back home, climb into bed, and pull the covers over her head, convinced she should never try again."

"Wow." He gave me a strange look. "You take this Lucy thing seriously, don't you?"

"Yeah." I sighed again. "I need help. Maybe a twelve-step program."

"No. You just need what the cowardly lion needed. Courage."

I chuckled. "Maybe."

"Definitely. So we'll put you on the list?"

"For courage?"

"No, goofy. To sing a solo."

"No way." I shook my head. "Oh, but speaking of the show . . ." I diverted him by talking about the PowerPoint I'd put together for the big night. Surely that would interest him. "I've got some great photos of the families in Nicaragua we'll be helping, along with photos of our team members sort of interspersed. I think I did a pretty good job."

"Do you have them with you?" he asked.

When I nodded, he extended a hand and I reached into my purse for the flash drive. He stuck it in his laptop, and seconds later the PowerPoint—okay, maybe it wasn't as great as I'd thought—ran on the new overhead screen.

"Do you mind if I . . ." He looked my way, his nose wrinkled.

"You want to fix it up?" I asked.

"Well, I know how to make the transitions work a little smoother. And it'd be fun to kind of go back and forth between the Nicaragua kids and the Texas kids. Maybe show that, in God's eyes, they're all one big, happy family?"

"Ooo, Armando, that's a great idea. I wish I'd thought of it."

He began to work on it, his hands moving so fast I could hardly keep up. "You have to remember I'm from one big, happy family." He chuckled. "Well, big, anyway."

Minutes later, he showed off the transitions, and I gasped as the screens shifted from one blessed face to another. Remarkable. The boy was a wonder with technology, no doubt about it. In that moment, I could almost envision him working at the church full-time. Heading up our media department.

We have a media department?

We would have one, if he'd consider it.

"Is there anything you can't do?" I teased.

"Hey, that's why they call me a jack-of-all-trades." For whatever reason, he didn't smile as he said those words. Clearly he didn't see them as complimentary. I thought back to Bella's description of him and realized just how that description might label a person. But in reality, he was multifaceted, and that wasn't a bad thing. His ability to do many things well impressed me on multiple levels, particularly when I saw how generous he was with the gifts he'd been given.

Time for a heart-to-heart.

"Armando, I wonder sometimes if you see how valuable you are to people."

He crossed his arms and sat back in the chair, giving me an inquisitive look. "What do you mean?"

"You're good at a lot of things."

"Good at a lot, great at nothing." His gaze shifted back to the board, and he fumbled with a couple of the levers. "People don't remember you when you're mediocre, that's for sure."

"But you're not mediocre. In fact, you're *great* at many things. I wish you could see that."

He glanced my way, giving me a sheepish look. "Trust me, it's not for lack of trying on my part."

"What do you mean?"

"I mean, it helps to be told once in a while that

you're good at something. For people to let you know that they're proud of you."

"Well, I'm proud of you." I meant it. Every word.

He didn't look convinced.

I put my hand on his shoulder. His rock-hard shoulder. "Armando, the problem is you're incredibly blessed. You can do so many different things, and do them all well. Choosing one thing that's better than another would be tough."

He glanced my way and smiled. "You're just saying that to make me feel better."

"No, I'm not. You're really good at the whole AV thing, but beyond that, you're good with people."

"I am?"

"Yeah." Didn't he see how great he'd been with his customers at Parma John's? How the teens had responded to him that night at youth group? "You might dislike the idea of growing up in a big family because you didn't get enough individual attention—or whatever—but you shouldn't. It made you the person you are."

"Sarcastic? Tainted?"

"Well, maybe a little of that too, but it made you root for the underdog, probably because you always felt like one."

Yikes. Had I really just said that out loud?

He sighed.

"I think you would be a wonderful friend to

Devon. You guys are a lot alike." I did my best not to sigh as I thought about the teen's decision not to go to Nicaragua. "He's in such a hard place right now."

"What do you mean?"

"There are problems with his mom. He hasn't really elaborated, but whatever it is has caused him to change his mind about going on the trip."

"No way." Armando looked genuinely distressed at this news. "Are you sure?"

"Yeah." I glanced at the clock on the wall—11:20. "I thought about swinging by their place today. Even brought some brownies to take over to his mom. Kenny said I could take my time. He's watching the shop."

"Can I go with you?"

"Don't you need to get back before the lunch crowd?"

"My brother's got his kids helping today, and my sister Sophia is there too. I want to go with you to see Devon. I'll even drive."

Great. Another trip in the red pickle jar. Hey, at least there was less of me to squeeze in this time. With my hips shrinking, I'd eventually fit just fine. Until then, I'd grin and bear it.

I double-checked Devon's address, and we headed off to see him. As Armando drove, I chatted about the upcoming fund-raiser. We arrived at the apartment complex, and I drew in a deep breath as I looked it over.

"You sure this is the right address?" Armando looked nervous.

I glanced at the paper in my hand. "Yeah. This is it." No wonder Devon wasn't keen on anyone driving him home after church. Talk about a rough neighborhood.

"Stick close to me." Armando grabbed my hand as we walked together toward the apartment complex.

Minutes later we rapped on the door and waited a second until someone called out, "Who is it?" in a gruff voice. A female voice.

"Friends from church," Armando called back.

The door eased open, and a bleary-eyed woman stared at us. Her dark brown hair stood in a messy twist atop her head, and her mismatched clothes looked as if they hadn't been washed in ages. For that matter, the smell emanating from the room made me wonder if anything had been washed. Somewhere there was food that needed throwing out. *Ick.*

My heart went out to Devon as I realized how tough his living conditions were. No wonder the kid kept his distance from others.

"What do you want?" Her words sounded as slurred as I suddenly felt as I breathed in the putrid aroma from the room.

"We . . . well, we came looking for Devon," I said. "Just wanted to stop by for a visit."

"Devon!" she shouted, catching me off guard.

He appeared seconds later, his eyes growing wide when he saw us standing there. "Hey." The teen looked mortified. I didn't blame him. We'd put him on the spot by coming without an invitation, and now I felt awful about it. No doubt he did too.

He stepped outside to meet us and pulled the door closed. "Did someone die or something?"

"No." I released a slow breath. "What makes you think that?"

He shrugged. "I don't know. No one's ever come to my place before. Figured something horrible must've happened."

"Not horrible. Unless you think chocolate is horrible." I lifted the bag of goodies and offered a smile. "I wanted to stop by to visit, and I brought these for your mom."

"Really?" He took the bag and peered inside. "Brownies?"

"And chocolate chip cookies. And éclairs."

"Man." I could read the excitement in his eyes.

"Go ahead and have one," I said. "But leave the rest for her."

"Okay." He reached inside the bag and grabbed a brownie, then shoved it in his mouth. "Mmm."

He offered one to Armando, who took it with a crooked grin and a "Thanks, dude."

Devon opened the door and hollered, "Hey, Mom. They brought you a present." She appeared a moment later, her gait less steady than before, if such a thing were possible. When she saw the bag, a grin appeared. Only then did I notice the dental issues. My heart went out to her right away.

After she took the bag, Devon closed the door again and stood with us on the balcony. "So, why did you really come?"

Armando leaned against the wall. "We're worried about you, Devon. One minute you're going on the missions trip, the next you're not. One minute you're hyped about helping with the fund-raiser, the next you act like you're not interested. What happened? Did someone say or do something to change your mind?"

Devon looked down at his worn shoes and remained silent for a moment. When he finally spoke, his words were strained. "Look, you see how it is." His gaze lifted, and he looked Armando in the eye.

"Yeah." Just one word from Armando, followed by a shrug, but Devon seemed comfortable with it.

"If you're worried about coming up with the money for the trip, don't be," I said. "That's why we're having the fund-raiser. It won't be an issue, I promise."

Devon released a sigh. "It's not that. I'm worried about leaving her alone. She . . ." He glanced back toward the closed door. "She can't be by herself. Not for more than a few hours, anyway. She's not in very good shape. You know?"

Clearly the boy wasn't talking about her weight or measurements. But he didn't take it any further, so I didn't ask.

"What if I said that my mom would look in on her while we're gone?" I asked. "Would that make you feel any better?"

"No." He shook his head. "I don't think my mom would let her in, to be honest. She's a loner. She won't let anyone in. No one but me, I mean. And she depends on me for pretty much everything." He dove into a story about a pastor who had once tried to help by sending a cleaning crew to the apartment. Apparently that scenario hadn't ended well for anyone involved. "So, she's kind of weird about being around other people."

"She wouldn't have to be around anyone, really. My mom could just stop by and visit for a few minutes at the door. Maybe bring her lunch or something. Nothing high pressure or anything like that. Just food."

He raked his fingers through his messy hair. "No one's ever done anything like that before. Not sure how she would react. She does like food, though. And she hates to cook. Like I said, she depends on me for pretty much everything, even that."

Man. What teen boy enjoyed cooking his own meals? Well, other than the Rossi boys, anyway.

"My mom's a great cook," I said. "I could ask her just to drop off the food, say a few words, and then leave. I'm sure she would be happy to do that. And she always makes enough for two meals anyway."

"Might work." Devon shrugged. "But I just don't know how comfortable I feel leaving for ten days. You know? What if I come back and she's . . ." He shook his head, and I could read the pain in his expression. "I would feel awful if something happened to her and I wasn't here to protect her."

I wanted to tell him that God hadn't put him on this planet to protect her in that way—that he wasn't called to be an enabler. But it wasn't my place to do so, was it? And what did I know about such things? Nothing. No doubt I'd put my foot in my mouth and live to regret it. Right now I just needed to keep my mouth shut.

"Hey, I have an idea." Armando snapped his fingers. "Let's get her to come to the talent show. Then she can meet everyone, and she'll feel better about people stopping by to check in on her."

"No way will she come."

"I'll ask her myself." I stepped toward the door, but Devon put his hand up.

"You don't understand. She's high right now. And she'll be high the night of the talent show. Unless she's passed out cold on the floor, which is option B. Get it?" He glared at me and I backed down.

"Devon . . ." Armando looked more than a little concerned. "Let's see what we can do about getting her some help. Long-term help, I mean. Please."

Devon's expression tightened, and I could tell he was growing weary of this conversation. "She won't take it. Trust me. She's signed in to those programs before and nothing ever sticks. This is just how it is, man."

"No, it isn't 'just how it is.'" Anger rose in Armando's voice. "Trust me when I say that things can change. People can change." The passion in his voice took me by surprise. "Just because you've watched someone roll around in their—their junk for years doesn't mean you give up on them. Yeah, you want to sometimes, but at least keep praying and hoping that she has a chance at a better life. She does, you know."

Devon shrugged. "I guess anything's possible. I've just been with her for years and know the routine, trust me."

"I'm not saying you can fix her," Armando added. "I know a lot of people tried to fix my problems for me when I was at my lowest. But don't stop praying for her. And do what you can to let people help when they offer."

Okay then. Looked like Armando had a calling on his life to preach. And wow, was he ever good at it. In a nonthreatening way, no less.

Devon nodded. "Hey, I won't stand in your way

if you want to offer. But she's going to object."

"Let me think about this awhile," Armando said. "I might know someone who can help. I . . . I know people."

I could read the compassion in his eyes. That, and concern for Devon.

"We're headed out to Starbucks," Armando said. "Come with us?"

We are?

"In that?" Devon pointed to Armando's sports car.

"Yeah. In that."

"Sounds good. Hang on a sec." He hollered inside, "Hey, Mom, I'll be back in a few."

Her slurred response was tough to understand, but it didn't keep Devon from sprinting toward the car and climbing into the tiny seat in back. How he folded himself into such a small space, I couldn't say, but I was grateful he had the good sense to offer me the spot in front.

We laughed and talked all the way to Starbucks, where Armando treated us to whatever we wanted. I got a Frappuccino, and Devon went for a mocha caramel something-or-other, along with a piece of chocolate chip banana bread.

Really, Lord? They have chocolate chip banana bread?

I resisted. Okay, except for that one little bite I stole when Devon wasn't looking.

Still, most of my focus remained on the two

guys as they chatted about everything from cars to boats to the upcoming missions trip. By the end of our time together, Armando had almost convinced Devon he should go. And by the time we dropped the teen back off at his apartment complex—his hands filled with more goodies for his mother—Armando had promised to take him fishing one day after the talent show. He even offered some random story about how I might join them.

We pulled away from the apartment complex just as the sun started to set over the water. I gazed out at the gulf, watching the waves rolling in and out and thinking about how life was like that— how one minute we walked with God, felt the tug of his love, and the next we turned and did our own thing. I couldn't help but think of Armando, of the strides he'd made in his life. And if today's conversation with Devon was any indicator, there would be strides in Devon's life as well. Thanks to his new pal.

Out of the corner of my eye, I took a peek at the handsome Italian heartthrob driving the car. This was no good old boy. Not by my aunt's definition. This guy was the real deal. If I'd ever doubted it, today he proved himself to me—and to Devon—once and for all.

A moment of delicious silence rose up between us as Armando snapped off the radio. "You want the truth?" he asked a short time later.

I turned to look at him. "Of course."

A half smile lit his face, and he glanced my way. "I had a really great childhood. I don't know why I act like my house was such a pain to grow up in."

"Aw, Armando."

"I didn't always get the attention I wanted, but when I see a kid like Devon, it makes me so ashamed that I ever complained. Or walked away from what was a pretty good life."

"There's nothing to be ashamed of. We all deal with things in our own way. There's no shame in that."

He shrugged as he turned the corner, his car now headed toward the church just a block away. "Trust me, I have a lot to be ashamed of. I wasn't the best kid. In fact, I was usually the one acting up to get attention. In a house as full as ours, I figured it was the only way to get anyone to look my way."

"Seriously?" As an only child, I totally couldn't relate to that.

"Yes. So I got in trouble at school. Deliberately failed tests. That sort of thing."

"No way. All to get attention?"

"Yeah." He pulled into the parking lot at the church and turned the car off. "Definitely not proud of it now. But that didn't stop me then. I kept it up through my college years. Dropped out after a couple years. Gave up on jobs." Pain flickered in his eyes. "You ever heard that expression 'self-fulfilling prophecy'?"

"Of course."

"Well, that was me. I've been my own self-fulfilling prophecy. It's embarrassing to admit, but it's true."

"Oh, Armando." I placed my hand on his shoulder. "You've got so much going for you."

"I do, which is what makes my decisions—until now—so stupid." He looked at me, and I could see the frustration in his eyes. "I've stayed out on the fringes, away from all the family activities. I guess they think I like it that way. Maybe I thought if I didn't really connect, they would come looking for me."

Shades of the prodigal son story swept over me.

"And I guess in their own way, they tried." He winced, and for a moment I thought I saw a shimmer of tears in his eyes. "My parents had a lot of what Aunt Rosa called 'come to Jesus' meetings with me." He sighed. "I have no idea what I was running from. It's not like I'm happier in Houston working in nightclubs. I'm not. In my heart, I think I want—need—to be back here permanently. With my family."

My heart pretty much burst into its own rendition of "Oh Happy Day" at that news. "Then why don't you just tell them you're coming home for good, instead of for a month or two to take Jenna's place at Parma John's?"

"Too proud, I guess." He leaned his elbows on the steering wheel, his gaze at the cross on top of our little church. "I think I've played this game for so long that I don't know how to stop it without looking like an idiot in front of them. I'd like to just come back and work with the family. Hang out with great people . . ." He paused and offered me a tender smile. "Like you."

A rush of joy washed over me, and I reached to take his hand. "Thank you. I like hanging out with you too." I gave his hand a little squeeze.

"Even though I'm a bad boy?" He rolled his eyes as he spoke the words.

"I never said you were bad. And if you want the truth, we're all bad in our own way. The Bible says we all fall short. Ya know? That's why we need God's grace and mercy."

"Yeah, well, I've fallen way short. You only know the half of it." He sighed and glanced out of the window. "My story's not as far from Devon's mom as you might think. I've . . . well, I've done a lot of things I'm not proud of, things I don't really like to talk about."

"No need to talk about it." I shrugged. "Unless you want to, I mean. But you're probably not as far off as you might think. And I know your family pretty well. They want you to come back home. I have a feeling your mom would throw a welcome-home party if you told her you were coming back to the island for good."

"Kill the fatted calf and all that?" His right brow elevated mischievously.

"Would that be so bad?"

"Nah. But I'd prefer the Mambo Italiano special, along with some of Aunt Rosa's garlic twists." He smiled. "And some more of that Italian cream cake we made. Man, that stuff was good. You're quite a baker, Scarlet."

"So you've said. But a girl appreciates hearing things like that again." I gave him a little wink. "Thanks to you, I'm baking another one for Hannah's wedding. I'll save you a big slice. Might even make a small cake just for you as a thank-you for what you just did with Devon back there."

"I love that cream cheese frosting." He hesitated as he gazed into my eyes. "It's great." He paused, and his cheeks turned red. "You're great."

"Th-thank you."

"So, if I do come back for good, would you ever think about . . ."

"About what?" My heart began that funny little pitter-patter thing that only happened when I got excited. Nervous. Hopeful.

He released a slow breath. "I know I'm not the kind of guy you'd probably consider."

A feeling of compassion swept over me. "Oh, I don't know. I'd say you're *exactly* the kind of guy I'd consider."

He looked my way, a hopeful expression on his face. "Really?"

251

"Really." I paused, thinking it through. "Armando, I appreciate the guys who have consistently walked the straight and narrow. But there's something to be said for a man who turns his heart toward home after seeing life on the other side of the fence. Your conviction is strong. And I see you fighting to be the man God wants you to be. That makes me really proud."

"The man God wants me to be." He echoed the words and then stared up at the cross once more. "Do you have any idea how long it's been since anyone called me a man?"

I wanted to respond, but words wouldn't come. I leaned over and laid my head on Armando's shoulder. We sat together, completely silent, staring at the cross until the sun went down. I couldn't remember when I'd spent a better evening.

18

Sweet Talker

You're the frosting to my cupcake.

                                        Author unknown

A terrible storm hit the island on Wednesday. I spent most of that day taking care of customers. Armando dropped by the bakery for a few minutes, but with so much going on, I barely had time to say two words to the boy. Er, man. He offered me the sweetest smile in the world, swallowed down a couple of brownies—on the house, of course—then headed back to Parma John's to work.

Back to Parma John's. I did my best not to sigh aloud as I thought about him coming home for good. I thought about it the following morning when the sun peeked through the clouds and the weather cleared, though he didn't stop in for his usual breakfast sweets, which I found a little odd. I thought about it that same afternoon, when he didn't come by on his break. I thought about it every time I pondered that evening's talent show rehearsal. Thank God Armando would be there to run lights and sound. Otherwise I wasn't sure how this would go down.

After closing up the bakery for the day, I stopped off next door at Parma John's, where I found Bella working behind the counter. She carried little Rosa-Earline on her hip and scolded Tres, her precocious preschooler, who sat at a nearby table using a fork to massacre a yellow crayon.

I greeted her with a smile. "Well, hello, stranger. Interesting to see you here."

"Hello to you too." She offered a grin, then moved her little girl from one hip to the other, her long curls tumbling in a messy array on her shoulders. "It's been a long day, and we have an even longer weekend to come."

I looked around, confusion setting in after a moment. "Isn't Armando here?"

"No." A look of concern crossed her face. "He said he had to go into town for a few hours. That's why I'm here, actually, because he couldn't be. Well, that, and I have a meeting with Gabi to look over sketches and talk about ideas. She should be here soon."

"Gabi?" The name didn't ring a bell. And what was Armando doing in town? "Do you mean he's gone to Houston?" A sinking feeling came over me. Surely he remembered we had a big night ahead. Right?

"I guess." She turned to take care of a customer's check, then looked back at me and shrugged. "Oddest thing. He left in a big hurry but didn't bother to tell anyone where he was going—or why. Strange."

"I sure hope he remembers that we've got our rehearsal tonight."

"I don't know." Bella waited on another customer, then turned back to me. "It didn't come up. I do know that D.J. talked to Bubba about the rehearsal. He plans to be there, even though Jenna's not doing very well. She's on bed rest until the baby comes, you know."

"Right. I've been praying for her."

"Please keep it up. The doctor said her blood pressure is too high, and that worries me. Worries Bubba too, I think." Bella glanced at her watch. "When is the rehearsal again?"

"In an hour and a half."

"Ugh." She looked at the long line of customers streaming in the door. "Well, I hope Armando makes it back in time."

"Yeah. Me too." With a wave of my hand, I dismissed any concerns. He would make it back. No problem.

Still, it seemed a little odd that he'd gone into Houston.

Not that I really knew that much about what he did in Houston. He'd been pretty closemouthed about that part of his life, hadn't he? But I hadn't asked either. It wasn't like we were a couple, necessarily. Oh well. I'd better focus on the upcoming rehearsal.

A familiar young woman entered the restaurant carrying a sketchbook. Bella greeted her with a smile, then turned to me.

"Scarlet, you remember Gabi, right?" Bella nodded at the beautiful woman to her right.

I did recognize the petite, dark-haired beauty. "Yes. You work at the bridal shop, right?"

"That's right." Her lovely Hispanic accent sounded like water trickling across rocks. "I measured you for your maid of honor dress for Hannah's wedding."

"Oh, right. The woman with the measuring tape." I groaned inwardly, realizing this girl knew my measurements. No one else on planet earth knew them. Even I didn't know them. Still, she didn't seem terribly shaken by my numbers, whatever they were.

"Gabi's helping me plan ahead for a fall wedding," Bella said. "She's got the best designs."

"You're a designer too?" For whatever reason, I thought alterations were her bag.

A shy smile crossed her face. "I try my hand at a few things. Hannah's dress is my first real creation."

"Wait . . . you designed Hannah's dress?"

She nodded. "But don't tell my boss, okay? He doesn't know I'm doing this on the side."

"Gabi works for Demetri Markowitz at Haute Couture bridal."

"Ooo, I know him. Not the nicest guy in the world."

"Hence the need for silence." Bella quirked a brow.

"Well, mum's the word then. But Gabi, if Hannah's dress is any indication, your designs are light-years better than Demetri's."

Gabi's gaze shifted to the ground. "Thank you."

"She's got a lot more too." Bella opened Gabi's sketchbook, and we looked through it, oohing and aahing at every page.

"I can't believe you haven't sold all of these to a famous design house," I said after a few minutes.

Gabi shook her head. "I really don't know if I want to go that route. I kind of like being here in Galveston. If I got an offer from a big house, I'd end up having to move to New York or something. I don't want to leave my mama and my grandmother. I've lived on the island all my life."

My imagination kicked in—along with a lot of jealousy—and I pictured Armando falling for this dark-haired beauty. Yes, the two of them would end up married with a couple of gorgeous, dark-haired, non-chubby children.

Stop it, Scarlet.

I smiled weakly as I gazed back down at her sketches. Gabi was beautiful. And talented too.

After a while, Gabi glanced at the clock and

gasped. "I have to get back to the shop. My boss is so particular." She looked panicked. "Promise you won't tell anyone about my designs?"

I promised, but I wondered why it mattered. Did she really fear for her job?

She disappeared from view, and I glanced at the clock. Was it really after six? No way. I'd better get on the road.

I'd just headed to the door when I saw Rosa coming in. She offered a broad smile and put her hand on my arm. "Scarlet, good to see you again, sweet girl. You're looking great."

"Thank you." I couldn't help but smile. "Good to see you too, Rosa. How's Laz doing? Recovering nicely?"

"Yes, but he's feisty. Ornery." She laughed. "The man was never very good at resting and relaxing, so this whole recovery thing is really getting on his nerves. And I probably shouldn't say it after coming so close to losing him and all, but he's getting on my nerves too." She clamped a hand over her mouth, then pulled it away. "Is that awful?"

"Nah. Probably 100 percent normal."

"Good." She patted my arm. "So glad I caught you. I had an idea I'd like to share with you, honey. I really think you're going to like it. In fact, I'm sure of it."

I glanced at my watch, a little concerned about the time. Still, I couldn't disregard her, especially after all she'd done for me. If she wanted to talk, we would talk.

Rosa carried on, clearly oblivious to my concerns about the late hour. "You're trying to raise money for this trip to Nicaragua, right?"

"Yes."

"And you're also hoping to draw customers to your shop. Though I don't think you need to worry about that. Now that you've won that bake-off, they'll come in droves."

"They already are." I gave her a thumbs-up and smiled.

"Perfect. Well, here's my thought. As good as your cakes are, I know something that's even better. We've all been talking about it, and we're in total agreement that your sticky buns are the best on the island."

Okay, I almost choked at that comment.

She clapped her hands together and grinned. "So why not host a sticky buns extravaganza one morning next week? Let people know it's for the fund-raiser. All proceeds can go to the missions group." She grinned. "And just so you know, Laz and I want to fund this venture. We'll provide whatever supplies you need to bake as many as you like."

"Oh no. Please." I couldn't allow them to do that, not with Laz in such frail shape.

"Honey, we can never thank you enough for what you've done for us. Covering my spot on the show—and winning—has been the icing on my cake, as it were. You've blessed me so much. And I know how much this trip means to you. Armando has talked about it nonstop."

"He has?" That surprised me.

"Well, sure. He's so proud of you. I've never heard him go on and on about anything like this."

"Really?" Knowing that made me feel better. It also reassured me that he would turn up for tonight's rehearsal.

She continued to share a detailed explanation of how the sticky buns fund-raiser could go down, and I thanked her for the suggestion. I gave careful thought to her words as I headed off to the church. The fund-raiser idea was a good one, but how could I put together something else with all I had on my plate? Seemed impossible, at least in the moment.

One day at a time, Scarlet. One day at a time.

First I needed to get through tonight's practice. Then work like a dog tomorrow morning on Hannah's cakes. Get them clear-coated and refrigerated. Spend tomorrow evening with Hannah in full-out maid of honor mode. Enjoy the wedding rehearsal and rehearsal dinner. Then spend as many hours as I could—*When? In the middle of the night?*—decorating her wedding cake.

All while running a bakery.

No problem. I could do this. As long as tonight's rehearsal went well.

I arrived at the church to find Uncle Donny in his older-model pickup truck waiting outside. He climbed out, carrying a large saw. Okay then. Looked like the show was on the road. Literally. He warmed up, making all sorts of unusual noises.

Out of the corner of my eye, I caught a glimpse of a shiny Cadillac pulling up. The three Splendora sisters spilled out, dressed in all their glittery splendor. Twila's sequined top was positively blinding. It didn't help that the evening sun hovered so low overhead, catching the sequins and dazzling me with their brightness. Jolene looked pretty snazzy in her green satin dress, and Bonnie looked downright delicious in her cotton-candy-pink capris and top.

The ladies greeted me first and then turned their attention to Donny. Bonnie Sue in particular seemed smitten. Of course, the other two ladies had husbands. But that didn't stop them from gushing over him. On and on they went, singing his praises and giving me the scoop on his upcoming saw solo.

Alrighty then.

"You know Donny's quite the hero in Splendora." Bonnie Sue's eyes sparkled as she looked his way. "His truck stop got a big write-up in our local paper. So did his rendition of

'Amazing Grace,' which he played on his saw at the grand opening."

I nodded, unsure of how to respond.

"And speaking of write-ups in the paper, I saw that your gig on television made the papers." Donny waggled his thick, gray brows. "Very nice promotion for your business. And for your aunt's too, I noticed."

"Yes, I think she's pleased with how things turned out."

"Well, no doubt. You did her proud. And the Rossis too. I'd say you're everyone's little darling right about now." He gave me a playful wink.

"Thank you so much." I managed the words, but my thoughts shifted at once to Armando. Was I his little darling? A couple of nights ago, I would've said yes. No doubt in my mind. But he certainly hadn't stayed in touch today, had he? I glanced at my phone, wondering if maybe I'd missed a call from him. Nope.

Oh well. He'd be here soon.

He'd better be, anyway. We couldn't very well manage this rehearsal without him, now could we?

I led the way into the sanctuary and glanced at the clock—6:35. Good. We still had twenty minutes before the others arrived. Well, all but Kenny, who entered the room right behind me.

I found my father straddling a ten-foot ladder at the front of the sanctuary, where he had apparently pulled down several wet pieces of Sheetrock.

They lay strewn all over the stage, creating an unexpected and horrible mess. From the looks of things, we were going to need every minute to get this mess cleaned up so that no one got hurt.

"Dad?"

He glanced down from his perch and released a groan. "I know, I know. Terrible timing. But that storm blew in more than a strong wind. Apparently there's a leak in the roof. The roofers came earlier and patched it, but I couldn't afford to pay anyone to replace the Sheetrock, so I'm doing it myself."

Kenny looked up at him. "I'll help you, sir."

"Son, I don't mean any harm by this statement, but how are you going to help with that bum arm of yours?" My father muttered something under his breath and climbed down from the ladder to begin the task of picking up the wet Sheetrock pieces. He glanced Kenny's way. "No, you just do me a favor and help my girl here. She's going to have a doozy of a time trying to work this rehearsal around the mess I've made."

And I did have a doozy of a time, starting with my feeble attempts to get the new lightboard up and running while they worked on cleaning up the mess. Talk about clueless.

Armando, where are you? Didn't you promise to come early?

The Splendora sisters got involved at one point, Twila leading the way. "I've worked

263

hundreds of lightboards in my day, honey." She did a little magic on the board, and voilà! We had lights! Well, sort of. Turned out she only knew how to get the board running, not how to work the individual levers and knobs. Oh well. A little light was better than no light at all, right? Except for the fact that it highlighted the gaping hole in the ceiling and wet Sheetrock on the ground.

I kept checking my phone to see if Armando had called. Nothing. In the meantime, Kenny worked alongside my dad at the front—er, top—of the sanctuary. I could hear hammering and sawing going on but didn't pay much attention. With the kids now in attendance, I needed to stay focused on them.

Or not. Something else stole my attention for a minute. At ten minutes till seven, Kenny approached the sound booth, looking dejected.

"What's wrong?" I asked.

"I think I messed up your dad's saw." He sighed and plopped down onto the seat next to me.

"What do you mean?"

"That's what I get for trying to help him with a bum arm. I busted the teeth out of his good saw."

"Aw, man." I looked at my father, who remained perched atop the ladder at the front of the church, saw in hand. "No, wait. It's fine. Rest easy."

"But I . . ." Kenny looked over at the saw he'd just placed on the sound table, his brow furrowed. "If that's not your dad's saw . . ."

I looked at it and shrugged. Then I realized what Kenny had done.

"Oh no!" we both cried out at once.

I gasped, then clamped a hand over my mouth. This was awful.

Ironically, Uncle Donny chose that moment to approach. He grinned as he glanced down at the saw. "There's my little Lucille. I thought she'd gone missing."

"Lucille?" Kenny paled.

"Yep. Named her after my precious wife, who passed away years ago. What a godly woman. Such an inspiration. Always left a song in my heart." He picked up the saw and held it close, as one would hold an infant. "This blessed instrument has been with me for years. I think you'll be tickled to hear the beautiful music Lucille and I make together."

"O-oh?" Kenny looked as if he might be sick at any moment.

After giving the saw a closer look, Donny appeared concerned. "Wait a minute. What's happened here?" He gazed at the saw up close. "Lucille? Darlin'? What happened to you?"

He turned back to face us, and Kenny rose. "Sir, I'm sorry. I had no idea I was using your saw to help Pastor Lindsey. I really thought it belonged to him. Surely you can see how easy it would be to mix them up. To me, one saw looks like any other."

"Are you saying that you . . ." Donny's eyes misted over. "You used my little Lucille to actually cut something?"

"Yes, sir. Well, sort of." Kenny groaned. "I didn't know. And I accidentally—"

"You . . . you broke her teeth?"

Fear registered in Kenny's eyes, along with embarrassment. "I didn't mean to, sir. And if I'd known she was your . . . your . . . instrument, I never would have used her in the first place. I just got so distracted helping Pastor fix the busted ceiling."

Uncle Donny looked so sad, I thought he might cry. And Bonnie Sue? Well, she approached looking as mad as a hornet. She headed Kenny's way, tongue clucking. "Young man, you've decimated my man's saw?"

"I didn't mean to, ma'am."

Poor Kenny. He would never live this down. I could tell he would go on beating himself up over it for some time.

And one more thing: if I had any question in my mind about how Bonnie Sue felt about Uncle Donny, she'd just answered it. She was smitten, as Armando would say. Then again, Uncle Donny didn't look as enthused. But he wouldn't be, would he? Not with his attention so fixed on his busted saw and all. No doubt he couldn't see past Lucille's teeth to any other woman in the room.

After a moment of quiet reflection, Donny

looked at Kenny and sighed. "No worries, son." The older fellow patted him on the shoulder. "I have a whole case of saws at home. Never you fear. I'll be back on the night of the show with Prince William. He's my favorite. I only brought Lucille here to practice on because I don't want to run the risk of anything happening to my favorite."

Ack. I knew he was just trying to make Kenny feel better, but judging from the look on Kenny's face, it wasn't working.

Uncle Donny cradled the saw like a baby, and I was pretty sure I heard him say, "You picked a fine time to leave me, Lucille," as he walked down the aisle.

Of course, hearing the name Lucille put me in mind of Lucy. I had to wonder what she would do on a night like this, when Ricky didn't show up and the show unraveled right in front of her. She would probably cry those big, gut-wrenching, overly dramatic tears of hers. And then the scene would end with the cheerful background music playing over and fading away, offering the television audience hope for funny episodes yet to come.

And so, as always, I took my cues from my heroine. I slinked away to the ladies' room, where I spent a few minutes in one of the stalls, a washed-up mess. I boohooed big, dramatic tears that would've made Lucy proud. Then I tried calling Armando. He didn't answer, but someone else did.

A female someone.

A female someone named Cynthia, who claimed she didn't know where Armando was.

Well, perfect. If that just didn't make my night, I didn't know what would. And so I blubbered all over again, this time for being such a fool over Armando Rossi. For thinking that he cared about me one whit. What a blithering idiot I'd been, putting my heart out there to be stomped on.

After a while, Mama came and found me. She offered a few encouraging words, helped me dry my tears, and sent me on my way with a "What would Lucy do?"

I told her very plainly that I was already doing what Lucy would do . . . and Mama just hugged me.

Fine. Lucy would dry her eyes and get back to work. She was a consummate pro, after all. With that in mind, I pushed aside my angst and made up my mind to focus on the kids once I made it out of the restroom. Well, the kids and the adults who had agreed to participate.

Only one problem: the trio of Splendora ladies found their way to the ladies' room before I could leave. They'd somehow figured out I'd been crying, and they offered to hold an impromptu prayer meeting to see me through. Now, I'd prayed in a multiplicity of places before, but never pressed up against a bathroom sink. Not that I minded, necessarily. In spite of the awkward setting, the ladies prayed the house down. Er, prayed the stalls down.

I headed back out to the sanctuary to assume the role of director. Somehow we forged ahead, and by 7:10 everyone was there. Well, everyone but Armando, who was still MIA. I had no idea why he didn't show but decided he wasn't worth crying over. No man was . . . right?

Is he really a man? No, he's acting like a boy. Just not showing up? Childish!

To be honest, I didn't really know him very well. Maybe he wasn't as ready to change and settle down as I'd thought.

We began the rehearsal, and Kenny did his best on the lightboard, but he didn't really have a clue what to do to emphasize the various acts. Without Armando's soundboard, we ended up with a squeaky, squealy sound, but we were kind of used to that, so it didn't matter so much. Still, I felt disappointed. Keenly.

"Bummer," Devon said when a squeal pierced the room. "Thought it was gonna be better than that."

"Me too," I muttered. At least my dad had gotten the mess taken care of. Sure, we had a gap in the ceiling, but unless it rained, we would probably be okay there. I hoped.

Thank God for Kenny. He worked alongside me from start to finish, keeping the show going and bouncing back and forth from the soundboard to the stage. All of this with a bum arm. God bless him.

Jolene stopped by the sound booth to whisper a little something-something in my ear. "If you don't marry that boy," she said with a wink, "I'm going to. He's a peach, that one."

I wanted to remind her that she was already married, but decided not to. How could I argue with what she'd said? Kenny was a peach, all right. And together we made a fine pear. Er, pair. We worked side by side as in days gone by, and we managed to get the job done. I breathed a sigh of relief, knowing things would turn out okay in the end. The audience members would be pleased. Yes, with the exception of the technical stuff, the program was really coming together.

Okay, there was that one incident with Bubba, who had accidentally brought the wrong track for his song. And the seniors' choir had a rough time getting their harmonies together. Still, we were on a roll. And if Armando ever showed up, we'd have an impressive show, no doubt about it.

Only, he didn't show up. I looked at the back of the auditorium at least twenty times during the rehearsal but never saw him materialize at the soundboard. So I checked my phone at least a dozen times. Asked Kenny three or four times what we should do in Armando's absence. I fended off questions from Devon, who seemed even more disappointed than I was.

My already troubled mind began to play tricks on me. Maybe Armando had been in an accident. Maybe Cynthia—whoever she was—ended up with his phone and truly didn't know him at all. That possibility left me nervous. What else could it be, though? He'd proven himself reliable in every way. Yes, an accident was the only thing that made sense. I closed my eyes and could almost envision him driving his sports car off the causeway bridge and into the bay.

Lord, keep him safe, I prayed silently. *And forgive me for judging him. Please let him be okay.*

That prayer stayed in my heart for the rest of the evening, from act to act, minute to minute. Many times I found myself offering up a silent but frantic prayer for the Almighty to spare Armando's life.

When the rehearsal ended and everyone left, I called Bella, who groaned when she heard the news of Armando's absence. "I'm so sorry he's let you down, Scarlet." Her sigh resonated over the phone line. "And I guess it's awful to say I'm not surprised. He . . . well, he does this kind of thing sometimes, and when he took off from the restaurant today, I had a weird feeling he would stay gone. He's kind of . . . well, kind of a loner. Marches to his own drumbeat."

"You should have warned me." *You should have given me a heads-up from the beginning that he might bail just when we needed him most.*

"I'm really sorry." She groaned again. "I've been hoping and praying that my brother would change. I actually thought I was seeing a difference, but maybe I was wrong. Again, I'm sorry he let you down." She paused. "I guess you could say he put us all out. And on a lousy weekend too. I'm so exhausted right now. I hope I can get through this wedding, to be honest. Still, I'm not terribly surprised that he's done this. I hate to say it, but I'm not."

"I see." My disappointment shifted to frustration as my thoughts reeled backwards to the day of the cake challenge over a week ago. Had he really kissed me? That lousy good old boy? The one my aunt had tried to warn me about? Yes, and look where it had landed me. In charge of a fundraiser with no one to run sound. Or lights.

Okay, now I was delirious. I needed to get some sleep.

Ending the call with Bella, I pondered my options. Sleep. It was the best plan. Tomorrow was a new day. I'd bake Hannah's wedding cake. Go to Hannah's rehearsal. Play the role of maid of honor with a smile. And pretend that today had never happened.

If I could just stop being frustrated with Armando long enough to do all of that.

19

Butter Me Up

Forget love—I'd rather fall in chocolate!
                                    Sandra J. Dykes

I spent Friday morning working frantically, not just on the cakes for Hannah's wedding but on products for my bakery as well. Customers still flooded the shop after reading in the paper that I'd fainted on television, so I couldn't jump ship. I needed to keep baiting them until the show aired in a couple of weeks.

With that in mind, I filled my cases with sugary delights of every kind. Kenny and I took turns waiting on customers and bouncing back and forth between the kitchen and the register. I never could have survived without him and reminded myself of that at least a dozen times.

Hannah called approximately twenty times by midafternoon, filled with concerns about tonight's wedding rehearsal and tomorrow's big day. Typical day-before-the-wedding stuff. I did my best to console her and to reassure her that everything would come off without a hitch. In other words, I played my role as maid of honor with flair and ease.

Until she asked how the cakes were coming. How could I tell her that I was only just now baking the cakes? She knew me better than that. By now I should have them baked, clear-coated, and chilled. I managed to convince her that things were under control with a hearty "Going great!" but secretly wondered how I would ever get them done if this train didn't slow down.

One thing struck me as odd. Aunt Willy never showed up on Friday morning. Not that we'd planned a get-together or anything, but I truly expected her to turn up at the bakery, dressed to the nines, what with Hannah's wedding being such a big deal at Club Wed. But she didn't.

I thought about that as I left the shop around 4:30 to head home for a shower. I pondered it as I dressed for the rehearsal. But by the time I reached Club Wed, I'd put Auntie out of my mind altogether. Once I saw Hannah and Drew, I shifted gears—into maid of honor mode. The next twenty-four hours were all about the bride and groom.

Well, mostly.

We gabbed in the foyer of Club Wed, then headed into the chapel for the rehearsal. I greeted Hannah's sisters, and before long Bella called us to attention, now in full-out wedding coordinator mode, right down to the clipboard in her hand.

She placed us in order at the back of the chapel and gave us instructions on how to make our entrances up the aisle to the front, starting with the bridesmaids and ending with me. The other girls would be walking down the aisle with their husbands as groomsmen. Me? I would make the trek alone. Nothing like drawing a little extra attention to the maid of honor and pointing out the fact that she had no fella in her life. Yippee.

Off they went, one skinny bridesmaid at a time, each with a hunky man on her arm.

Deep breath, Scarlet. It's going to be okay.

When my turn came, I headed off . . . alone. I'd just taken a couple of steps with a pretend flower bouquet in my hand when a familiar voice sounded to my right.

"Scarlet, I need to talk to you."

I glanced over to see Armando standing in the sound booth, and my heart quickened. Just as quickly, my anger rose to the surface.

Forget it, buddy. You don't stand me up one night, then pretend nothing happened the next.

I shook my head and kept walking. No way was he ruining this night for me. He'd messed up one special evening; he wasn't going to do the same for another. Staying focused on my best friend was critical. I wouldn't think about anything other than her right now. Besides, we were in the middle of a rehearsal. He knew the routine.

I tried not to look back at him after I passed by,

but I found it difficult with those puppy dog eyes pleading with me.

"I'm sorry," he whispered. "I really am. But there's a reason . . ."

I didn't want to hear his reason, and this wasn't a good time anyway. Right now I needed to focus on my best friend. Tonight was her night. Well, hers and Drew's. I glanced up at the groom-to-be standing at the altar. How wonderful he looked. How loving. Sweet. Dependable. How . . . unlike Armando.

Ugh. Don't think about Armando.

Hannah's sisters lined the front of the church. Trim. Svelte. Pretty. Practically perfect in every way. I felt odd in comparison and silently fretted about what I would look like tomorrow afternoon, being so much different in appearance than the others. Would the wedding guests pick up on the fact that my dress wasn't like the other girls'? Probably, but at least I could tell everyone I was the maid of honor, right?

Not that anyone would be looking my way. No, all eyes would certainly be glued on Hannah, who now appeared at the back of the chapel on her daddy's arm. I couldn't tell who was more teary-eyed, my BFF or her father, who sniffled all the way up the aisle. You would've thought this was the real deal, not just a rehearsal.

I watched my best friend make her way toward us and couldn't help the tears that flowed. I hadn't planned for them, of course, but there they were. Shoot, was my mascara running? Nah. I'd used waterproof.

Hannah took her final steps up the aisle on her father's arm, looking half nervous, half excited. Out of the corner of my eye, I caught another glimpse of Armando in the sound booth. The guy was definitely in his element. If only he'd been in his element last night too. Then maybe I wouldn't be so angry right now. I would look his way and smile instead of scowling inwardly.

I really, really don't like you right now, Armando Rossi. Just see if I ever talk to you again!

My father took his role front and center to run the rehearsal. He smiled at Hannah and spoke several sweet words over the couple. The whole thing made me tearful, not just because Hannah was my best friend, but because I couldn't stop thinking about how my father would react when it came time to perform my wedding.

Likely he'd blubber all the way through it.

Likely we both would.

I almost lost track of what was happening until my father asked, "Who gives this woman to be married to this man?"

Hannah's dad squeaked out, "Her mother and I do," dabbed at his eyes, and released his hold on her arm and placed it in Drew's. I wasn't sure Drew could see through the puddle of tears in his own eyes. He gripped Hannah's arm so hard it looked a bit painful. Not that she complained.

At this point Bella intervened and asked for someone to stand in for the bride. "No point in accidentally marrying the couple a day too soon," she said. Drew didn't look as if he minded that idea at all, but Hannah pouted a bit, probably just for fun. Still, it seemed it would be for the best. What if they accidentally said their "I dos" tonight instead of tomorrow? Then what?

I took a little step backwards, silently willing them to choose anyone but me. With my luck, Bella would ask Armando to play the role of the husband-to-be. Thank goodness Hannah's parents decided to take the place of the bride and groom, and we chuckled as they came to the "till death do us part" phrase.

"Better get this right, Dad," Hannah called out from her spot on the front pew. "I want to see you two married from now until when Jesus comes back."

This got a chuckle out of everyone in attendance. But the way I was feeling, Jesus could come back right now. I'd be thrilled not to have to deal with my mixed-up feelings toward Armando any longer.

I blew out a slow breath and released a silent prayer to God to relieve me of my disappointment and frustration. Perhaps keeping my distance from Armando would be for the best. He could go back to doing whatever it was he did before he met me, and I would go back to trying to love Kenny.

No, I wouldn't. It certainly wasn't fair to Kenny to string him along when I didn't care for him. Besides, the guy had eyes in his head. He could see that I didn't respond to his attentions the way he wanted me to.

Pay attention, Scarlet! You don't want to miss your best friend's wedding rehearsal. She needs you.

We carried on with the rehearsal, and it ended on a high note, with the groomsmen giving a rousing cheer as Hannah's parents melted into a passionate kiss at the "I do" point. Bella gave some final instructions, then announced the rehearsal dinner, to be held in half an hour at Gaido's on the seawall.

Frankly, I could hardly wait to get through the rehearsal dinner and back to the bakery, where I planned to stay up all night decorating a cake . . . and eating as many sticky buns as I could to wash away the churning in my stomach.

20

How Do You Like Them Apples?

She tells enough white lies to ice a wedding cake.

Margot Asquith

I couldn't help but notice that everyone was coupled up as they headed out to the rehearsal dinner. Everyone but me, of course. I tagged along on their heels, feeling the weight of my aloneness as never before. Perfect. Just the way I wanted to end an already difficult evening. Nothing like driving to the dinner by myself.

I made it to the lobby of Club Wed without drawing any attention to myself. Well, except for the part where I muttered all the way.

I heard the sound of a bird trilling off in the distance. I looked up to discover the Rossis' pet parrot, Guido, in his cage. The colorful bird appeared to be singing some sort of song. I took a couple of steps toward the cage, and the bird hollered out, "Go to the mattresses!" then began a machine-gun sound. Freaked me out a little. Then he lit back into his song, and I leaned in to make out the melody. Ah yes, "Amazing Grace." Interesting.

I thought of Armando, of all he'd been through over the past several years. How he'd shied away from his family. I thought of the grace God offered. Why couldn't I offer the same grace now? Why not go back into the chapel and have it out with Armando and then forgive him for letting me down last night? Listen to his explanation? Talk it through? Ask him to go with me to the restaurant? That's what a normal person would do.

Then again, I'd never been accused of being normal, had I? No, I had not. And so I headed out into the dark parking lot, ready to make my way to Gaido's . . . alone.

Oh well. I'd make the best of this. And I'd have a great time. No matter how awful it was.

At the last minute, Hannah came sprinting toward my car. "Can I ride with you?" she asked.

"What about Drew?" I looked around, confused by her request.

"His mom doesn't drive at night anymore, and he offered to take her."

"But don't you want to—"

"They're in her Mini Cooper. I hate being pressed into that tiny backseat. The last time I tried it, I couldn't walk for hours afterward. Can't risk that right now. I've got the most important walk of my life tomorrow—straight into the arms of my groom." She giggled.

Now, that I could relate to. Well, the car part,

anyway. Not the walk down the aisle toward the groom part.

I gestured for her to join me in my Jeep, and before long we were on our way, laughing and talking about how the rehearsal had gone. My stomach rumbled, and I could hardly wait to have dinner.

We pulled into the restaurant parking lot, and I groaned when I saw Armando's red sports car. Who invited him? Okay, so he was working sound for the rehearsal. Hannah probably invited him to be polite. Well, never mind all that. I would avoid him at all costs and remain focused on my best friend. She deserved the evening of her lifetime.

I bit back a yawn as I climbed out of my car. Somehow I had to make it through this dinner, consume enough caffeine to keep me going, and head back to the shop to decorate the cakes for Hannah's wedding. There would be no time tomorrow morning to do anything other than deliver and stack the cakes before I dressed and dove into maid of honor mode once more.

Armando called out my name, and I glanced his way, unsure of what to do.

Hannah must've heard him too. She glanced at Armando, then back at me. "I think he wants to talk to you, Scarlet."

I shrugged. "There was plenty of time to talk last night at our rehearsal."

Okay, there really wasn't time to talk last night, not with the ceiling falling through and Uncle Donny's saw being de-teethed and all, but that was beside the point, wasn't it? Point was, if the guy wanted to talk, he knew my number. He could've called.

Armando approached, a sheepish look on his face. "Are you going to avoid me all night?"

"Maybe."

At this point Hannah caught a glimpse of Drew and headed inside to meet him. She gave me that "take your time" look. Great.

Armando touched my arm, and I tried to ignore the rush of emotion that coursed through me as he spoke. "Scarlet, I'm really sorry about what happened, but there's a perfectly logical explanation, if you'll just let me explain."

"Oh?" I tried to act nonchalant. "Is that so?"

"Yeah." Armando moved closer to me. "See, I went to Houston to—"

"I know you were in Houston," I said. "I called your phone."

"Oh, I know. I—"

"I talked to Cynthia." That should shut him up.

"Cynthia?" He looked perplexed at the mention of her name.

"Yeah." I raised my eyebrows. "Cynthia. The girl who answered your phone. I talked to her last night, so I know you were . . . were . . ." Actually, I didn't know what he was doing. Only that a girl named Cynthia answered his phone. Better stop right there before I said something I might regret.

He shook his head. "Scarlet, listen, I can explain all of that. And you know me well enough to know I wouldn't just stand you up like that. I know how important this fund-raiser is to you. To your whole church. That's what I—"

I took a couple of steps toward the door of the restaurant. "I don't know you that well." I spoke the words through clenched teeth. "Maybe I just thought I did."

He looked genuinely distressed at this proclamation. He shoved his hands in his pockets, his gaze shifting downward. "I was there for you at the cake challenge, wasn't I?"

"Yeah, but—"

Now he looked me directly in the eye. "I got the new lightboard for your church, and I'm loaning you the soundboard too. I'm not a bad guy."

Okay, he had a point there too. And he obviously wanted to tell me what had happened last night. Why couldn't I just relax and let him? Instead, I reached for the handle of the door. Armando grabbed it first and opened it for me. I rushed inside, ready to be done with this. Just one more thing I needed to say.

"Armando, listen, this is Hannah's night. I really need to stay focused on her. Can we have this conversation another time? After the wedding, maybe?"

"But it won't take long to explain." The door closed behind him. "You're going to feel really bad when you hear where I was."

"I doubt it." I glanced across the restaurant to see if I could locate the others. Ah yes, there they were. In the back on the left. The maître d' approached, but Armando gestured for him to give us some time. Great.

"Look . . ." He leaned in so close I could smell his cologne.

Do. Not. Get. Distracted.

I turned away from him toward my BFF, who glanced my way with a concerned look on her face.

"After we met with Devon the other day—after I saw how bad off his mom is—I decided to ask a friend of mine if she had room at the halfway house called Sheltering Arms in South Houston."

"W-what?" I looked at him, confused.

"Yeah. I don't really call her Cynthia, though. I've always known her as Miss Cindy. I got to know her when I was staying at the men's facility down the block. And by the way, she's old enough to be my mom. Oh, and did I mention that she's married to a pastor? They've been in ministry together for over thirty years."

I swallowed hard and felt my pride slither down my throat.

"Anyway, I left the island and drove all the

way to South Houston to see if she could get Devon's mom into her program. We worked it out." He put his hand on my arm. "She's got room for her, so I set the whole thing up. Devon's mom can check in as soon as she wants. We just have to talk her into it now, but I think Devon can do that. I plan to go by his place tomorrow afternoon after the wedding to give him some pointers for how to approach her. I really think we can make this work. I do."

Still, none of this made sense. "Why didn't you just come back to the island and tell me all of this in person?"

"I left Sheltering Arms at 5:45 to come back home, and I got caught in traffic. I wanted to call, but that's when I realized I'd left my phone back at the facility. So I had to turn around and drive back to Houston to get it."

Well, that made sense. Sort of. "And then?"

"Then . . ." He shrugged. "Then I got caught in even more traffic and didn't make it to Miss Cindy's place until an hour and a half later, which totally ruined my night. When I got there, she told me I'd missed a call. When I made the drive back to Galveston, I called you."

"I didn't have any calls from you."

"Check your phone. The call went straight to your voice mail. You must've been on the phone with someone else at the time, but I definitely left a message."

I reached for it, anger setting in. How dare he say he'd called me?

A quick glance at my phone sent a cold chill down my spine. I'd somehow overlooked the voice mail. His call had come through at the very same time I'd ratted him out to his sister. Ugh.

"I even came by the church, but by then you guys were all gone." He gestured for the maître d' to seat us. "But I did catch Devon. He was walking home. Did you know he walks all the way?"

"N-no." I had no idea.

"Yeah. I took him home and told him all about the program. He's talking to his mom to see if she'll do it. I prayed all the way home last night, and I have a real peace about it. Oh, and I think I've also got Devon convinced he should invite his mom to the talent show. She can do that first and then join the program. Might help her to see that her son is in good hands while she's away."

Shame washed over me as I realized just how off base I'd been about Armando.

We followed the maître d', who led the way to the wedding party in the back of the room. I needed to shift gears now, to think only of Hannah. But my thoughts kept drifting back to what Armando had done for Devon. I'd totally misjudged him, and now I felt like a fool.

I somehow made it through the dinner and was all smiles every time Hannah looked my way. I even managed to give a rousing maid of honor speech, though emotions grabbed hold of me and tears flowed a couple of times. By the time we left the restaurant, I was a mess. Emotionally, I was spent. Physically, even more so.

Still, I had a wedding cake to decorate. How in the world could I do that now, with nothing left in me to give?

Armando seemed more than a little concerned about my well-being. This I discerned from his ever-present hovering. He seemed especially worried as I headed out to my car. We stood under the overhead light as I fished for my keys. When I found the remote, I pressed it, and the locks on my Jeep clicked open.

Still, Armando would not leave my side. "Scarlet, let me drive you back. You're exhausted."

"That's sweet, but I might need my car to make a run to the store."

"A run to the store? At this time of night?"

"Yeah. I'm not going home, anyway. I'm going back to the bakery."

"At eleven o'clock on a Friday night?" He looked genuinely perplexed by this.

"Yes." I offered a nod, followed by a yawn. "I'm going to be up all night working on Hannah's wedding cake. With everything going on, I didn't make as much progress as I'd hoped. So I have no choice."

"Is Kenny helping you?"

"No." I shook my head. "He promised to run the shop for me tomorrow so I can focus on Hannah, so I don't want him to know I plan to stay up most of the night."

"At the bakery?" Armando looked alarmed. "You're going to be there by yourself?"

I nodded. "I'm sure it'll be fine. It's a safe area."

"A safe area? The Strand? In the middle of the night? Scarlet, you're not going to do this alone. I'm going to come and help you."

"No, it's okay." I put my hand up. "The cakes are baked and have the clear coat on them. They just need to be iced and decorated. Well, after I make the cream cheese frosting. Which will require a trip to the grocery store for cream. And cream cheese." I glanced at my watch, wondering how long all of this would take.

"I'm going to do all of that with you." Armando's pat on my arm brought me comfort. "There's no way I'm letting you tackle all of this by yourself in the middle of the night."

"Really?"

"Really." He took my keys from me and opened the passenger door, ushering me inside. Once I settled into the seat, he leaned in and gave me a peck on the cheek. "And by the way, you look amazing tonight."

"I . . . I do?"

"Yeah, that dress is perfect on you. Love the

color with your eyes." He traced my cheek with his finger. "I think Lucy would've approved."

That got a chuckle out of me. No doubt she would have. I'd stolen the design from her, after all.

We stopped off at the store for cream and cream cheese, and then Armando drove me back to the bakery. We arrived at 11:35. He grabbed an apron and put it on, then tossed one my way.

"Okay, where do we start?"

"We . . ." I pulled the largest cake from the refrigerator and double-checked my milk supply for the frosting. "We have to start with the largest one. I plan to do a really cool scrolling design on this one but can't start that until the cakes are frosted." I yawned. "Which means we have to start by making the cream cheese frosting."

"I think we've already established that I'm pretty good at that." He gave me a wink, and my heart took to fluttering.

Yes, he was good at the sweet stuff, all right.

He grabbed my largest bowl, opened the packages of cream cheese, and dumped them inside. "Where's the recipe?"

I found it and we went to work, mixing and frosting alongside one another for the next couple of hours. Before long all four cakes were iced and scrolled, and I'd created some gorgeous gum paste flowers in varying shades and pressed them into their designated spots.

I stood back and looked at what we'd created together. My heart wanted to sing at the sheer beauty of it all. Then again, I could barely think straight, let alone sing. And if I did sing, Armando would probably bring up that whole "you've got to sing at the fund-raiser" thing. No way was I going there. Not tonight, anyway.

"We'll wait to stack them until we get to the church tomorrow morning." I paused and glanced his way. "You are going to the wedding, aren't you?"

"I'm not doing sound, but I'll be there as a guest." He smiled. "If you want the truth, I'm coming just to see how gorgeous you look in your dress. But don't tell the bride. I'm sure she'll look nice too."

Ugh. He would have to go there. That awful maid of honor dress.

"Can you come by the shop at nine and take the cakes to Club Wed?" I asked. "I really need to spend the morning with Hannah."

"What time is the wedding again?"

"Eleven o'clock." My heart quickened as I realized it was now two in the morning. Not much time to sleep, awaken, shower, dress, and prep for the wedding.

"Okay. I'll come by at nine. What about Kenny?"

"Kenny." I paused as I spoke my assistant's name. "He'll be here running the shop. Can't really expect him to load and stack cakes with only one arm."

"True. Well, don't worry about it. I'll get everything to the reception on time, I promise."

We finished putting the cakes into the walk-in refrigerator and then headed out to the front of the bakery for a cup of coffee. While filling the coffeepot, I caught a glimpse of my reflection in the mirrors behind the cases. The mixer had sprayed splatterings of cream cheese frosting into my hair. Go figure. Not that Armando seemed to notice . . . or care. Likely he would just call it all "accessorizing."

"I think this is going to be your best cake ever," Armando said. "And I'm not just saying that because I helped."

I gave him a playful wink. "Well, don't tell anyone, but I added an extra ingredient this time. I'm not sure if you noticed, but I used heavy whipping cream in the frosting instead of milk."

"Wouldn't have known the difference, to be honest. But what would your aunt say about that?" Armando waggled a brow.

A little sigh escaped. "She's so by the book." I thought about Aunt Willy, and an odd rush of fear gripped me. Reaching for my phone, I gave it a close look to see if perhaps I'd missed a call from her. Nothing. So strange. I would have to remember to call her in the morning to see if she planned to attend the wedding.

"Is she a devout recipe follower or something?" Armando asked, clearly oblivious to my concerns about Aunt Willy's MIA status.

"What?" I put the phone away. "Oh yeah. She follows them to a T, which is kind of funny, because I'm more adventurous. I've always loved coming up with new concoctions. A little of this, a lot of that." I chuckled. "You never know what you're going to get when you make up recipes like I do, but sometimes you end up with something really great that no one else has thought of. Like my sticky buns, for instance."

"Love your sticky buns."

I did my best not to flinch and just smiled instead. The boy would never know my dirty little nickname. Not if I had anything to do with it.

Armando drew close, a sly smile on his face. "So, if I'm understanding you correctly, sometimes you follow the recipe you've been given and the outcome is good. Other times you add a pinch of this and a dash of that, and you wind up with something so great that it takes your breath away."

"Right."

He pulled me into his arms, and my heart quickened. "Sometimes you take two things—or, in our case, two people—who don't seem to go together, and throw them into the same bowl, and you end up with something better than anyone could've expected." He followed these words with a tiny kiss on my cheek, which sent a delicious shiver through me, yummier than the frosting I'd sampled earlier.

"Oh, now I see." I did. I saw his boyish smile, his sparkling eyes, the little dimple to the right of those gorgeous, sexy lips. I saw the playful expression, the dark, wavy hair—hair that I wanted to run my fingers through. I saw the boy —no, the man—who had captured my heart. The same man who had come to my rescue not once but twice now—first on the cake challenge, and now on my BFF's wedding cake.

Cakes weren't the only things he'd rescued, though. No, he'd rescued my heart, hadn't he? Rescued it from mediocrity. Rescued it from being handed over to the wrong fella. He'd given it reason to sing.

Sing.

A little hum escaped my lips, and Armando grinned. "There you go again. Singing."

"Yeah." I felt heat rush to my face. "Sorry. Just can't seem to help myself."

"You go right on, you songbird, you." He gazed into my eyes and smiled. "Glad to see I have that effect on you."

At once the little melody ended, and guilt washed over me. "Armando, I feel awful about what happened last night. Just goes to show that I shouldn't have judged you."

"It's okay. Totally understandable."

"Still, I know you better than that. I should have given you the benefit of the doubt."

"From now on you can." He winked and placed several tiny kisses on my cheek. "Mmm. You taste like sugar."

"I'll take that as a compliment."

"Take it any way you like." He kissed me soundly on the lips—twice. I found myself a little giddy. Then again, with the smell of sugar in the air, I might be delirious.

Yep, I was delirious, all right. In his arms, I realized the sweetness of his kisses were enough to send me on a sugar high that could very well last the rest of my life.

"Do you realize how beautiful you are?" he whispered in my ear when the kiss ended.

"I have cream cheese frosting in my hair and gum paste under my fingernails."

"Yes, I know." He gave me a sexy little wink. "And you've never looked better."

"Gee, thanks."

"No, seriously. You're in your element, and that's one thing that makes you beautiful to me. You're doing what you were created to do."

So are you. I wanted to say the words aloud but didn't. He was doing the very thing I needed him to do right now—holding me steady. Being the anchor to my proverbial ship. Keeping my breathing under control.

I leaned into him, and our lips met for another precious kiss.

I heard a rap at the front door and looked up to see a Galveston County police officer standing there, mouthing the words, "Everything okay in there?" No doubt the man was worried, what with two frosting-covered fanatics standing in the bakery at two in the morning.

I nodded and gave him a thumbs-up, and he headed down the street to keep a watchful eye on the other businesses.

A little chuckle escaped me as I thought through the song now rising up inside my heart once again. Yes, everything was certainly okay inside of Let Them Eat Cake. In fact, I couldn't remember a time when things had been better.

21

That Takes the Cake!

I never met a cupcake I didn't like.
Author unknown

On Saturday morning, as I prepped for Hannah's wedding, I checked my phone once more to see if Aunt Willy had called. Nothing. I texted her, but she didn't respond. Seemed a little strange. Usually she called me several times a day. I really would've expected her to call and ask how things were going. But she didn't.

So I called her. Oddly, she didn't answer. This stirred my curiosity and, frankly, made me a little nervous. At this point I honestly gave a thought to calling 911 so that someone could check in on her. Maybe a drive up to Houston was in order. Still, how could I leave with so much going on?

Instead of panicking, I decided to call my mother. She was usually pretty good at panicking enough for the both of us.

Mama answered on the fourth ring, sounding a little out of breath. "S-Scarlet. I was just jogging around the house."

"Beg your pardon?"

"It's that new Wii Fit thingie. I put the remote in my pocket and jog around the house. Trying to get back in shape." She began a lengthy conversation about her cholesterol, which only served to get me more worried about Aunt Willy.

"Mama, have you heard from Aunt Willy over the past couple days?"

"No." A couple of quick pants followed her words, and I could tell her jog continued in spite of our conversation.

"And did you notice that she didn't send out her promo email the other night? She's never missed that. We always get those notices like clockwork."

Mama continued to huff and puff. "Actually, now that you mention it, I don't recall seeing it."

"And doesn't she usually call Dad at least once a day to complain about something? The weather? The price of gas? Some television pastor asking for her money? Anything. Everything."

"Yes."

"But she hasn't called today?"

"Hmm." Mama paused and appeared to catch her breath. "Maybe she tried your daddy on his cell. Hang on a second, Scarlet. I'll ask him." She was gone for a minute, then returned, now sounding as concerned as I felt. "That's odd. He says he hasn't heard from her for three days."

Ack. A sick feeling came over me. "Mama, you don't suppose . . ." I couldn't say the words aloud, but they flitted through my mind.

"I'll give her a call. And if she doesn't answer, I'll have her assistant check on her."

"Ooo, that's a good idea."

"I'm sure she's okay, honey," Mama said. "She's just been really distracted since the television show. Maybe she's resting. Or maybe she's taking a little vacation or something."

"Yeah. Maybe." Not that I'd ever known the woman to take a vacation, but anything was possible, I supposed.

"You focus on Hannah today," my mother said. "I'll have your dad keep trying to reach Willy. I'm sure everything's fine."

"Okay. You're probably right."

Mama was right about one thing. Today was all about Hannah, and I needed to stay alert, to meet her needs, whatever they might be.

I dressed in casual clothes and carried my maid of honor dress with me. When I arrived at Club Wed at 9:30, Armando had already delivered the cakes. Relief washed over me as I saw that they looked even better in the daylight. I made quick work out of stacking the layers and adding the ribbon, replaying last night's events as I went along. I found myself giddy, remembering the many kisses Armando and I had shared.

When I finished the cake, I looked it over with pride. "I think perhaps you were right, Armando." I spoke aloud, though no one was in the room.

"Armando?" Bella's voice rang out from

behind me as she walked in. "What's he done this time?"

I turned to face her and grinned. "Nothing bad, I promise. And I was so wrong about what happened the other night at the rehearsal."

"Oh? Do tell."

"When things slow down, I'll tell you the whole story. But in the meantime, just know that he came to my rescue in the middle of the night last night and helped me frost and decorate that cake. We wouldn't have had a wedding cake today if not for your brother."

"Well, God bless my brother." She gave the cake a closer look and then offered up an admiring whistle. "I think that's your best one ever, girlie."

"That's what he said. And I think he was right." Crazy what we could accomplish when we worked together.

"Hannah and her sisters are in the bride's room," Bella said. "That's where you ladies are getting dressed."

I giggled, in part because the phrase "Hannah and her sisters" put me in mind of the Woody Allen movie, and in part because I could only imagine how giddy my best friend must be on this, her wedding day.

A couple of minutes later I found Hannah in the throes of setting up her workstation—putting out makeup, jewelry, and so forth. Her gorgeous wedding dress, a beautiful beaded number hand-crafted by Gabi, was hanging in anticipation.

I dove into maid of honor gear, helping with her hair and locating everything from hairpins to safety pins. Next I kept vigil while one of her sisters did her makeup.

"What do you think?" Hannah turned my way, the look finally complete.

"I think . . ." A lump rose in my throat, and I did my best to speak above it. "You're as pretty as a picture."

She giggled. "I'll bet you say that to all the photographers."

"No. The only other photographer I know is Drew, and he's not pretty." I clamped a hand over my mouth and then laughed as I pulled it away. "I mean, he's very handsome, but I wouldn't call him pretty."

"Not to his face anyway." Hannah chuckled and eased the tension in the room. "But you're going to get to know another photographer today. Bella's brother Joey is in town visiting the family and is photographing our wedding. He'll be here in about thirty minutes to catch all of us in action, so you girls don't have long to get ready."

I rose and reached for my dress, sighing as I saw it hanging next to the other bridesmaid dresses. Oh well. No point in worrying about my size right now. Worrying wouldn't accomplish any-thing.

"Hey, speaking of photographs . . ." Hannah

stood and faced all of us. "Drew and I have a surprise for all of our guests."

"Oh? What kind of surprise?" I asked.

"Something special. We thought it would be fun, since we're both photographers." She clasped her hands together and grinned. "We ordered a photo booth. It's being delivered in a few minutes. They're going to set it up in the reception hall."

"A photo booth?"

"Yes," she said. "You know, like the ones in the mall. You go inside and make funny faces and it spits out your picture. Only this one won't cost anything." Her eyes sparkled with obvious delight. "We provided all sorts of props too. Hats, feather boas, over-the-top jewelry, even a king and queen crown. And it's free for the guests. Just grab whatever prop—or person—you like and slip inside to have your picture taken. You keep the pictures as a memento. Isn't that a great idea?"

"Yeah. Great." I nodded, but in my heart I groaned. Just one more way to capture this day in photographic form. If only I could've lost a few more pounds so that I would look like the other girls when I was in my dress. Ugh.

"Okay, well, hurry up and get dressed so you all can help me into my gown." Hannah turned back to face the mirror. "I'm going to go ahead and get my jewelry on while I'm waiting."

Her sisters did that usual girl thing where they

peeled down to their underclothes in front of each other, but I headed to the bathroom to change into my dress. I found myself more than a little intimidated and decided I needed some privacy. Once alone, I slipped out of my jeans and T-shirt and wriggled my way into the Lycra under-garments I'd purchased special for today. The bottom piece went on okay, but getting the top piece into place almost turned out to be my undoing. At one point I thought I might have to call for backup. How humiliating would that be?

I finally managed and was startled to see just how much smaller I looked with Lycra holding everything in place. Not that I could breathe. Then again, breathing was highly overrated on days like today, wasn't it?

Though gaspy, I knew I must forge ahead. I reached for the maid of honor dress, but as I slipped it over my head, it felt different from before. Odd. Once I got it on, I reached to pull up the side zipper and gasped when I realized the dress was too big. Not just a little too big either. *Ack.* Happy problem, but not on a day like today, with less than an hour to go before my best friend's wedding. And with the new photographer waiting? Now what?

I walked out of the stall and stood in front of the mirror, analyzing the situation. Bella chose that moment to enter. She buzzed from stall to stall, checking the toilet paper supply, but paused when she saw me standing there, examining my reflection.

"Scarlet." She stood alongside me and stared at my reflection.

"Houston, we have a problem." They were the only words I could manage.

"No kidding." She reached for the excess fabric on the sides of the dress. "Okay, don't panic."

"Do I look like I'm panicking?"

"No, not yet. We might be in luck. Gabi's here. She came just in case we need her to make any last-minute nips or tucks to Hannah's dress."

"Oh, this is perfect. She's the one who fitted me in the first place."

"Right. I'm pretty sure she can work some magic with this dress if we can just get her to a sewing machine. Hang on a second and I'll go get her." She sprinted out of the room and returned moments later with Gabi at her side.

"Bella says we have a problem." The petite young woman stood back and examined my dress. "Man. That's not what it looked like when I fitted you a few weeks ago, is it? Not even close."

"I guess I've changed a little since then." A nervous giggle erupted.

"More than a little, I'd say." She grabbed excess fabric from each side and pulled the dress tight. "Okay, we're talking at least two inches. Maybe three. Girl, you've dropped some weight."

"Guess so. Didn't realize it was that much, though. Most of my other clothes are loose fitting, so I haven't been paying that much attention."

"I always keep an emergency kit in my car. Pins, measuring tape, and so on." She looked more confident than I felt, which made me feel better about the situation. Just as quickly, her confident look faded a bit. "But I don't have a sewing machine."

"I've been thinking about that," Bella said. "My parents live next door with my aunt and uncle. My aunt Rosa has a top-of-the-line Bernina."

"You've just spoken the magic word." Gabi's face lit into a smile. "Okay, I'll be right back."

She headed out to get the pins and returned minutes later, sewing kit in hand. At this point, a frantic race to the altar—Hannah's, not mine—began. By now, all of the bridesmaids were gathered around me like baby chicks with their mother hen. Nervous chicks. The clock ticked down the hour. With the photographer due in ten minutes and the bride waiting alone in a separate room, we were truly in countdown mode.

Gabi pinned my dress, then signaled for me to take it off. I didn't want to pull it off in front of the other girls—especially girls as slim and trim as Hannah's sisters—but I had no choice. At least they got to see the Lycra-sized version of me. That brought some degree of comfort. Besides, all I could think of was Hannah. She'd been left in the bride's room alone to deal with her gown. Would she hate me for this?

Forgive me, Hannah! I didn't mean to ruin your wedding day.

"Where are your other clothes?" Bella's words startled me back to reality and reminded me that I was still standing in my undergarments in front of the others. Go figure. It hadn't even fazed me.

I gestured to the stall, and she grabbed my jeans and T-shirt, then tossed them my way. "I'm guessing it won't take her long, but you might as well put these on."

"Right." I wriggled into my jeans. They too felt looser, but then again they would, what with my thighs being compressed in the Lycra torture suit. The T-shirt felt baggy as well, but I didn't have time to worry about that.

"I need to do my makeup." Scrambling, I found my bag. "I feel like such a heel."

"Why?" Hannah's youngest sister asked.

"This is Hannah's day. I'm her maid of honor. She needs me."

"She's talking to Mama right now," one of the other sisters said, then rolled her eyes. "They're having 'the talk.' "

"The talk?" I gave Bella a curious look, and she raised an eyebrow. "Ohhh. *The* talk."

"Yeah, apparently Hannah's mother has been trying for weeks to have this mother-daughter chat, and Hannah has done her best to avoid it. But today she's a captive audience."

A giggle followed on my end. "Okay, well, maybe she doesn't need me right now, after all. I would have very little to contribute to that conversation." I reached for my makeup bag and went to work on my face, starting with the foundation. The other girls stood nearby, double-checking their makeup in the mirror alongside me. Before long Hannah's sisters headed off to check on the bride, leaving me alone with Bella.

As I worked, we chatted nervously, but I could tell something was up. Bella kept giving me a weird look. Was I imagining it?

No. She leaned against the counter and crossed her arms at her chest, falling silent.

"Spit it out, girl," I said as I ran the blush brush across my cheeks. "You've got something on your mind."

"I do." She hesitated, and I could sense her concern. "I've been wanting to talk to you about this for a while now but couldn't seem to find the right time. I wanted to wait until the others left to bring it up."

"You want me to bake more cakes for Club Wed?" *I hope.*

"Well, that too, but this is more personal."

I quirked a brow. "You having another baby? Do I sense a baby shower cake in my future?"

She threw a hand up in the air. "Bite your

tongue! My hands are so full right now I hardly have time to breathe, let alone run a business. So, no babies. Yet." She flashed a coy smile.

I pulled out my lipstick and ran it across my lips, then smacked them together. "What, then?"

Bella spoke to my reflection in the mirror. "Scarlet, let me ask you a question. I know you're on a diet and all that. You look great, by the way. Gabi was right about that, for sure."

"Thank you."

Her nose wrinkled. "Look, I get that you want to be happy with yourself, so please don't misunderstand what I'm about to say."

Okay, that really made me wonder what she was about to say.

She released a slow breath and gave me a pensive look. "I just wonder . . . do you feel lovable . . . just like you are?"

"Just like I am?" Ugh. Why did we have to go there?

"Because you are, you know. You're like Mary Poppins—practically perfect in every way."

That got a snort out of me, one that brought a certain degree of embarrassment. "Seriously? I'm far from perfect."

"What I mean is, it doesn't matter how you look. The number on the scale doesn't define you."

I looked at her reflection and did my best not to sigh. Standing there in her designer dress, she looked more supermodel than wedding coordinator.

Then again, she always did. Every curly hair was in place. Her clothes were impeccable.

I sighed. "You don't understand. You couldn't possibly." *What are you, a size 2? Have you ever been overweight a day in your life? No, I think not.*

"To some extent, maybe not. But I've got my own hang-ups. We all do. Still, you seem to be a little . . . fixated."

"Fixated?" I glanced at my chubby self in the mirror. "How so?"

"You talk a lot about weight. And diet. And calories. And carbs." Bella placed her hand on my arm. "I just want to make sure you realize you're gorgeous to the Lord. You don't have to change on his account. So I hope this isn't about that."

"Oh, I know that." At least, I was pretty sure I knew that. Still, this weight-loss journey wasn't about proving myself to anyone else. Not any-more.

"Bella . . ." I brushed my hands on my jeans and reexamined my reflection in the mirror. "I'm just really, really tired of being uncomfortable in my own skin. It's time for a change."

Her face lit into a smile. "Okay, then. That I can live with."

"And I want to be healthy," I added. "I want to live to see my babies and my grandbabies." I giggled. "And I want to be . . . sexy."

"Girl, you are."

"Maybe. Hard to tell at this stage of my life. But one day I want my husband to think I'm ravishing." Images of Armando danced in my brain—handsome, precious Armando. Suddenly I could hardly keep the giggles from erupting.

"He will."

"Yes, he probably will. And God already does." How could I make her understand that I'd already figured out all of that on my own? "But it's important that I feel as good about myself as I possibly can, which is why I'm working at it. I might never lose a ton of weight, and that's okay. I just need to know that I'm doing the very best job I can with the body God gave me. That's all. No more excesses." I put my hand up. "Scout's honor."

"No crash diets?"

"Never again, I promise."

"Good girl. Then I heartily approve." She sighed. "Though how you manage working around all of those sweets is beyond me. I look at cake and all I want to do is ask for the largest piece you have."

"Then you will have my largest piece." I laughed. "Just as soon as this ceremony is behind us. I think you're going to like the Italian cream cake I made for Hannah's wedding. It's your aunt Rosa's recipe."

Her nose wrinkled. "Her old recipe or the new one she stole from the web?"

"The new one."

We both laughed.

"I changed up a couple of things to make it even better," I said. "And it's so good, I might even have a piece myself. I can do that, you know. Without eating the whole cake, I mean. I really can have my cake and eat it too."

Whoa.

For the first time, I'd spoken those words *and* understood them.

"I can have my cake and eat it too," I repeated.

"Awesome." She flashed a smile, likely wondering why the phrase meant so much to me. How could she possibly understand the depth of the words? I'd only just discovered the truth of them myself.

Just then Gabi came bounding back into the room, dress in hand. "Did it!" she hollered, then tossed the dress my way.

"Girl, you're a miracle worker!" I proclaimed.

I scrambled out of my clothes, not the tiniest bit worried about my chubbiness, and she slipped the dress over my head and zipped it up. The three of us—Bella, Gabi, and I—stood back and examined my appearance in the mirror with the fitted maid of honor dress now in place, showing off my every curve and making me look like a plus-size model.

"Wow." Bella gave a little whistle. "I can't wait for Armando to see you looking like this."

Me either. Only, I wouldn't say that aloud. Not in front of Gabi, who stood nearby beaming like a proud mama.

The ladies headed off to see to the final details of the wedding, and I slipped into the bride's room to visit with Hannah. Thank God her mother had finished "the talk." Hannah stood there red-faced, looking completely embarrassed.

"Well, that was fun," she said and giggled. "Remind me to tell you later what she said." She shook her head and pinched her eyes shut. "Ooo, I wish she hadn't told me some of that. Now I wonder if I'll be able to think about anything else when I see Drew."

"Well, let's find something else to talk about. Like your dress, for instance. I know you're ready to put it on."

"Yes. My sisters have disappeared on me. But speaking of dresses, you look gorgeous. That dress was made for you."

Literally.

"Thanks," I said. "Now, back to you. I would love to have the honor of helping you into your gown. What's a best friend for?"

Hannah turned toward me, eyes misty. "She's for helping me through the toughest week of my life. I couldn't have made it through the last few days without you, Scarlet. Thank you so much."

"You're worth it." I gave her a little wink, then walked over and grabbed the wedding gown.

Gabi entered the room at that very moment and helped me get the bride into her dress, then we stood back and let out admiring whistles.

"Wow." The white satin dress took my breath away, but the intricate beading really took the cake.

Ha! Took the cake!

Hannah slipped her arm through mine, and we stared at our reflections in the mirror. "It's going to be your turn next."

"Nah." I shook my head.

"Yep. And you're going to be the most beautiful bride ever."

"Doubtful. Have you seen yourself?" I pointed to her reflection in the mirror.

"Yes." She swished this way and that, showing off the couture gown. "Don't you think Gabi did a great job with this? She's amazing."

I gave Gabi an admiring smile. "Amazing doesn't begin to describe it. She just performed a miracle with my dress too. I don't know how much you heard, but she's a whiz with a needle and thread."

"I heard a little." She gave me a wink. "All I have to say is, it's a perfect fit now."

"Yes." I stared at my reflection and realized just how much smaller my waist looked now that the dress had been taken in.

"My sisters think you're gorgeous, by the way," Hannah said.

"Really?" I smiled as I thought about that. Not that it really mattered what others thought. But it didn't exactly hurt either. "Hey, where are they?"

She rolled her eyes. "I have a sneaking suspicion they're doing something to Drew's SUV. I'm nervous just thinking about it."

"Ah yes. I believe I heard a little something-something about that." I wouldn't tell her how much forethought had been involved. She would find out for herself. Soon.

Right now, we had a wedding to get to.

"You ready for this?" I asked.

"Been ready for months." She released an "ah, love!" sigh, and we both giggled. Minutes later, her sisters returned, alongside Bella, who gave us our final instructions.

"Okay, the guests are here. Drew and the groomsmen are ready to make their entrance. And you . . ." She gazed at Hannah with a smile. "You are going to be the prettiest bride to ever walk the aisle at Club Wed."

"Oh, I'll bet you say that to all your brides." Hannah waved her hand as if dismissing the idea.

Bella nodded. "I do. But they buy it every time." She turned to face the rest of us. "Ready, ladies?"

I was, actually. Ready to stand before the crowd and honor my BFF. Ready to see Armando's eyes when he caught a glimpse of me in this dress for

314

the first time. Ready to have my photo taken in that goofy photo booth with the man who made my heart sing. Ready to dance the night away afterward. And ready to have a little sliver of Italian cream cake to celebrate it all.

22

Let Them Eat Cake

Never trust a skinny cook.

Anonymous

Hannah's wedding day came off without a hitch. Well, except for that one part where my dad accidentally botched up the groom's middle name in front of 250 guests, but everyone got a big laugh out of it. Surely the whole thing would make for a good story later.

Armando gushed over my maid of honor dress—and the girl in it. At least three or four times he sought me out to whisper flattering words in my ear. Not that I had time to absorb them, what with the Italian cream cake being such a big hit. I'd never received so many compliments for something I'd baked, with the exception of my sticky buns.

Thinking of sticky buns reminded me of Aunt Rosa's suggestion. As I made my way home from the wedding on Saturday afternoon, I thought through the possibilities. Should I really host a special fund-raiser featuring the sugary delights?

If so, I would need to put together a plan—in particular, a date—soon.

With that in mind, I decided to give Aunt Willy a call to fill her in, but I faced the same dilemma I'd faced over the past couple of days. She didn't answer.

When I saw my mother in church the next day, I asked if she had heard anything.

"Not a word, Scarlet." Mama's brow wrinkled. "Your father says he's going to drive up to her condo this evening. He's really getting worried. Would you like to go with us?"

"Yes." I released a slow breath, my concerns growing. "This is really scary."

"It is. But I'm sure she's fine. Maybe she just wants to be left alone."

"Maybe." Still, none of this made sense. "Were you able to reach Genevive?" Auntie's assistant would surely know how to locate her.

"No." Tiny creases appeared between Mama's eyes. "She didn't answer, but I doubt your father left a message. You know how he feels about answering machines."

"Right. Well, I'm going to try to call her before church starts."

I slipped away to the room behind the choir loft and made the call. Thank goodness Genevive answered the phone on the third ring.

"Oh, thank God, Scarlet. It's you," she said after I offered a quick hello. "I've been wanting to talk to you for a couple of days now to make sure your aunt is with you."

I felt my heart skip a beat. "No. That's why I'm calling. I was hoping you knew where she was."

A long pause followed on the other end of the line. "Oh, Scarlet . . . I haven't seen her for three days now. I've been so concerned."

"Same here. And my parents haven't heard from her either."

"I don't know what to think," Genevive said. "I've been trying not to worry, but what else can I do? Your aunt has never done anything like this before, so I can only imagine that something has happened to her."

"Maybe she was going on some kind of trip," I said. "Maybe a conference of some sort?"

"No, I have her itinerary right here in front of me. She's not scheduled to go anywhere for another two weeks." The concern in Genevive's voice was evident. "I'm just so confused. All this time I've tried not to fret. I figured she was with her family. You know? She loves you guys."

She . . . she does?

"I don't know what to think," Genevive said. "Except maybe I should start calling the hospitals, just to make sure. Nothing else makes sense."

"What about her car?" I asked.

"What about it?"

"Maybe you should check with the police to make sure it hasn't been stolen or something."

318

Visions of Aunt Willy tied up in a bad guy's basement stirred my imagination and my fears. Of course, we didn't have basements in Texas, but that was beside the point. What if someone had harmed her in some way?

A lump rose in my throat, and I fought to speak above it. "I love her, Genevive. I'll do anything to know she's okay."

"I know. Me too."

We ended the call just as the opening song began. I made my way into the sanctuary and took a seat on the second pew beside Armando, who looked happy to see me. It felt really good to share the church service with him, especially with his hand wrapped around mine, but I couldn't stop thinking about Aunt Willy.

I thought about her all the way through my father's message on love. I thought about her as we drove past the bakery on our way to Parma John's for lunch. I thought about her when my phone rang around two o'clock, just as we were leaving the restaurant. Ironically, it was Hannah, thanking me for all of my help with the wedding. Go figure. The girl was getting on a cruise ship to head off on her honeymoon and stopped to call me?

"Go enjoy your honeymoon, girl," I admonished. "Have the time of your life."

"Oh, I already have." She giggled. "Let's just say that Mama didn't even tell me the half of it."

Eew! I put a stop to that conversation at once, especially when Armando tried to figure out what we were talking about.

Hannah headed off to her honeymoon, and Armando and I headed off to his car. I'd just climbed inside when Bella came rushing toward us. She spoke through the open window. "Scarlet, I have news."

"News?"

"Yes." Her brow creased in obvious concern. "I know you're not going to believe it, but there's been a sighting."

"A sighting?"

She leaned into the window and whispered, "Your aunt Willy."

Relief flooded over me. "You found her?"

"Well, D.J. did. He drove up to Splendora this morning to pick up the kids from his parents' place, and . . . well . . . you're not going to believe it."

"Try me."

"He stopped off at his uncle Donny's truck stop to fill up his truck, and there was your aunt."

"Wait." My breath caught in my throat. "My aunt was in Splendora, Texas?"

"Not just in Splendora," Bella said, "but at Donny's gas station."

"It's not just a gas station," I said from memory. "It's a full-service rest stop for families, complete with food and the cleanest restrooms in the state."

"Somehow I doubt that's why she drove up there." Bella laughed. "Though they did appear to be talking about some sort of business transaction when D.J. walked in. Still, he said they were very . . . what's the word he used? Chummy."

"Chummy? My aunt and D.J.'s uncle?" The very idea gave me the giggles. Before long my giggles turned to full-blown laughter.

"And get this," Bella said. "D.J. said she was standing behind the counter. Even waited on a customer for Donny when he got busy doing something else."

"No way." My heart did a strange little twist at this news. Was Auntie in need of medication, perhaps?

Armando remained silent, but I could see laugh lines forming around his eyes.

"Honestly? Aunt Willy and Uncle Donny?" Was such a thing even possible?

I could hardly wait to call Mama and tell her. When I ended the conversation with Bella, I did just that. She seemed stunned, but she added her chuckles to mine. The whole thing seemed so out of character for Aunt Willy, and yet delightful too.

Armando and I sat in the car and talked through the Aunt Willy thing for several minutes.

"It's nuts," I said. "She's with a man?"

"What's so nuts about that?" He offered a little shrug.

"She's a self-proclaimed man hater, that's what. She especially can't stand guys who are macho or chauvinistic."

"And Donny comes across that way to you?"

"Not me. She . . ." How could I explain the whole shirtless, golf-cart guy thing to Armando? He would never get it. "She just said something to me once about thinking he was a good old boy."

"Nothing wrong with good old boys."

"Right. Except that she perceives them to be anti-women-in-business-for-themselves."

"Kind of weird. She's opposed to men who don't like their women to be in business for themselves, and she's the polar opposite—all business. Wouldn't you say?"

"What do you mean?"

"It's just my perception from the few times I've been around her. She seems to be all about business." He gazed at me. "Can I ask a personal question?"

"Of course." I gave his hand a squeeze.

"Does your aunt ever call you just to talk?"

I released a breath, wishing I didn't have to answer. "No. She calls to make sure I locked up the bakery or to double-check my orders. But she's never once just called to say, 'Hey, how are you?' or even tell me happy birthday. The woman is definitely all about the bottom line, trust me. About how well we're doing financially and all that."

"So this whole Uncle Donny thing is truly—"

"Bizarre. So bizarre, in fact, that I have to think the only reason she's up there is to do business with him." That really bothered me. Did she not trust me enough to know that I would give him the bakery goods I'd promised? "Anyway, she's never married, so she doesn't have a family of her own. And I never thought about it before, but you're right. She never calls to say, 'Hey, how are you?' or 'Why don't we spend the day together? Go fishing?' "

Armando snapped his fingers. "Hey, speaking of fishing, I still want to plan a fishing trip with Devon. Maybe we could take your whole family and include Devon in the mix. How would that be?" He chuckled. "Can you imagine your aunt Wilhelmina with a fishing pole in her hand, relaxing on the pier?"

I closed my eyes and tried to envision it. "Nope. First of all, we couldn't get her to sit that long. Second, if she so much as saw a fish, she would scream and toss it our way."

"I'm not so sure. I still think we should include her."

I bit back the laugh that threatened to erupt as I thought about Willy with a fishing pole in hand. Then again, she spent a lot of time fishing already, didn't she? Yes, she was always fishing for a piece of my pie. So far I'd given her my pride, my talent, and my angst.

My attention shifted back to Armando. Maybe he was right. Maybe once we got this fund-raiser behind us—once my sticky buns were all sold out and we'd pocketed enough money to send a team to Nicaragua—we could hit the pier and fill our nets.

Right now we had bigger fish to fry. A talent show awaited my attention. One with a saw played by a fella who obviously had the hots for Auntie. I had a feeling he wouldn't be singing "You Picked a Fine Time to Leave Me, Lucille" any longer. No doubt his tune had changed to something a little more romantic.

I leaned toward Armando and laid my head on his shoulder, realizing my tune had changed too. No longer filled with insecurities and fears, my heart now sang a crazy Elvis tune, complete with my own hunka hunka burning love.

23

Save Room for Dessert

In the buffet of life, friends are the dessert.
Author unknown

With Aunt Willy safely located, I turned my attention to the one thing that still demanded my attention this week—the Nicaragua fund-raiser. In spite of my exhaustion, in spite of my lack of sleep and physical strain, I needed to focus on the talent show. On Saturday night we would all gather in the sanctuary at the church with hopefully hundreds of audience members. The decision was made to push the sticky buns extravaganza off another week or so. We needed to get this talent show behind us.

I spent the week finalizing our list. By the time Friday afternoon arrived, I felt sure we were in good shape. Armando had the lights and sound in perfect running order and had even created a fun light show for the teen portions. I could kiss the boy. Actually, I did kiss the boy. Not just once but twice.

Not in front of Kenny, though. He seemed more distant than usual, and I felt sure he knew about my feelings for Armando, but we didn't discuss it. After the show I would bare my soul. Right now I needed to stay focused so that we could get through this. Too many things were riding on it.

Armando and I arrived at the church at 5:30 on Saturday afternoon and were surprised to see the trio from Splendora already there.

Jolene rushed our way, a frightened look in her eyes. "Scarlet, I'm glad you're here. We have a problem."

My heart quickened as I realized something had gone wrong. "What happened?"

"Twila's lost her voice."

"No." I looked at Twila, who leaned against the Cadillac, dressed in a glittery top and black skirt. She nodded, then pointed to her throat and mouthed the words, "I'm so sorry."

"It's okay," I said. "I'm sure we'll think of something."

"No idea what," Bonnie Sue said. "I mean, she's got no voice at all. Which puts us in a real jam. We've got three songs planned and now we can't do them."

Armando looked concerned at this news. No doubt. After all, the Splendora sisters were our money act. We'd even put an ad in the paper.

"What are we going to do?" Bonnie Sue paced the parking lot. "There are reporters coming and everything."

Twila shrugged and mouthed another woeful

"I'm sorry." I felt really bad for her but didn't know what to do, short of praying for a miracle.

"I have the perfect idea." Jolene snapped her fingers. "If Twila can't sing, you'll have to go on in her place, Scarlet."

"W-what?" I took a couple of giant steps backwards. "I don't sing."

"That's it." Armando looked thrilled by this news. "It's perfect."

"No!" I put my hands up in the air. "I . . . I can't."

"Of course you can," Jolene said. "Remember? We heard you awhile back, singing your heart out when you thought no one was listening."

"That's different," I argued. "I haven't sung in front of anyone since . . ."

"Since her aunt Willy said she was tone-deaf when she was in the third grade." My father's voice rang out from behind me. "But Willy was wrong then, and she's wrong now. The old gal is hard of hearing and doesn't know an angel singing when she hears it." He drew near and took my hand. "Scarlet, what she did to you broke my heart then, and it breaks my heart now. You've always had a beautiful voice. I only wish you could see that."

"You're my dad. You're supposed to say things like that."

"I'm not related to you," Jolene said. "And I concur."

"Me too," Bonnie Sue agreed.

"But I have it on good authority that Aunt Willy is going to be here tonight to hear Uncle Donny play his saw, and she's going to hear me."

"Perfect." My father clasped his hands together. "Then this is the ideal way to show her just how wrong she's been."

"But on such short notice?" I glanced at my watch and cringed. How could I learn the harmonies of three Gershwin tunes in such a short time and still direct the show?

"You go with the ladies to practice." Armando placed his hand on my arm. "Your dad and I will make sure everyone gets settled in for a run-through in the sanctuary."

"You sure?"

He nodded and gazed intently into my eyes. "Trust me."

"Oh, I do." *No need to prove yourself, sweet boy. You've more than accomplished that of late.*

I tagged along on Bonnie Sue's and Jolene's heels into the choir rehearsal room, where Twila took her place at the piano and pounded out my part. I did okay on "Someone to Watch Over Me" but struggled a little on the other two songs. Before long, however, I managed to get them down. Mostly. I still cringed, wondering what Auntie would say when she heard me singing in public.

By the time seven o'clock rolled around, I'd somehow been able to meet with the participants, change into my MC dress, and touch up my lipstick. I stood before the people and greeted them, though the vast number crammed into our small sanctuary almost took my breath away. And it didn't help that a reporter from the *Galveston Daily* sat in the front row with a notepad in hand.

Oh. Yikes.

Still, the show must go on and all that. We opened with one of the teen boys playing a rousing number on his guitar, which got everyone hyped up. From there, the teens did their human video about addiction. I couldn't help but notice there wasn't a dry eye in the place.

When it came time for our trio to perform, my legs felt like lead. I somehow stood in front of the crowd, but I felt completely nauseous. Honestly, if Bonnie Sue and Jolene hadn't been there on either side of me, I probably would've fainted. Or thrown up. Something.

But as the music kicked in, a strange calm settled over me. And as the first notes were sung, as my mouth opened and the harmony I'd just learned poured out, I found myself relaxing. By the time we hit the second song, I was having fun. And by the time the audience begged for an encore, I felt like diving into a solo rendition of "I Believe I Can Fly." Not that "I Believe I Can Fly" was on the agenda, but I would've sung it if asked.

Which is why, five minutes later, when I sat down on the front pew and Twila opened her mouth to thank me—when I realized she was in full voice—I almost lost it.

"You could have sung?" I whispered, trying not to make a scene while little Gracie Williams sang "Happy Birthday, Jesus" from the stage.

"Yeah." Twila hung her head. "Sorry about that. Guess I told a little white lie, but I've already asked the Lord to forgive me." She patted me on the back. "If it makes you feel any better, I do have a sore throat, and my voice was really scratchy this morning. But the other ladies don't have a clue. They really think I'm voiceless."

"Still . . ."

"Honey, you needed the boost," she whispered. "You needed to see for yourself that you still had it in you to do it."

"I suppose."

I thought about her words as the show continued. Really, the whole "stand up in front of the church and sing" thing had felt good. Really, really good. Once the nerves passed, anyway. And the harmonies had come, no problem.

Guess you were wrong, Auntie.

Either that, or my voice had grown and developed since third grade.

I stole a glance her way when I stood to introduce Donny. She had that "I'm so proud of my man" look on her face. Totally threw me. But I had to remain focused on the show.

Donny made his way to the front, the usual

aroma of gasoline a little fainter than usual. He looked pretty spiffy in his button-down shirt and khaki pants. Auntie must've dressed him. Well, not literally, but she must've given him some advice. And the scent of an expensive cologne wafted by as he gave me a little hug before starting his number. Alrighty then.

I took my seat, completely mesmerized.

My awe continued as the man pulled out his saw, which he introduced to the audience as Prince William. He even included a funny little story about how the saw had acquired its name.

Then the song began. I listened, completely spellbound, as Uncle Donny played "Amazing Grace" on his saw. If you had told me that a saw could sound like this, or that a man could usher in the presence of God using a common tool from his shed, I would've said you were crazy. But the moment was undeniably holy.

I thanked God that Uncle Donny hadn't been able to play for us last week at the rehearsal. Had I known this was coming, it would have been less powerful, no doubt.

I glanced across the room and took in my aunt's face. I'd known the woman for over twenty years, of course, but had never seen any emotion on her face—other than frustration or angst. What I saw now took my breath away.

Tears.

Lots and lots of tears.

As I listened to "Amazing Grace" peal forth, a few tears of my own started. I wasn't the only one. I could see Armando's eyes welling over. And my mother's. And . . .

I could hardly believe it, but as I looked across the aisle, I noticed Devon's mother had come. My heart quickened at once as I noticed the tears in her eyes. They started as a little trickle down one cheek, but before long full-fledged tears streamed like a river rushing past its banks.

Devon slipped into the space beside his mother and put his arm around her shoulders. By now she was visibly sobbing. This stirred my mother to action. Mama hurried toward the woman's pew and slipped into the spot on the other side of her. Soon the sobs were under control. Still Uncle Donny continued on, now playing "In the Garden," one of my favorite hymns. From there he shifted into "Softly and Tenderly."

Uncle Donny continued to play, his eyes closed. I was pretty sure at one point that I heard a heavenly angel choir chime in. *Lord, are those angel voices, or are the people singing?* The people were singing. Most, anyway.

I glanced back at Armando, who seemed completely mesmerized by all of this. No doubt. We had been ushered into the presence of God, and it caught us all completely by surprise.

So this is what heaven will be like. I smiled as I thought about how comfortable I felt in the Lord's presence, like a daughter curled up at her daddy's knee. I wasn't distracted by weight issues and men on golf carts. This holy moment had nothing to do with people being successful in business or feeling like they had no value. In this place, all of those things were irrelevant. Here, I focused on praising God. Worshiping him.

When Uncle Donny finished his song, the crowd rose in spontaneous applause. Now, I'd seen a lot of things in my day. Mostly in other churches. In our little church, folks rarely rose and cheered. But with the Splendora sisters shouting "Hallelujah!" and "Amen!" my heart wanted to sing.

This is what heaven is going to be like, Lord. All of us, from all denominations, worshiping together and enjoying your presence.

Sister Twila took to dancing a little jig in the aisle, which, under ordinary circumstances, probably would've thrown my conservative pastor father into a panic. Not now, however. He was too busy with his arms up in the air, praising the Lord. And Mama? Well, Mama was pretty busy too as she prayed with Devon's mother, who continued to weep.

I somehow managed to make the transition from Donny's songs to the final act—a beautiful aria by Bubba, another anointed moment. I had to admit, the whole evening had been orchestrated by God—every single bit of it. I wouldn't change a thing, not even my role in the trio.

When the event came to its rightful end, the offering plate was passed, and I could see folks reaching deep into their wallets. I didn't stress over how much money came in. God had this one covered. I could sense it.

After I dismissed the audience, people lingered, many of them congratulating Uncle Donny and the others who had performed. I made my way back to Armando, who remained at the sound-board, now talking to Devon's mom. I waited until they were finished, then slipped my arm around his waist and whispered, "Thank you" in his ear.

"What are you thanking me for?" he asked. "You're the one who pulled all of this together."

"Maybe, but the lights and sound were the icing on the cake."

"Icing on the cake." He grinned. "Hey, that reminds me, don't you guys have refreshments in the fellowship hall? I'm starving."

"Sure do. That's where everyone's headed now. I brought all the sweet stuff I could manage."

"You brought the sweet stuff, all right." He pulled me close and pressed a kiss into my hair. "You're here, after all."

I giggled.

"By the way, I told you that you could sing," he said.

"You did." I offered him a smile.

"That first time in my car. When you were singing along with the radio. I realized it then."

"I didn't know you were paying attention."

His eyes narrowed, and he leaned in to whisper his response in my ear. "Oh, trust me, I've been paying attention to every little detail from the moment I first laid eyes on you."

I gave a nervous giggle and glanced around, happy to see we were the only ones still left in the sanctuary. Well, almost.

More nerves kicked in when I turned to see my aunt and Uncle Donny standing behind me in the aisle. I couldn't remember the last time I'd seen her in a church, but knowing she might offer a critique of my singing made me nervous.

She reached to pat my arm. "Scarlet, that was lovely."

You could've knocked me over with a feather. Still, I wasn't sure if she was referring to the whole evening or to my singing in particular.

"Maybe when I die, you ladies can sing at my funeral."

I did my best not to groan at that proclamation. Apparently her words didn't sit well with Uncle Donny either. He crossed his arms at his chest and gave her a scolding look.

"What, old man?" She glared at him.

"You know."

"I don't. I'm not a mind reader." She rolled her eyes.

"All this foolishness about dying." He reached to grip her hand. "I've had enough of it."

"It's not foolishness," she said. "We're all gonna die. Surely you know that."

"Yes, but maybe you're only focused on it because you're not sure where you're gonna go after you die. Is that it?"

Whoa. Go, Uncle Donny!

Auntie squirmed and pulled her hand from his. "I really don't think we need to have this conversation. Not standing here in the aisle of a church, anyway."

"Sure we do." He grinned, a beautiful, godly grin. "And no better place than the aisle of a church, sweet girl. You're in the safest place in the world to start living life to the fullest."

She glanced around, and I could read the embarrassment on her face.

Donny slipped his arm over her shoulder and gazed straight into her eyes. "I say you get past your fear of dying and focus on living. How about that? Focus on the time you have left . . ." He gave her a wink. "And who you get to spend that time with. Start thinking about it as a gift, not a curse."

"Curse?" She sputtered like a car running low on gas. "The things you say."

"No, the things *you* say." He brushed one of her curls out of her face. "You say a lot of things you really don't mean, and it's time to admit it."

"Well, I—"

"What you're really saying—whether you admit it or not—is that you're scared. You're scared of being alone, and you're scared of what's on the other side of the great beyond. But you don't have to be afraid of either of those things. We can take care of that right here, right now."

She seemed to wilt at this proclamation. I'd never seen Aunt Willy gaze at a fella with such admiration, but she did now. And as he drew her into his arms, as he planted kisses in her wispy curls, she melted like butter left out in the sun.

The duo faded into a quiet conversation about the Lord, and before long I saw Auntie bow her head. Now, I'd always believed in miracles. Mostly for other people in faraway countries. But I'd never witnessed one firsthand until that very moment.

Overcome with emotion, I turned to Armando. He pulled me close and held me. "It's been a good night," he said.

"A very good night." I glanced up at him and smiled. "I'm so proud of you, Armando. Proud for the role you've played in Devon's life, and his mom's too."

"She's going to do the program." He gave me a little wink.

"I knew you would convince her."

"Don't think I had anything to do with it." He pointed up. "He did."

"Well, God used you along the way. Don't discount yourself." I paused, deep in thought. "You've been such a great influence on Devon. I can't wait to see what the Lord has in store there. It's gonna be great."

"We'll take that fishing trip. That's one thing I'm determined to see happen."

"Oh, I'm sure. Regardless, I just love the idea that Devon's got you to confide in now. He's never had that before. When I think about the impact you could have in his life, I get so excited. You've already given him hope that he can make something of his life."

"Well, he can. He's got skill."

"See what I mean? You recognized that in him, and now he believes it too." I hesitated, my heart heavy. "I only wish you could see it in yourself as well. You've got skill, Armando. Lots of it. And I for one am very proud of you. You've made a huge difference in the life of this church, in the lives of the kids going to Nicaragua, and specifically in my life."

Armando messed with a couple of levers on the lightboard, then flipped a switch to shut it down. He looked up at me, his nose wrinkled. "Do you mean that?"

"I do. Nothing would be the same if you hadn't gotten involved."

He stepped away from the board. "Can I ask you a question then?"

"Sure."

"Is it too late to sign up?"

"Sign up?"

"To go to Nicaragua. Is it too late to sign up? I'd really like to go."

"You . . . you would?"

"Yeah. You're going to need someone to help with the boys, right?"

"Right." I swallowed hard. I could hardly believe Armando actually wanted to go to a third world country to minister to kids. Was I hearing things?

He paced the aisle, finally coming to a stop in front of me. "Say it again."

"What?"

"That I have value."

"You—you have value, Armando." Frankly, it broke my heart that he had to ask. "And God wants to use you. So I'm thrilled that you want to go to Nicaragua. We're going to have the best trip ever."

"We are."

He reached to flip off the overhead lights, and the sanctuary faded to dark. I could hear the joyous voices of people coming from the fellowship hall. Seconds later the trio of Splendora ladies erupted in song—Twila leading the way. Go figure. Then the strains of Uncle Donny's saw added the perfect background.

I knew we should join them. Of course we should. But right now, nestled into the arms of a good old boy from Galveston Island, I couldn't seem to convince myself to leave the sanctuary, no matter how hard I tried.

24

Baked to Perfection

A pinch of patience, a dash of kindness, a
spoonful of laughter, and a heap of love.

Anonymous

The week after the church fund-raiser, we held a
sugar-filled fund-raiser extravaganza at the
bakery. I did my best not to think about my backside as the day progressed, but I found it difficult,
what with so many people talking about sticky
buns and all. Strangely, Aunt Willy didn't show up
for the big event. I'd expected her to be there with
bells on. Nope. She didn't show. Of course, nothing
she did—or didn't do—these days surprised me
anymore. No, since that night at the church, the
whole Wilhelmina world seemed to be tilting off
its axis. The rest of us simply watched it transpire
and wondered what would happen next.

Not that I had time to be thinking about Auntie
today. Our bakery had done great business in the
past, but nothing like this. By the day's end, we'd
brought in over 2,100 dollars for sticky buns
alone. Once folks heard about the fund-raiser, they
offered crazy-high money for the sweets. This all

proved to be great news for the missions trip. We now had all of the money we needed to take the group to Nicaragua. I could hardly wait.

At the end of the day, my family, along with several of the Rossis and the Splendora trio, gathered around the little tables to finish off the sweets. I even had a sticky bun myself. To celebrate, of course. I lifted it high in the air and made a proclamation, a motto I'd recently adopted: "Reach it, raise it!"

"What's that?" Bella asked, taking a nibble of a brownie.

"Never heard that expression," Jolene said, clutching a cookie in each hand. "Something new?"

"It's a sermon my dad preached a few weeks back." I glanced at my father and smiled. "He said we should think like high jumpers when we set goals. Then when we reach them—"

"And we will," my father chimed in.

"We can raise the rung, as it were. Set the next goal a bit higher. Raise the bar. So that's my plan with next year's missions trip. Reach it, raise it. We'll take more people on the trip, and we'll plan for an even larger fund-raiser. Who knows, we might have to rent a hall to accommodate more people."

"Ooo, sounds great," Mama said.

"Reach it, raise it." Bonnie Sue grinned. "I love it!"

"Me too," Twila added. "Count on us to sing

next year. I, um, well, I promise not to have laryngitis."

Jolene punched her in the arm. "Like you ever did."

Bella grinned. "I like this 'reach it, raise it' slogan, Scarlet. Sounds like a good business plan too. I think I could use a dose of that enthusiasm with Club Wed. We've been thinking about expanding. Maybe starting a facility in Splendora."

"No way!" This really got Bonnie Sue in a tizzy. "Maybe I'll be your first customer!" She dove off into a conversation about her upcoming wedding, at which point Twila reminded her that one needed a husband in order to make a wedding happen.

"I've got someone in mind," Bonnie Sue said, then crossed her arms. "Sorta."

"I love the idea of expanding Club Wed," I told Bella. "And I think the motto fits. Setting goals is critical, no matter what you do. I just know one thing—if you don't set any goals, you surely won't reach them. And if you never challenge yourself to go farther, you won't. So . . ." I looked at my audience and raised my hands as if leading a choir.

"Reach it, raise it," we said in tandem.

"Yep." I nodded. "And you get that sermon absolutely free. I won't charge you a penny for it."

We all laughed.

I noticed Bella looking at me. The others kicked

off a lively conversation about the missions trip, and she gestured for me to join her in the kitchen. I followed along on her heels, wondering what was up. Something big, if one could judge from the serious expression on her face.

When we arrived in the messy kitchen, she leaned against the counter, and her eyes flooded. "Thanks for giving me some time alone," she said.

"Is everything okay?" I asked.

"More than okay." She paused, her eyes still brimming. "Scarlet, I just want to thank you."

"Thank me? For what?"

"For caring about my brother."

"Ohhh." I grinned. "Well, that's easy."

"It hasn't always been," she said. "But lately I see such changes. Mama says that watching the transformation in Armando over the past few weeks has been a lot like watching the tide come in. It's all happening so gradually that you don't even realize it. One minute you're standing there looking out at the water, and the waves are way out there so far they're nowhere near your toes. The next minute you look down and the water's up to your ankles."

I loved the water analogy but kept quiet, sensing that she had more on her mind.

"That's how it is with Armando," she said. "I mean, we've waited for years to see the Lord work these kinds of changes in him. I guess maybe I'd given up hope that he was ever going to be any different." A tear trickled down her cheek.

"I didn't know him before," I admitted, "so I only see the awesome, godly man he is now." At this proclamation, I felt the sting of tears in my eyes.

"Who he was before . . ." She shrugged and reached for a rag, then began to wipe down the counter. I joined her, and we worked together. "Who he was before was a lost young man. He was raised in church, sure, but I guess he was just bored with it all. He got off into . . . other things."

"I think I know a little about that," I said. "We've talked some. But it's all turning around now."

"I'd say." Bella grinned. "And my parents aren't the only ones who are thrilled. I couldn't be happier for him . . . and for you." She dropped the rag and wrapped me in a sisterly embrace. "I'm just so grateful."

"Hey, don't look at me," I teased. "I'm not the one who brought about these changes. God is."

"He used you, silly."

"Maybe a little. But I don't want you to worry about Armando ever going back to the way he was before. He's got so much to offer."

"He's always had a lot to offer." She sighed. "You know, I love my family, but they never really gave Armando much of a chance as a kid. They were so busy running the restaurant and then the wedding facility. He kept acting up and getting in trouble and stuff. Honestly, I think he was crying out for attention."

"He was." My hand flew to my mouth, and Bella looked my way, her eyes growing large.

"You've talked to him about all of this?"

"He . . . well, he talked to me. Told me a little about growing up in such a big family."

"It was rough." She sighed. "I love my parents. And my relatives. But when you're surrounded by a mob—and I use the term loosely here—the chances of getting individual attention aren't great. I've told you the story about the day my dad decided to hand over the wedding facility to me to manage?"

"No."

"Horrible. I didn't think I could do it. And I totally blew it a thousand times before the business took off."

"What made the difference?"

A smile lit her face. "D.J."

"D.J. saved your business?"

"Well, not exactly. But falling in love with someone who supported me really helped. And he helped me out at a very critical moment, which just convinced me that he cared even more than I knew."

I pondered Bella's words as she continued to share her heart. For whatever reason, the conversation put me in mind of Aunt Willy. How many times had I told myself she would never change? In so many ways, she and Armando were as different as night and day. And yet they had both been prodigals who'd wandered away and done their own thing.

"It's just so good to see my brother back home again," Bella whispered. "I wasn't sure he would ever be content being back on the island for good. But that's changed. Now he's happy working at Parma John's." She looked my way and smiled. "And we have you to thank for that too."

I heard a little sniffle from the doorway and glanced that way. Bella's mother stood there, eyes filled with tears. She walked toward me and wrapped me in her arms. "I'm not sure how to thank you," she said.

"No thanks necessary," I responded. "He's a great guy."

"Who's a great guy?" Armando's voice rang out from the doorway. "What's going on in here? Why wasn't I invited to the party?"

"Oh, trust me, you're the guest of honor." I walked over and took his hand, then gave it a squeeze.

"Really? Well, that's great. Did you bake me a cake?" he asked.

"Sure did. Italian cream cake with cream cheese frosting."

"Yum." He licked his lips. "Do I get to blow out candles?"

"Um, no. No candles. But you can have the first piece. Just follow me." I led the way to the bakery, where the others appeared to be in a daze. Probably too much sugar. No doubt they would still indulge in a piece of Italian cream cake if I offered it. So I did.

Twila, Jolene, and Bonnie Sue were the first in line. After Armando, of course. I noticed that Kenny lagged behind. He'd been really out of sorts lately. I didn't blame him. We'd finally had that heart-to-heart, and he'd taken my news well, but things had been odd ever since. When everyone settled down to enjoy the cake, he began to pace the shop, obviously nervous. All the pacing was making me nervous too.

"Kenny?" I offered him a piece of cake, but he refused to take it. "You okay?"

He released a slow breath. "I, um, I need to tell you something."

"Should we . . ." I gestured to the kitchen. "Do we need to be alone?"

He shook his head. "No, it's probably better if I say this in front of everyone."

Oy.

I swallowed hard and tried to imagine what he might say.

"It's about your aunt," he said a moment later.

Everyone in the room grew quiet at this point, especially my parents and the Splendora ladies.

"W-what about her?" I asked.

His face turned red. "Maybe you'd better sit down."

I did. "Tell me, Kenny."

He paced the room, then turned back to face all of us. "She got married."

"She . . . what?" my mother and I both squealed at the same time, and then the other ladies chimed in, especially Bonnie Sue, who looked as if she might be ill.

For a minute there I felt sure I'd misunderstood, so I posed it as a question. "Did you say that Aunt Willy got . . . married?"

He nodded. "She and Donny ran off together. Well, not really ran off. They're in Splendora."

Bonnie Sue began to wail. Twila and Jolene did their best to comfort her, but the tears continued.

I shook my head as I tried to envision my aunt in the piney woods of east Texas. Crazy.

"She's setting up a bakery in his gas station," Kenny explained. "I think they've already started that process, actually."

"It's not just a gas station," I said. "It's a full-service rest stop for families—"

"With the cleanest restrooms in the state of Texas," my parents chimed in.

We all laughed.

Well, all but Bonnie Sue, who now ranted about how her wedding at the new Club Wed facility would have to be postponed until a future date.

I couldn't picture Aunt Willy living in Splendora, clean restrooms or not.

Obviously, neither could Bonnie Sue, who glanced my way and muttered, "She stole my man."

Twila popped her on the head with one of my menus. "Bonnie Sue, Donny was never your man to begin with. And you certainly don't want a fella who's in love with someone else."

"True." Bonnie Sue rubbed her head. "But I was sure he was the man for me." Tears trickled down her plump cheeks, and she sighed.

"God will bring the right man," I said. "In his time." Boy, if anyone knew that to be true, I did.

Bonnie Sue did not look convinced. In fact, she looked downright angry.

She wasn't the only one who looked a little put out. My father rose and joined Kenny in pacing. "I just don't know why my sister wouldn't tell me this herself. No offense, Kenny, but why did she share such personal information with you instead of her own family? Doesn't make a lick of sense."

"Well, that's the next part that's going to be hard to hear." Kenny gazed into my eyes. "Willy wants me to take over her shop in Houston."

My heart suddenly felt as heavy as lead. "What? Are you serious?" I couldn't imagine running Let Them Eat Cake without Kenny. We might not be a couple, but we were still a team. A baking team, anyway.

"It's the opportunity of a lifetime," he said. "How could I turn her down?" He dove into what a great thing this would be, and I realized he was right. Someone as talented as Kenny deserved his shot at running his own place. I would miss him terribly, but I couldn't hold him back.

The others in attendance took turns congratulating him when he finished. My mother gave him a hug and told him he would be missed. So did my father. Armando shook his hand, and I heard an audible sigh from Kenny at that point. I managed to get him off to the side after the others went back to talking about Willy and Donny's marriage.

"I'm going to miss you, Kenny. I really am. You're so great to work with."

"Scarlet, I love working with you. But . . . it's hard. Being here, I mean." He glanced across the room at Armando. "I'm not saying you shouldn't fall in love with whoever you like. Just saying it will be easier to swallow from the north end of Houston. And besides . . ." He grinned. "Your aunt offered me a salary I couldn't refuse."

Crazy. And all this time I'd thought Willy didn't care for Kenny. Apparently it was just the facial hair, not the man himself.

Suddenly I was filled with pride for him—kind of like a mama hen looking out for her chicks. Yes, I'd be up a creek without a paddle when Kenny left, but he was right—this was the opportunity of a lifetime for him, and I'd be crazy to stand in his way. If anyone deserved special recognition, he did. And I had no doubt he would be the best head baker Crème de la

Crème had ever seen. Auntie was right to hire him.

We finished our celebration about thirty minutes later, and Armando helped me close up shop. We ended the evening with the sweetest kiss ever, and I sent him on his way to help his family tend to Uncle Laz, who had remained at home by himself most of the evening.

Before leaving the bakery, I decided to make a quick call to my aunt. She answered on the third ring. "H-hello?"

"Aunt Willy, sorry to call so late. Were you sleeping?"

She gave a tiny giggle. "Um . . . no."

"Is there something you want to tell me?"

A lengthy pause followed on her end. "I'm assuming by now you've already heard?" The words were more statement of fact than question.

"I have, actually. And . . . congratulations."

"Thank you. How did your father take the news?" she asked. "Does he think I'm off my rocker?"

"No, he's thrilled for you. Shocked, but thrilled."

"Good. I'm so relieved. And did Kenny tell you the rest?"

"He did," I said. "That part was a little shocking too, but I'm happy for him. He's going to be a great asset to your business."

"Oh, I agree." I heard her breathe a sigh of relief. "I'm just glad you're not angry with me, Scarlet."

"Not at all. In fact, we all want to spend some time with you and Donny when you've got a day you can give us. We want to have a family day."

"Family day?" Aunt Willy sounded as if she couldn't quite figure out what I meant by those words.

"Yes, we want to go to Pleasure Pier for the day. Maybe invite the Rossis along."

"Oh, I've been wanting to go there anyway." My aunt's voice became more animated by the moment. "See, I had this idea—"

"With all due respect, I'm not talking about a marketing day, Auntie," I said. "I'm talking about a real family day, one where we ride rides and eat cotton candy and buy nonsensical gifts for others. A day where we spend too much money doing arcade games and spring for a fishing expedition off the end of the pier."

"F-fishing?" She paused. "I've never been fishing."

"Then it's about time. And I have it on good authority your new husband loves to fish."

"So he says." Her voice drifted away.

"Well, I think you're going to love it too. There's nothing more relaxing." I dove into a conversation about a fishing trip my father had taken me on as a child, but I could tell I was losing Auntie. Time to reel her in (pun intended).

"Aunt Willy, the main thing is we need to spend

time together doing something that's not business related. No bakery talk."

"I don't know if I can do that," she admitted.

"I might have a hard time stepping away from business chatter too," I said, "but I'm willing to give it the old college try if you are. I think our family members would appreciate it."

No doubt they would. I couldn't remember the last time I'd sat down with my mom and dad to talk about something other than cakes and cookies. They were probably weary of the whole bakery chatter.

I knew that Willy wasn't, of course. She would never tire of business life. We had that in common. And I loved that we shared a passion for cakes. But now we needed a passion for something more—each other. Our relationship was about to be sweeter than any cake or cookie.

Not that she saw much value in a cookie, but whatever.

Our relationship was going to be the proverbial icing on the cake, and though it was long overdue, I had a feeling the Lord would use it to reach out to others in our community. Yes, it would probably grow our businesses too, but I couldn't think about that right now. All I wanted to do was focus on the woman on the other end of the line, the one who had poured life and soul into my business because she believed in me.

After teaching her how to fish, of course.

25

Sweetened by Life

C is for cookie. That's good enough for me.
Cookie Monster

On the third Saturday in July, my family met up with the Rossis at Pleasure Pier, where we had the time of our lives riding rides and playing games at the arcade. I kept a watchful eye on Aunt Willy, who strolled the pier with her arm looped through Donny's. I'd never seen her look happier.

I couldn't help but notice that married life had changed her not just emotionally but physically too. A rosy glow lit her cheeks—one that didn't require excessive amounts of makeup—and her smile rivaled the sunshine streaming the mid-afternoon skies over the Gulf of Mexico.

Aunt Willy came close and gave me a giant hug. She whispered, "I'm transformed" into my ear.

I gave her a curious look. "Transformed?"

She gave my hand a squeeze. "Oh, honey, I don't know if you'll ever understand, but I've lived my whole life putting business first. From the time I was twenty-three, when my mentor passed away so unexpectedly, I was the one in

354

charge of the store." Her eyes flooded with tears quite suddenly. "You have no idea how hard I've worked to prove myself."

Oh, I might have some idea.

Out of the corner of my eye, I saw Armando stand up a little straighter as he listened in on our conversation.

"I never really felt like I was as good as my brothers and sisters," Auntie said. "Always wanted to prove myself to my mother."

"You . . . you did?"

When she nodded, Armando came a little closer.

"You have no idea how tough my mother was. Nothing I ever did was good enough. If I got a B+ on a test, she insisted it should've been an A. If I came in second place in the spelling bee, she asked me why I wasn't first. I'm telling you, I think I started baking to prove something to her," Aunt Willy said. "But she died before she could see my first bakery open. She never even lived to see me make a success of myself, so it's all kind of bittersweet."

Armando stood in front of her. "But you kept trying to prove yourself, right? Even though she was gone, I mean."

A little sigh escaped Aunt Willy's lips. "Yes, but it seems so silly now. So pointless. My mother— God bless her—never believed in me. She said I'd never amount to anything, but I refused to believe it. So by sheer will and determination, I set out to prove her wrong. I grew that bakery to a great success."

"You certainly did." I offered her an encouraging smile.

"It's just so ironic," Willy said. "The very person I needed to prove myself to wasn't even there anymore to see how great I was doing." She offered a little shrug. "Not that I could've fixed Mama, anyway. I know that now. She had her own set of problems, and I wasn't meant to take care of them."

"It's funny you should say that. I've always been in the fixing business too," I said. "I honestly thought that fixing people was as easy as baking a cake. You add all the right ingredients and hopefully it turns out. But you can't force change on a person. I know that now."

"I'm old, Scarlet." Willy's gaze shot out over the water, and her words drifted away on the afternoon breeze.

Okay, I couldn't argue that, but I didn't know what to say in response.

"When you're old like I am, you don't want to change. You get settled in your ways. And when you've lived the kind of life I have—all work and no play—you're especially settled." She released a sigh. "Sometimes I feel like I've waited my whole life for something special to happen to me."

"Something special? You've been on television. You have one of the top bakeries in the state. You've been in magazines. I'd say your life has been very special."

"Externally, I suppose it has appeared that way. But in here . . ." She pointed to her heart. "Well, it's a different story."

"Oh?"

Aunt Willy nodded. "I went through a lot of hurt," she said. "Not just stuff related to my mom but in general. Had my heart broken a couple of times. Once in a major way. Even then, I think I wanted to prove something with the business— that I didn't need anyone else in my life. Didn't need my mother. Didn't need a husband. Didn't need . . . anyone."

She sighed. "I don't mind admitting it's been a very solitary existence. As much as I love my business, it doesn't really love me back, and it certainly doesn't wrap its arms around me when I'm tired." She shrugged. "Of course, sometimes it feels like it's a noose around my neck, but I'm finally figuring out how to wriggle out of it."

"Aw, Aunt Wil—" I caught myself just in time as I slipped my arm around her tiny waist.

She grinned. "And that's another thing. I love it when you call me Aunt Willy."

"You do?" *No way.*

"Yeah. I see that it's a term of endearment. Personalizes it. Wilhelmina is so formal, anyway.

I'll never understand why my mother named me that in the first place. Just showing off by giving her child a fancy name, I think." She chuckled. "At least, that's what I've always said."

"Well, I'm tickled pink that you like to be called Aunt Willy," I said. "I've had a doozy of a time trying to remember not to say it. Just comes naturally to give you a nickname."

"Nicknames are great." She smiled. "Never really had one as a kid, even though a few people called me some choice names over the years. But I see the value in a nickname now, and I also see the harm." She paused and gazed into my eyes. "Which brings me to my next point. Scarlet, I owe you an apology."

"You do?"

"Yeah. That whole sticky buns thing was way out of line."

"Sticky buns?" Armando's brow furrowed. "She bakes the best sticky buns on the island."

"Right." Aunt Willy nodded. "But I think she knows what I mean."

I knew, all right. But to hear her apologize meant the world to me. It startled me too, and I was convinced the world must've tilted off its axis for her to be standing here in front of me, saying all of this.

Stranger still that her story felt—and sounded—so much like Armando's. Raised in a big family. Overlooked as a kid. Feeling like the odd man out.

Striving to prove herself by striking out on her own.

Yep. Willy and Armando were two peas in a pod. A generation or two apart, of course, but two peas in a pod. I'd just opened up my mouth to share this little revelation with them when I realized the two had entered into a heart-to-heart. I backed away and let them talk, knowing that the Lord could take it from here. He certainly didn't need my help.

Another revelation. I'd spent much of my time trying to help God help others. In reality, I could trust him to do it on his own, without my input. Looked like maybe I'd been trying to prove myself too—to him and to Aunt Willy.

Maybe I deserved to join the conversation after all. I took a couple of steps back in their direction just in time to see Armando place a fishing pole in my aunt's hands.

"Do I . . . do I have to?" she asked.

I nodded and quoted a Scripture about being fishers of men. That got Uncle Donny tickled as he walked up behind us. "She's already caught herself a man," he said, then slipped his arm over her shoulder.

"That I have." She tried to hand me the pole, but I wouldn't take it.

"You've caught a man, all right, Willy, but you need time to just sit and rest." This time the admonition came from my father, who approached with Mama's arm looped through his. "So take a seat. Hang tight to that pole and see what the Lord brings you."

She settled into the spot next to Donny, and before long he'd baited her hook. Actually, I had to think he'd baited her hook weeks ago when the rest of us weren't paying attention, but that was probably an analogy for another day. Today he sat beside her, pole in hand, gabbing about his many years as a consummate fisherman. Auntie hung on his every word.

Until there was a tug on her line.

A whoop went up from Aunt Willy, loud enough to startle a family standing nearby. "I got something!" she called out. "It's a big one!"

Uncle Donny helped her reel it in. Turned out she'd caught a clump of seaweed. We all had a good laugh, and she settled back down again, this time completely relaxed and looking like a woman who fished for a living. Go figure.

I sat on the edge of the pier and dangled my legs over the side. Armando headed off to fetch Devon, who'd run into a friend at the concession stand. Turned out the teen had a great passion for sharing the story of his upcoming Nicaragua trip.

He drew near with Armando minutes later. When Armando reached for a pole, Devon looked my way and grinned. "You gonna clean it if he catches it?"

"Nope. That's why we brought you along. I'm just here to observe."

He got a laugh out of that. Settling in next to me, he grabbed a pole and baited it. Looking up at me, he asked, "Did you hear about my mom?"

"That she's in the Sheltering Arms program?" I nodded. "I think it's great, Devon."

"I think it's gonna stick this time." He flashed a smile. "I talked to her this morning and she sounded good. She's not ready to bail or anything, which is totally cool. Usually by now she's skipping out."

"I'm believing God for a complete recovery," I said. "I'll keep praying until it happens."

"Thank you." He tossed his line out into the water. "Did you hear the rest?"

"About you moving in with Armando?"

"Yeah." Devon nodded. "I wasn't sure what was going to happen after I got the eviction notice from our apartment."

My heart swelled with pride at Armando's generosity. Having a teen stay with him at his new condo? I could hardly imagine the two living together, but Armando's huge heart for this kid went above and beyond the call of duty.

"He gave me a job too," Devon said. "I'm working at Parma John's now."

"Are you serious? Now *that* I hadn't heard."

"Just happened." Devon laughed. "With all the Mambo Italiano pizzas I want. As long as I make them, anyway."

"Oh, Devon, I'm thrilled."

"Me too."

He gazed back out at the water for a moment before flashing me another smile. "You know, I never told you this before, but I used to think your church was boring."

"So why did you come?" I asked.

He shrugged. "People, I guess. There were nice people there. And they cared about me."

"What do you think now?" I asked.

He paused, and I noticed something tugging on his line. "Now I like it. I mean, it's growing on me."

"Face it, we're all growing on you."

"True, true." He began to reel in the line, and we all gave a celebratory holler when we saw the fish dangling on the end of the hook. He took it and wriggled it loose, then dropped it into the bucket at his feet before baiting his hook again.

The afternoon sun hovered in the sky, beaming down streams of sunlight over our little group. It reflected off of the water, making it hard to see. Still, I managed to watch as Devon tossed his line back into the water once more. Then I rose and brushed my hands on the legs of my jeans.

Armando stepped into the spot behind me and slipped his arms around my waist—my ever-shrinking waist. "Now it's your turn," he whispered in my ear.

"My turn?" I pivoted on my heel to face him. "What do you mean?"

"Grab a pole, little Lucy. Ricky wants to take you fishing."

"Hey, I just came out here to watch."

He shook his head. "Nope. You're not getting away with that."

"I'm not?"

He laughed. "Don't you remember that *I Love Lucy* episode where they went deep-sea fishing?"

"Yeah." I sighed. "But I can't believe you remember that one. It's not one of the more famous ones."

"I've done my research," he said. "I figure if you're gonna fall head over heels for a nutty redhead, you'd better know what she loves."

"What I love, eh?" I bit my lip to keep from saying, "You know what I love most, right? You." Instead, I just smiled and took the pole he offered, then followed along behind him to a private spot on the end of the pier. "Any idea what we'll catch today, Ricky?"

"Actually, I think I've already caught the one thing I needed most." He planted a little kiss on my cheek. "Hope she doesn't want me to toss her back."

"Out there?" I pointed to the gulf. "No thanks. I love to swim, but not that much."

We had a good laugh at that and settled into our spots.

As I gazed out onto the Gulf of Mexico, pole in hand, all of life slowed down. I put the bakery out of my mind. My concerns over the upcoming trip, my customers, losing Kenny, cakes that still needed to be baked . . . all faded away. The sounds of the seagulls overhead provided just the right backdrop for this precious moment. All around me family members chatted and laughed, talking about everything from the weather to upcoming get-togethers. It sounded like music to my ears.

When I felt that first little tug on my line, I couldn't help but holler. I didn't mean to startle Armando, but I did. He almost dropped his pole as he turned my way.

"Got one?" His eyes widened in boyish delight.

I nodded, my own eyes wide. "Yep. Got one!"

I stared into Armando's gorgeous chocolate-brown eyes, distracted as always by their beauty, and realized I'd snagged one, all right. He was the Ricky to my Lucy, my perfect complement. And I wouldn't dream of tossing him back, no matter what troubles life might throw our way.

26

Sweets for the Sweet

Kissin' don't last, cookin' do!

Author unknown

The Monday after our fishing trip, I found myself battling a sunburn. A bad one. Still, work beckoned. I headed to the bakery, my thoughts sailing a thousand different directions at once. With Kenny leaving to work for my aunt, I needed a long-term plan. Maybe it had something to do with my hypersensitive skin, but I couldn't seem to think straight. Couldn't come up with anything.

Thank God for Mama. She agreed to help out a couple of days a week. I needed someone full-time but would settle for what I could get. It didn't hurt that Mama already knew my work routine. Mostly, anyway.

She arrived at the bakery at nine that morning, ready to dive in. Kenny and I showed her the various recipes, and she helped with the brownies and several simple iced cakes. By noon, the glass cases were filling up with things she'd made.

"I can't believe it." She gave the cakes an admiring look. "Not bad for my first day."

"Not bad at all." I chuckled. "And now you don't have to use the Wii Fit as often, Mama. You're going to get plenty of exercise here, trust me."

"I don't mind a bit." She flexed her arm, showing off a would-be muscle. "In fact, I think maybe the Lord's been preparing me for this all along. I'm just sorry I don't have more time to give you, honey, but your dad really needs me up at the church."

"I know. I'm just so grateful you're here now." I gave her a hug. Working with my mother even part-time would be fun. We'd always been more like sisters than mother and daughter.

Around two o'clock that afternoon, Armando showed up. He looked pretty spiffy. Instead of his usual Parma John's apron over jeans and a T-shirt, he wore a button-down shirt and dressier jeans. Talk about cleaning up nice.

"You headed somewhere important?" I asked.

"Maybe." His eyebrows elevated mischievously. "Why do you ask?"

"Because . . ." I slipped into his open arms. "You look like a million bucks."

"Well, thanks. You look pretty amazing yourself."

I glanced down at my dirty apron and sighed. "Seriously?"

"You couldn't look any prettier if you spent all day in the beauty salon. I love you like this."

My heart did a girlish flip-flop at the "I love

you" part. None of the rest mattered. He loved me. He really, really loved me.

"I came by to see your mom in action." He glanced around. "She's here, right?"

"She's in the kitchen."

He walked behind the glass cases and peered into the inner sanctum, then looked back at me with a smile. "Looks like she's in her element."

"She is. I think she's really enjoying this."

"I'm glad. You're really going to need the help now that Kenny's about to leave."

"True." I sighed. I wanted the best for him, but every time I thought about handling the bakery on my own—even with Mama's part-time help—I felt a little nervous.

I took a seat, ready to share my thoughts with someone who could understand. "Mama has agreed to come a couple of days a week, but she's already so busy working in the office at the church. I guess I'll have to hire someone."

It really needed to be someone with a lot of baking experience, anyway. Mama could bake, but she didn't know much about the bakery biz. Or waiting on customers. In fact, she was a little on the shy side, which might prove to be problematic.

"You might not need to hire anyone at all," he said. "I had an idea that just might work."

That certainly captured my attention. "What's that?"

"Well, we've hired Devon to work at Parma John's. He's already started."

"Right. I heard he's doing a great job."

"He is. I'm really proud of him." Armando paused and shoved his hands in his pockets. If I didn't know any better, I'd say the boy looked nervous. "Anyway, he's there now, and my brother, of course. And Jenna's coming back in a couple of months."

"In theory, anyway. Now that she has two little ones, she could change her mind at any moment and decide to be a stay-at-home mom."

"It's possible. But I think we can manage. So . . ." He puffed his chest out. "I've located the perfect person to work with you."

"You have?"

"Yes." He grinned. "Me."

The breath went out of me. "You? You're going to stop working at Parma John's and work at the bakery?"

"Not exactly. I have a plan to merge our two worlds. Something that will remedy all of that."

"A plan?" None of this made sense. His family would be upset if he left them high and dry at the pizza parlor to help me out. Wouldn't they?

His gorgeous brown eyes sparkled as they honed in on mine. "Here's my idea." Armando paced the bakery. I could read the excitement on his face.

"Armando, you're making me nervous."

With a wave of his hand, he dismissed my

concerns. "Relax. It's all good. Well, I hope you'll think it's good."

Talk about piquing a girl's curiosity. *What are you up to, Ricky? Lucy's dying to know!*

He pointed at the wall, where I'd painted the words "Sweets for the Sweet" in beautiful script. "What do you see there?"

"I see a saying that makes me smile. It also makes me want chocolate, so I try not to read it very often."

He rolled his eyes. "Beyond that."

"I see a wall?" I tried.

"Right. A wall." He smacked it with his hand, then crossed his arms at his chest as if trying to tell me something.

"And . . . ?"

"It separates us." He leaned against it and offered a smile.

"Are we speaking literally or symbolically here?" I asked. "It would be good to know, going into this conversation."

"Literally." He patted the script and then looked back at me. "Do you know what's directly on the other side of this wall?"

"Parma John's?" I asked.

"Well, yes, but what specifically in Parma John's?"

"No idea. The kitchen?"

"No. I thought that at first too, but I was wrong, thank goodness."

"Thank goodness?"

"Yes. It's a bare wall with nothing on it. A couple of tables up against it, but nothing to prevent us from making an opening . . . right about here." He pointed to a space in the center.

"Wait. You're putting a hole in my wall?"

"I'm connecting our worlds, Scarlet."

Connecting our worlds? I walked over to the wall and ran my hands over the words. I tried to envision the whole thing gone.

An opening?

"You want the two businesses to become one? Is that what you're saying?"

"Yes." He threw his hands up in the air triumphantly, then brought them back down again. "Well, no. You would still be Let Them Eat Cake and we would still be Parma John's. But I wouldn't have to walk so far to see you." He gave me a delightful smile, and I grinned, convinced he was just saying all of this to be silly.

"Walk so far to see me?" I said. Okay, that cracked me up. "I'm right next door."

He pouted. "But there's a wall of separation between us, and it needs to come down. Don't you agree?"

"I guess. But what does my aunt Willy think of this idea?"

"Haven't asked her yet, but Uncle Donny offered to be the one to broach the subject. He's next door talking to her right now."

"I see." Weird.

"I think we can help one another if we merge forces," Armando said. "We've never had a lot of luck with our desserts, but you've got the best sweets in town."

"Thank you."

"You know it's true."

"Well, thank you again." *What are you up to, Armando Rossi?*

He patted the wall, a look of contentment coming over him. "So, what do you say? Can we open up the place? Merge forces?"

I paused to think through his idea. While it sounded great to me, I really had to wait on my aunt. Her opinion was the one that really counted.

"Oh, and one more thing." He flashed a sly smile. "While we're taking walls down . . ." He dropped to one knee, and I half expected him to pull Uncle Donny's saw out of some toolbox he'd hidden under the table or something. Maybe he would start to take the wall down right now.

Instead, he reached for my hand.

"What are we doing?" I asked. With a tilt of my head, I gestured to several incoming customers, who now looked on, intrigued.

Turned out there were more customers than I'd realized. Strange. Hadn't noticed my dad before. When did he get here? And Bella? She must've snuck in when I wasn't looking. And Hannah? No way.

Armando's voice reeled me back in. "Scarlet . . ."

"Yes?"

"I'm not just asking if you want to merge businesses."

"You're . . . you're not?"

"Nope." His gorgeous eyes flashed with merriment. "I'm asking if you want to merge lives."

"Merge lives?" I echoed, trying to make sense of this. Only one problem—with so many people looking on, I couldn't think straight. "Sorry, I'm a little confused."

"Then let me unconfuse you." He reached into his pocket and came out with a little box. At this point the customers and family members behind me took to cheering. Then I saw Aunt Willy enter on Uncle Donny's arm. They looked on as Armando opened the box and pulled out a little —no, make that huge—diamond ring.

My breath caught in my throat. "Armando."

"I asked you a question, Lucy." He waggled his brows. "Ricky's waiting for an answer."

A nervous chuckle escaped me.

"If you say no, you'll have some serious 'splainin' to do."

He grinned, and I found myself fixated on that gorgeous face. "Oh, Lucy's not saying no. No way, no how."

"So that's a yes?" He lifted the ring out of the box and dangled it in front of me.

"On one condition." I put up my hand to stop him. "You have to let me sing at the Copa Cabana. Now that I've had a taste of stardom, I think I enjoy the spotlight too much to let it go."

He laughed. "Honey, you can be the headline act. I'll even put in a stage at Parma John's so you can perform as often as you like."

Okay, that was a little much. Still, the idea intrigued me. I giggled and extended my left hand. "In that case, Lucy says yes."

He slipped the gorgeous marquise-cut diamond onto my ring finger, and a huge cheer went up from the crowd. Armando rose and swept me into his arms. He planted kiss after kiss on my cheeks, his lips finally finding their way to mine. As he swept me away to worlds yet unknown, I felt giddy with delight. No baked goods on earth could come close to the sweetness I felt in Armando's arms.

Here, in this place, I really could have my cake . . . and eat it too.

Author's Note

What joy to write this fun book about a cake decorator! I've been the mother of the bride four times over and have coordinated many other weddings besides. After spending nearly six hundred dollars on cake at daughter number one's wedding, I vowed never to do that again. Daughter number two trusted me enough to make and decorate her cake, and I've been at it ever since! Though I don't work as a professional cake decorator—the stress would kill me—I often gift brides with their cake. There's something so exciting—and tasty—about the process. It's also a fun way to relieve stress.

Speaking of tasty, I've spent the last two years of my life losing weight and getting in shape. I've lost nearly one hundred pounds! That's why I decided to work the "getting comfortable in my own skin" plotline into Scarlet's story. Yes, I still occasionally have a nibble of cake. No, I don't eat the whole thing. I must admit that cake baking is tougher work now that I'm trying to avoid sweets!

Adding Armando to this story was an afterthought, by the way. Initially I'd plotted the story with a different hero. As I thought it through, however, the truth surfaced: this needed to be more than just a story about two unlikely people meeting and falling in love; it needed to be a story about two people with individual struggles and issues who overcame them and fell head over heels for each other.

Oh, and the whole Nicaragua thing? I went on a missions trip to Managua, Nicaragua, in 2003 with a fabulous team of believers. How did we earn the money? We put on a show, of course. And who headed all of that up?

Do you really have to ask?

Acknowledgments

To my editor, Jennifer Leep. This tasty story would never have found a home if you hadn't believed in Bella in the first place. I'm tickled to see how far her story has come and how many people she's brought with her. It's all because of you, girl! It's all because of you. Thank you too for walking with me through the illnesses of my grandbabies. Putting family first slowed down the process, but I'm thrilled that the story still came together with my sense of humor intact, in spite of the trauma.

To my sales and marketing team at Revell. Bless you for your continued support. You are the wind beneath Bella's wings. You help her— and me!—soar.

To my readers. You helped me dream Bella back from the great beyond. If you hadn't come knocking at my door for more, these stories wouldn't exist. Thank you for encouraging me and giving me a reason to believe that Bella was more than a fictional character from Galveston. She has become a living, breathing entity, a staple in my life and my writing journey.

To my grandbabies. Nina has worked very hard to lose weight and get in shape so that she can dance at your weddings. I hope my hand is still steady enough to decorate the cakes. If not, call on Scarlet. I hear she's quite the cake decorator. While you're at it, ask her to sing. She does a great rendition of "I Believe I Can Fly."

About the Author

Award-winning author Janice Thompson enjoys tickling the funny bone. She got her start in the industry writing screenplays and musical comedies for the stage, and she has published over ninety books for the Christian market. She has played the role of mother of the bride four times now and particularly enjoys writing lighthearted, comedic, wedding-themed tales. Why? Because making readers laugh gives her great joy!

Janice formerly served as vice president of Christian Authors Network (CAN) and was named the 2008 Mentor of the Year for American Christian Fiction Writers (ACFW). She is active in her local writing group, where she regularly teaches on the craft of writing. In addition, she enjoys public speaking and mentoring young writers.

Janice is passionate about her faith and does all she can to share the joy of the Lord with others, which is why she particularly enjoys writing. Her tagline, "Love, Laughter, and Happily Ever Afters!" sums up her take on life.

She lives in Spring, Texas, where she leads a rich life with her family, a host of writing friends, and two mischievous dachshunds. She does her best to keep the Lord at the center of it all. You can find out more about Janice at:

www.janiceathompson.com
or
www.freelancewritingcourses.com.

Center Point Large Print
600 Brooks Road / PO Box 1
Thorndike ME 04986-0001 USA

(207) 568-3717

US & Canada:
1 800 929-9108
www.centerpointlargeprint.com

Lincoln Township Public Library
2099 W. John Beers Rd.
Stevensville, MI 49127
(269) 429-9575